SUFFERING THE FIRE

BARRY HOTSON

Cillian Press |

First published in Great Britain in 2014
by Cillian Press Limited. 83 Ducie Street, Manchester M1 2JQ
www.cillianpress.co.uk

British Library Cataloguing in Publication Data.
A catalogue record for this book is available from the British Library.

Paperback ISBN: 978-1-909776-04-3
eBook ISBN: 978-1-909776-05-0

Published by
Cillian Press – Manchester - 2014
www.cillianpress.co.uk

From the front page of the *Ulcethorpe Evening Argus*,
Tuesday 13th August 1974

DISASTER AT BOROUGHCLIFF

The flames are still burning and the smoke is still billowing after last night's terrifying explosion at Boroughcliff. The Performance Intermediates chemical works there has been all but flattened. The huge fire – believed to be the largest ever in peacetime Britain – is unlikely to be extinguished before tomorrow, with the Humberside Fire Service battling with brigades from Yorkshire and Nottinghamshire. Local residents face another night in emergency shelters. Nearly a hundred houses in the village overlooking the site were damaged in the blast, whose effect was felt over twenty miles away.

It is thought that sixteen operators and technicians have been killed, based on the number of bodies recovered and men still missing, but no names have yet been released. Eleven more men have been seriously injured, with three in a critical state.

The Boroughcliff site was established before the war to make ammonium sulphate fertiliser using coke oven gas from the Ulcethorpe steelworks as the raw material for ammonia. Its expansion into a major petrochemical complex to manufacture an intermediate for nylon is much more recent, with the new facilities in operation since 1972.

Works manager Alec Masters, 32, refused to comment on the cause of the explosion, other than to suggest the possibility of sabotage. He announced that company specialists would be working with HM Factory Inspectorate on a detailed investigation. However this will be hampered by the complete destruction of the control building and loss of all processing records. He admitted that the manufacturing process involved the use of over a hundred tons of highly flammable cyclohexane, but stressed that all equipment and procedures were suitable for the risks involved.

A little fire is quickly trodden out,
Which being suffer'd, rivers cannot quench.

William Shakespeare: King Henry VI Part Three

ONE

The coffin glides towards the blue curtains – heavenly blue, you might say. My only feeling is that I'm almost free.

The holy muzak can't hide the noise of the roller conveyor any more than turning up the volume masks the hum of an amplifier. Or maybe it's my ears, always tuned for warnings: noises at the wrong time, in the wrong place, with the wrong tone.

I look sideways to Lou and down to Emily and Hannah sitting between us. They're still intent on their final sight of Mum's polished oak shell. It's a blurred view for them. I had my one-off paroxysm when the hospice rang.

Mum's been declining to an early death ever since Boroughcliff – thirty-one years of wasting away. Now she's got what she was waiting for: her release from bereavement's grief. Why didn't she ever recover? The disaster stole Dad from me too; and yet the way it turned out, I lost them both: a dad crushed and burnt to death, and a loving mum replaced by an irritable and depressed recluse. I struggled to please her the whole time – but not any more. Now I'm released too; I can focus on the new job, prove my talent, make my name – and show Lou she's wrong.

The curtains are parted and then the coffin's out of sight. People don't know what goes on back there, later – the technology: fuel-air ratio, furnace temperature, stack gas analysis, emission control. It's the black hole at the crematorium: the invisible part between the corpse in the coffin and the grit in the casket. Maybe they don't think, because of the Holocaust link: 'cremation' and 'extermination'.

"Michael!"

Lou's pressurised whisper penetrates my trance. It's time to leave; and as I get up and turn into the blue-carpeted aisle I see someone who's come in late sitting alone in a row at the back: a small professorial man in his fifties whose hair is still a good match for his tie. It's Ivor Hughes, the firebrand safety writer, the bane of weasel-worded politicians and roughshod-riding corporations. He was guest speaker at last year's GPSC meeting in Barcelona. I only knew his name before that. It's much more famous than his face – the sign of someone worth listening to.

Yes, I know who he is; but what the fucking hell is he doing at Ulcethorpe Crematorium this Monday morning in December 2005 at Marlene Paine's funeral?

He sees me staring, and gives a little nod and one of those closed-lip smiles I've been practising all week. And as I stand blocking Emily's exit my scalp's prickling with the answer. I'm shrinking and he's growing. He's that Ivor, from thirty years ago – the reporter with the beard who dated Mum and took us both out in his Mini Cooper. He hasn't got a beard now, but it's the same man. It's only him turning up here that's made me twig.

Memory's a pile of old videotapes without labels, and he's picked one out for me and put it in the player fast-forward. It's showing a time I'd forgotten; when Mum wiped away her grief for a while and started to live, and I was... well, even with nightmares, not so sad. But then he left her and she retreated back into her shell and made things hard again for me. Why the fucking hell has he waited until now before coming back – and come back when she's dead? Something doesn't add up. He owes me a bloody explanation.

I'm moving again now; the shockwave's decaying. The other mourners – now fifteen of them with Ivor Hughes – are still sitting like patients in a surgery waiting for the doctor's call. The order of service doesn't go beyond this. Maybe it should've done. I haven't got everything right – that muzak, for another thing. I should've given a fuller spec. I'm always aiming for perfection, because of Mum. It's not often I miss.

Anyway, viewing the floral tributes is next. Mum's sister Pam and her entourage already know, and I can tell the rest at the door; and I'll need to thank the priest (or is it priestess?) and the funeral director's men. She knitted up a pretty decent address about Mum from the strands she pulled out of me. I'd have had to eulogise with white lies. Hannah could've done it if she'd been a couple of years older. The girls had a very generous perspective on Mum.

I stick back on my sad smile for general consumption, and avoiding any focus on the pairs of sympathetic eyes lead my trio of lovelies up the aisle and out into the raw wind rasping down from The Ridge through the copse of skeletal trees.

"If you lead the way, darling, I can stand here and say our thank-yous and point people in the right direction," I tell Lou. And now I've another motive: I don't want Ivor Hughes to escape. I've a quiz book of questions for him. I went in there to bury the past, and now I want to exhume it for some long overdue pathology.

"Yes, OK Mike; but where? What is the right direction? I don't see the wreaths."

"They're through that gate in the hedge," I explain with a hand signal. I don't know how she managed before satnavs, but I love all her facets: the arty, the sporty, the mumsy, the glammy – and the scatty, of course.

"I want to stay with you, Daddy," Emily pleads, clinging to the sleeve of my funereal Crombie in the stripy mittens that Mum knitted her. They're her little homage to her grandma. And she's been missing me while I've been up here, it seems.

"No, go with Mummy and Hannah, sweetheart. I'll only be a minute or two."

Aunty Pam and husband Brian and their family retinue emerge first from the chapel – one of those typifying the aggressive style of post-war crematorium architects, with its sawtooth gables trying to puncture the louring sky. They're the only other family mourners. Mum's brother Graham wasn't disposed to leave Rupert and their costa-lot villa in the winter. Once my cousins Robin, Rebecca and

9

Helen were like a brother and sisters to me, but Dad's death and Mum's isolationism severed our contacts and they've since receded far into the distance. They all follow Lou and the girls in a silent crocodile – but without the tears.

Then I'm explaining things to newly widowed Mrs Baldry – or Wayne's mum as she used to be before my primary school pal failed the eleven-plus and we drifted apart – and Mum's nearest neighbours Mr and Mrs Furr and Mrs Ruston, who've congregated in a foursome with a hundred-and-twenty-one years of knowing Mum between them, I've calculated. They all opt for the viewing but pass on the lunch at Owerston Hall.

"That's for family, love. I don't think it's for me, if you don't mind," says Mrs B, shoulder-hunching and shivering after the warmth of the chapel; and the others nod in agreement.

I've soon swapped farewells with the sexy Reverend Anne Shipman and her organist – it's priest apparently in the Church of England, but I think priestess suits her better. They hurried off to a burial on their home turf – well, underneath it. Why have I been ogling her – seeing kiss-me lips and a sanctified come-hither? I never noticed in her study last week. I've also had another dose of Lindop & Son's soothing linctus. It's the unctuous son in charge today, smothering with scripted sympathy like he's worried I might complain of short measure and call in Trading Standards. I said I'd collect the ashes on Wednesday. His men are stowing their trolley now, and I'm still waiting for Ivor Hughes.

It would've been the year after Dad died when he came into our lives – I was nine. He was writing disaster anniversary features for the *Argus* and interviewed Mum for one of them. I don't know what attracted her to him, but I was very anti at first, despite the allure of his car. Dad had become my hero and I didn't want anyone usurping his position or diminishing what little attention I was still getting from Mum. Anyway, they started to hit it off, and it triggered her renaissance – unless that happened before. I need time to replay that video at normal speed to work a few things out.

I hear the Daimler woken to go home, and purring at its cosseted life. What the hell's Ivor Hughes doing in there? Praying? I walk into the vestibule to take a look. He is praying – well, his head's bowed. Now I feel like a snooper, and slink back out.

The hearse has started its snail's pace uphill to the gates, canopied by the leafless branches. They're flailing themselves free of twigs as well now. The road's newly surfaced, but the temporary 10 mph signs are superfluous. I wonder what's the quickest speed it's ever been. And then I turn back to face the door and see him striding out as if he wants to overtake it – but he's looking towards me and has an outstretched hand.

"I'm Ivor Hughes, Michael. I was a friend of your mother once. I'm so sorry for you."

We shake hands, and he adds his left hand, doubling and prolonging our contact. It's like he's staking a claim and wants to hang on to me until the paperwork comes through. His eyes are moist, and I don't think it's because of the wind.

"Thank you," is all I reply, retrieving my hand.

"Sympathetic words are a poor salve at a time like this, I'm afraid. Done to death, most are, if you'll excuse the pun."

I smile and he's relieved; but I'm not up to saying anything yet. The Ivor in those remote scenes has become this man – well-known and yet a stranger – who's come to pray and cry and lament Mum's passing in a way that puts me to shame. But why? It doesn't make sense – and neither does his seeming attraction to me.

"Thanks for waiting. I needed a bit longer in there, see. I had a lot on my mind." He pauses – maybe to think about some of it again – before resuming. "Even after thirty years I recognised you as that young car spotter with hair as black as mine, but you probably don't remember me."

"I do now." My words are starting to flow. "I recognised you too, but in two stages: first as Ivor Hughes the safety guru and then as the Ivor with the beard and the Mini Cooper – the same man."

And despite the crow's-feet at his green eyes and the few grey hairs I can now see flecking the black, he could almost be the shaven double of the Ivor with the Mini Cooper still. Maybe my brain's manipulating its first image of him in preference to accepting the new one – the mind's eye tricking the optic nerves somehow. Poor Mum must've aged over forty years in the same time. He wouldn't have recognised her.

He looks wistful. "I've a Mini Cooper again, but it's not the same. I feel dwarfed by it... I didn't know I'd become a celeb. I can't believe that."

"Not to the wider world, maybe; but I'm an engineer. I heard you talk at a Global Process Safety Club do."

Now he's looking like he's unwrapped a precious gift. "There's a good thing then. I didn't expect that. It's something else we've got in common. Are you a safety engineer then, Michael?"

"Not any more; I've gone beyond. I'm a distribution manager now – but still with Omega Oil. It's a chance to realise a few ambitions." I can see his disappointment; I've taken his gift away. "Look, we're in the garden looking at the flowers and tributes, and then there's a buffet lunch. I'd like you to join us." It seems a good way to keep hold of him for my grilling about the past.

"There's a pity, but I've got other plans now. Sorry, and all that. I'm seeing one or two people I knew when I lived here – people I've kept in touch with."

Now I'm disappointed, and it probably shows, but his slick continuation was already up his sleeve.

"But my evening's free. Why don't you and your beautiful family come and have dinner with me?"

"Louise is taking the girls back home this afternoon – we live near Chelmsford – but I'd very much like to." It's Louise when I speak, not Lou, but she doesn't object to Lu-Lu at intimate moments.

"That's excellent. I'm staying at Owerston Hall. I expect you know it."

I nod and smile. "It's our lunch venue."

"There you are, then. Let's say eight o'clock, shall we? I'll meet you in the bar."

He puts his hand in the pocket of his short navy raincoat, and I glimpse a private satisfied smile – more like someone stowing an entrance ticket he's won than feeling for his driving gloves. But then he looks up and does smile at me, and sticks a firm hand on my shoulder.

"Bear up, Michael," he says, before turning away.

I swivel to watch his brisk step to his car. It's British racing green with a white top. I'm sure those were the colours before; I can see him slamming its door outside 10 Kilvert Road the first time he called.

I'm about to follow to check the mobile in my car for messages but decide against. Today's one day I'm allowed to relegate work to second place. As I enter the garden I can hear him zooming off, shot blasting his wheel arches with loose chippings. I tut-tut in mock dismay at a safety campaigner infringing the speed limit.

The swishing blades of Siberian air are blunted in here by a three-metre high hedge of yew fit to grace a stately home – but they're not deodorised. We're leeward of Corus today, and steel making is tainting the air. And tonight I'll be jolted awake by its percussion and look out of the window and see a furnace tap painting the sky red; and tomorrow there'll be more grit on my car and smuts on people's washing (if they dare hang it out). But despite all that I still like the place. It breathes, it snorts, it growls; it's got a life. I can't blame Ulcethorpe for fouling my childhood.

The mourners and wreaths are at the far end of the quadrilateral under the oak pergola that runs all round like an abbey cloister. It might bring a holy solemnity to some, but the blanched wood is more like the ribcage of a dinosaur to me. Anyway, the scene's an attractive composition: the variety of ages, groupings and poses; and the coloured accessories to some of the women's sombre coats like streamers and splashes from the floral drift at their feet.

Hannah's crouching in a ladylike way to read a card out to the Furrs. Lou and Emily are making a foursome with Mrs Ruston – whose jaunty black beret belies her wrinkles – and Mrs B, whose grey hair

13

straggles like a worn out mop. And Brian's doing his own stooping over a large tribute of scarlet roses. I've a camera in the car, but this isn't a wedding. People don't do photos at funerals, and I don't want to start a trend.

I catch Lou's eye with a wave and she waves in return, but Pam walks over to meet me.

"Who was that little dark bloke, Mikey? He hasn't come in." She never misses a trick.

"Ivor Hughes."

I'm glad I've got an aunt like her: lively, humorous, sixty-five going on fifty, always bouncing. Mum might've been the same if she'd escaped the depression and done make-up and hair tinting and stuff – and given up smoking and avoided the cancer, of course. And Pam's been fantastic since Mum went into the hospice, coming over twice a week from Sheffield while I drove up at weekends.

"Yes?"

"Well, that's who it was."

"Who is Ivor Hughes, then? Don't prat around – not today."

"Sorry." Pam's also a good sport, but I shouldn't be teasing now. It's part of the relief I've felt since that phone call in the middle of the night: my release to freedom – but I can't be telling her that. "He was a man friend Mum had after Dad was killed. Maybe you didn't know."

"That was him? I knew, but I'd forgotten the name. Why ever would he turn up? And how would he know? How weird."

"Yep, I agree. I'm seeing him tonight; I hope to find out."

Her eyes focus inwards on to some spot in her mind, and she offers the hushed commentary appropriate at a funeral.

"He sounded really nice. She made out it was only platonic, but I knew it was more – I could hear the excitement underneath. I was over the moon for her… They'd been to a party and she'd bought a super dress for it; and they were going out for the whole day – the next weekend, I think, with Michael, with you. But then she went quiet about him – evasive, even… I pushed her but all she'd say was

14

it hadn't worked out; she couldn't trust herself to judge men. And she shut me up if I ever asked about it again… And there were no more boyfriends; no more of anything much."

It all resonates with my hazy impressions. Yes, the super red dress – but it wasn't super. There was another word, an odd word. And before the red dress I remember her red blouse, matching the red berries in The Rowan Way.

Pam switches from the past to the present. "And thirty years later he turns up again, when it's too blooming late. I can't believe it. You've been reminiscing with him, have you?"

"Not really. We were talking shop. I know him. Well, know of him."

"Mikey, you're having me on again."

"No, honestly. He's well known in my walk of life – or what was mine in CSS. You know, process safety and risk management and all that boring stuff. He's from the valleys, butty; a right little maverick, he is."

"That's a lousy accent. Just tell it to me straight."

"I am. I recognised him as Ivor Hughes the safety expert, I thought what the fuck is he doing here, and then I twigged. Let's move back, shall we. I need to circulate before the neighbours disappear."

We join Brian, who's been loyally reading the tributes on the wreaths. "Who's Ivor, Mike?"

"Bloody hell, Brian." But I quickly interpose an apology. "Sorry. Sorry, Bri. It's only that he seems to be taking over – in my mind, I mean. It's my fault, not yours. Pam'll tell you about him. Anyway, why do you ask?"

He's a good foil for Pam, stolid and successful; but rather too keen on passing on his lifetime's knowledge and experience so it's not wasted. He's looking miffed now. "The card on those roses: *Marlene, you is, you is, forever. Ivor.* That's why."

"Let me have a look," says Pam, bending over the wreath. "He must've been very keen," she muses. "'You is, you is': it reminds me of that song in *Porgy and Bess* – 'Bess, you is my woman now, you is, you is'. And red roses – how romantic. And how sad."

15

"Anyway, I'd better talk to the Ettisham Park folk. I can catch up with you all at lunch, but they're not coming," I say, to excuse my move towards Lou. With her Scandinavian looks and blonde hair flowing from under her fur hat she could be an oligarch's wife – but she's mine. What've I done to deserve her?

"Daddy, that was more than two minutes," Emily complains.

I muss her equally blonde hair, which is pinned up into a pleat. "Sorry, sweetie."

"Daddy, don't."

"Ooh, sorry again. I had to talk to a man." I turn to Lou. "Did you notice that small dark chap when we came out?"

"No, Mike. I was looking at the back of your coat collar. It's not turned down properly." She makes the necessary adjustment. It's odd that an art lover like Lou sometimes fails to see the bigger picture.

Mrs B gives verbal support. "That's right, Louise, look after him. They need it."

"Well, you've missed him now," I continue. "He was Mum's boyfriend after Dad died. It didn't last long."

"I wouldn't have thought she'd been into boyfriends and things," says Lou.

"No, darling, but you didn't meet her until years later. She was different for a short while then."

"I remember it," says Mrs B. "She bought a red dress for him – a real bobby-dazzler."

That was the word.

After asking after Wayne – a warrant officer at Tidworth long settled into army life – I move on to give Hannah support with the Furrs and Mrs Ruston, not that she needs any. In many ways she's like me, looks included – the Spanish heritage from Granddad Searle's Beer ancestry – and is even tough enough to resist peer pressure. She phones and texts but doesn't blog or Bebo; she prefers board games to games consoles; she'll download music but wouldn't shop on line. She steers a course of her own.

16

"Hannah's just telling us she's at Grade six, Mr Paine," says Mrs Ruston, the awe in her voice proving her understanding of ABRSM piano exams.

"Yes, she's way in front of me now."

"That's because you don't practise enough, Dad."

"I don't have the time in this job, sweetheart." And in case Lou heard, I add, "Not yet, but I will."

"And what do you want to be when you grow up, Hannah?"

This comes from Mr Furr, who's demonstrating that the tonsure of a monk and a grey walrus moustache don't hit it off together. Another shivering pensioner, he probably wishes Homburgs and trilbys were back in fashion on a day like today. And then he's completely floored by her striking answer.

"I'm going to be a human rights lawyer and be in charge of Liberty when Shami Chakrabarti retires."

Before we leave I stoop to read the kindest thoughts and deepest sympathies and most affectionate remembrances from Mum's few friends and relatives. It's time we invented some new phrases. There's a wreath from Graham, at least, with godetias and gaillardias in those hot España colours; and it's arrived with a cryptic message: *Lena, why didn't you come to us? All our love, Gray and Rupert.* Come for what? A holiday? To live with them? She'd never mentioned it. He must've become totally out of touch with what she'd become.

My mind's on these questions – possibly unanswerable unless Pam knows – as we scurry towards the chapel on our way to the car park. I've Lou and Hannah hugging an arm each and Emily's skipping ahead – not the right form of motion for a crematorium, but I've let it pass.

"Mike, why cremate your mum and not bury her with your dad?" says Lou.

It's rather late to ask this now, when it's a fait accompli – or almost. Maybe I should've discussed the pros and cons with her before, instead of doing it off my own bat as usual.

"Because she always wanted a cremation, as long as I can remember.

17

And near the end she told me again, 'don't put me in the cemetery with your father'."

"That's an odd way of saying it. What about the ashes?"

"She didn't say, and I didn't want to upset her by talking about it. I was hoping there might be a mention in the will."

"Couldn't they be scattered here?"

"Yes, but I was thinking of Dad's grave, mixed in with the chippings. I ought to go there to pay my respects, and check the council are earning the maintenance money."

"I've never seen a grave, Daddy," says Emily.

"It's ages since I've seen his – or his mum's. But there's no time today."

Gravestones and tablets are clinging things. They're the way the deceased clutch at you, demanding remembrance on their territory. However much they live on in your mind, you avoid their memorials at the risk of a guilty conscience. I'm feeling guilty now. Cremation and then a scattering of the ashes is the answer – a real scattering, not just a sprinkle on the grave.

'Don't put me in the cemetery with your father': yes, it does sound odd – more like a strong aversion to Dad than to being buried. Yet she never criticised him. But then she hardly spoke about him at all.

I've assumed not talking about their husbands is the norm for widows – not wanting to stir up the sediment of their married lives for fear of clouding the present with ancient grief. But who knows? I never pressed Mum, anyway; and now when it's too late I wish I had. The sum total of what I'll ever know about Dad is already in my head, and I feel deprived without the whole story – something like when I read *The Mystery of Edwin Drood*. But with Dad I know about the ending, his horrific crushing and incineration; all the blank pages come before. At least, with Ivor Hughes' advent I might discover something more about Mum.

TWO

Visitor parking is empty now, apart from our two cars. "Who's going with Mummy and who's coming with me?" I ask.

"I'll go with Mum," says Hannah, releasing my arm. I guessed she would, to spread the Paine brains.

"Goody, goody!" Emily skips on to my Beemer as I zap open its doors. I think she wants to catch up on time with me.

"How do I get there, Mike?" asks Lou.

"Follow me."

"But if we're separated."

"We're not going to be separated." And I twist to kiss the gleaming lips and breathe the scent of my Cossack princess. "There, I've glued us back together." I often think I'm living the last line of a fairy tale: marrying Lou and living happily ever after – I hope.

"Silly. Now where is it?"

"You go out of town on Ettisham Road, and Owerston's the first left turn after the speed derestriction. It's about a mile and then you take the road to Pellingham. The Hall's down there after you leave the village. There's a big sign."

"After you leave Pellingham?"

"No, Owerston. That's why it's Owerston Hall, darling. The postcode's DN21 4UC if you want to use your toy."

"Write it down, Mike."

"No, I can remember it, Mum." Hannah's taking charge.

But we make the journey without GPS navigation, the smug grin of the Prius and the tense face at its steering wheel prominent in my rear-view mirror all the way.

Lou chose the car. She's not interested in petrol-electric hybrid technology but she knows about global warming. It's one of the scientific things she's added to her portfolio of art and style. Omega's car policy doesn't restrict on CO_2 yet, but I did take note, and chose a diesel 525 with a pretty good rating.

I signal early for Lou and turn off Radio 1. I'd have had Composer of the Week on, or a CD, but let Emily choose.

"Oh, Daddy!"

"We're there now, sweetheart." And I can't take any more of the racket – yet another sign of impending middle age.

Owerston Hall's been a hotel since its sell-off by some descendent of Edward Everard, the steel baron – the man who put Ulcethorpe on the map with the agglomeration of five villages into one town.

I used to stay when auditing or reviewing projects at our Whittonsea refinery. It's Victorian gothic, and in brick and stone a scaled-down reminder of the V&A I walked past during those four years in the 80s after persuading Mum that Imperial College was the best place for a chemical engineering degree. It was also the furthest away.

The hotel rooms are like honeymoon suites: canopied beds, thick drapes, William Morris wallpaper, antique furniture – that sort of thing. My buddies from Houston lapped it up, but really it was OTT for single guys (and that's 'men' in my lexicon). It's £140 plus a night, but quite painless on the Omega AmEx.

Mum moaned about me not staying at Kilvert Road. I always visited, but couldn't face a night there with her in that mausoleum replaying scenes from my childhood: feeling miserable and unloved and puzzling how to please.

After parking next to Pam's gas guzzling RX8 – more technology, but no longer cutting edge – I wait for Lou to reverse in alongside before we open our doors. Then we're exposed to that wind again, which really is cutting edge.

"Mum said you've stayed here, Dad, and it's really wicked," Hannah says, impressed.

"Yep, a few times."

"Why didn't we stay here, Daddy?" asks Emily.

"Because we were fine at Grandma's."

She's not convinced; I see a very protruding pout. "Next time, may we come here?"

"Yep, if we come to Ulcethorpe again." But there'll be no need, so I won't have to shell out.

Lou consoles her with a hug and we march up the steps, through the half-glazed doors and on to the marble and slate chequerboard floor in the lofty oak-panelled hall.

"Oh, look! That's gross!" says Hannah.

The Everards' famed philanthropy didn't extend to the animals of Africa, the stuffed heads of a good few of whom are mounted on the walls. With some of the weaponry of the natives – assegais, knobkerries and shields – and two glass cases of memorabilia, it's like a display in a fusty old-fashioned museum. Apparently these trophies from long dead big game hunters came with the house like sitting tenants. I'm used to them but it's a shock to the girls.

"Ooh! Poor things," Emily adds. "Daddy, I don't like it here, after all."

The young woman with cropped white coiffure at the desk is similarly static – like a marble bust in a white blouse and grey jacket, but her eyes are grey. She swivels them from Emily to me as a sign she's alive and not just a stunning exhibit.

"I'm Michael Paine. I've booked a funeral lunch here."

Her lips soften. "Good afternoon, sir. You are in Ancholme room. It is to right at end of corridor." And she points out our way.

I thought as much: Eastern European, probably Polish, and probably with a doctorate in astrophysics, but earning more on reception here. I take a chance and show off with one of the phrases I learnt on due diligence at Gaz Slaszka: "Dziękuję bardzo."

I was right. "Proszę bardzo," comes back – and with a smile. Directions followed, phrases explained and coats deposited we join the others.

* * *

I was told the room could accommodate thirty with ease – but not all comfortably seated, it turned out, with only two sofas and four armchairs. But other than that minor glitch – the third time today my planning's been shown up – everything else here has been excellent. But it comes at a price, of course.

"Shall I get you one as well?" Brian asks, as he brings a coffee over to where I'm standing.

"No thanks, Bri; not during the day."

"So what does your empire consist of, apart from petrol stations? I've only had details third hand, via your mum and Pam."

"Well, actually I'm not responsible for the filling stations, only for the fuel getting there. They come under retailing. I'm Southern Distribution – it covers our main fuel depot at Brentfield, the pipelines from it, another smaller depot, and the tanker fleet."

"Oh. Quite a mixed bunch, then."

"Yep. But the depots are just storage and pumping – pretty routine stuff. It's the logistics side that's difficult."

"Now, Brentfield; that's west London, isn't it?"

"You're thinking of Brentford. No, it's near Brentwood in Essex."

"Well, anyway, that's where you keep most of the petrol?"

"Yep, but not just petrol – there's diesel, kerosene and fuel oil as well."

Brian breaks off to drink some coffee, as if he's preparing for a long cross-examination. He's an accountant, and was finance director at a Sheffield cutlery firm that's still in business, so he knows his onions. Like me, he realises the devil's in the detail. I sense him wanting to get to grips with the flow of fuels around the country and on to the forecourt. I'll have to oblige, and yet I wish I was cross-examining someone myself: Ivor Hughes. My mind keeps springing back to his last minute arrival. There's no sense in it. Why would he come?

Brian clinks his cup on to his saucer and resumes. "Right. So how do you bring it all in?"

"We've got a big pipeline from each refinery – Wiremouth, where I used to work, and Whittonsea. They send down everything in batches."

"Oh, underground pipes; I assumed rail tankers."

"Not to my depots. And we don't use rail for supply either, only road. There're fifteen-hundred miles of these pipelines criss-crossing the country, Bri."

"I hadn't realised."

"And millions of tonnes pumped through each year. You're not the only one not to know."

"So how much petrol etcetera do you have at this Brentfield?"

"It varies, but over ninety-thousand tonnes when we're full up."

"Christ! It's a huge site, then. All that could make a big bang and bonfire – bigger than Boroughcliff."

"It's all under tight control. You don't have to worry."

"Maybe that's what Alec Masters was telling someone at the Rotary Club over a gin and tonic while your dad was agonising over whether that leak would explode. That was his name, wasn't it – the works manager who went on to higher things?"

"Yep… If he was saying that it would've been typical: bullshit covering incompetence."

"Well, Mike, now you've got the chance to demonstrate your competence – show how you run a tight ship."

"I will do."

"Good. And you said you had other pipelines, as well?"

"Yep. Two smaller ones – to a second depot on the Medway, and for aviation fuel to Stansted."

"Mm. Much more to it than I thought. And then there's all the road transport."

"Which'll be on contract soon, thanks to me. An aspirin for the headaches of fleet management, I hope. I've been negotiating a deal with a bulk liquids outfit called Tankerfreight alongside my traffic manager – before he's pensioned off. I'm having to leave it to him while I'm up here." But it'll be my head on the block if we get it wrong.

Mum picked a bad time to die.

"Contract delivery's nothing new, Mike. I'm only surprised Omega's not done it before. Provided it's only the fringe specialisms, contracting out can work very well. But there's always the idiot that wants to go further – contract out manufacturing itself, some would."

I smile at Brian's witticism. He's out of touch. It's common practice already, and spreading like a tsunami wave.

"Anyway, this promotion – a step to greater things?" he asks.

"That's what I want."

"Like what?"

"UK Logistics Director… then maybe into operations management… then even a European Something-or-other. Who knows?"

"Mm. You're aiming high. You've got it all mapped out."

"Yep."

"What does Louise think about it?"

"In favour." I know it's a fib, but she can't hear me with all the chatter. She'll see it my way in the end.

"Well, best of luck, then." And he slaps my arm and smiles and moves away.

I've been hoarding the stress of the tanker contract like a miser, not letting Lou have a glimpse. I didn't want her knowing I wasn't in total control. From the start she's been lukewarm about the move, not encouraging, like I expected – worried whether I could hack it, I suppose. She said I should be proud of the job I was already doing – she was. Maybe I should've opened up to Brian on a couple of issues still bugging me – on the tanker fleet valuation, for one – and got some sound advice, but I missed the chance.

* * *

Now Robin and Rebecca and their families have departed and I'm on one of the sofas. Emily's giving my knee pins and needles and partly blocking my view of Helen sitting opposite. It's staggering she hasn't a man in tow, with her looks. Pam's been saying how she's a dead ringer for Mum in her early thirties, and remembering the photos from before Dad died, I don't disagree. We've been mainly talking about Mum. After all, it is her day. How she never recovered from Dad's death – all those nevers, in fact: never socialising, never working, never driving, never holidaying, never truly living at all; with just that one bursting *Very* light dispelling the gloom when Ivor Hughes came on the scene. But also how on rare occasions she could resurrect the spirit of her earlier self – chatty, interested, lively, sympathetic – and shine through her Capiz shell defences when offered the right spark: my Albert Hall graduation, our Swaledale wedding, the girls' births, and Pam and Bri's ruby anniversary.

"I'm lucky, Michael. I only saw her at her best, and so that's how I'll remember her," says Helen, leaning to put her empty glass on the table beside the sofa.

The drinks are finished. "I think it's time to go," I announce, and jog Emily off my knee.

I get up gingerly in case the numbness undermines my leg, and Helen stands at the same time. Without warning she takes advantage of our closeness to give me a consoling hug. It's a shock, but not just because of her tenderness and my tremor. For an instant, as her face closes with mine, she's Mum and I'm me with my O-level results slip. It's one of those rare moments in my life when she showed some love – albeit compromised by reticence. And I've a sense of other hugs years earlier, proper enveloping ones. I wish I could remember them.

After donning our funereal coats we're now in the darkening reception hall. The girls are flicking through glossy magazines at a side table to avoid eye contact with the wildebeests and their friends on the walls, and I'm establishing an acquaintance with the white sculpture – Alicia, now I'm close enough to read her lapel badge. I'm also parting with £600, or will be at the end of the month. But it's been worth it; and the thought of inheriting upwards of two hundred times as much after the house sale is fair consolation.

"You have been in Poland, Mr Paine?" Alicia asks.

Before replying I finish the Michael L Paine signature, grandiloquently extended from plain M Paine when I opened my student account to go to Imperial. Then I look up into her pale eyes, but they're impossible to read.

"Yes, on business: Katowice."

"On business; yes, it is not for tourists there."

"But we stayed in Krakow. That is for tourists."

She allows herself a slight smile, but it doesn't seem to be for me. "It is my home. You see Wawel?"

"Yes, but we hadn't enough time. You've left a beautiful city."

This time she does smile at me. "Yes. Do I staple these for you?"

"No, thank you. But we made time for Auschwitz. Those words – 'Arbeit macht frei' – still chill me now."

"Yes, and me. I went when I was at school: Oświęcim by train and then a bus; and then, if that was not enough, another bus to Birkenau. I close my eyes and see it all again." And she does close her eyes, and presumably does see it all again.

And I see a beautiful death mask, which maybe isn't so inappropriate. It's only for a few privileged seconds. People are very vulnerable with their eyes shut. I feel like her master, and she's my slave.

She resumes her inscrutable stare, her defences reinstated. "Thank you, Mr Paine." She hands me the paperwork and my card. "Do widzenia."

"Do zobaczenia," I reply. It makes her lift her eyebrows. But if she's still on duty I shall be seeing her later.

"Practising your Polish? I heard you, Mikey," says Pam, as I approach the others.

"Just Berlitz phrases," I reply, moving on towards the door. "Come on, girlies."

"Dad!" Hannah objects.

"Sorry, sweetheart." They've both become touchy about certain endearments. Pet and poppet, the ones once used on me, are definite

26

no-nos now. "Pam, did you understand that card from Graham? 'Why didn't you come to us?'"

"No. I meant to ask you. She never said anything about invites to Spain."

"We'll never know, then. I shan't be asking him."

"I might, next time he rings."

Outside, the wind continues its swashing attack in the waning light. The grey and silver cars are almost ethereal in the gloom, but my red one still signals itself. Its colour follows Omega's safety advice on visibility reducing risk. I wrote it myself; but Lou would choose silver.

We exchange various combinations of handshakes, hugs, and kisses – after all, there're twelve farewell pairings – but other than with Pam I'm content with two handshakes. And then they're inserting themselves into the Mazda, Helen through one of the dinky rear doors that Emily tells us are really dizzy. I tune in to the turbine tone of the Wankel rotors, and we wave as they power past and disappear round the bush-cushioned bend in the drive, Pam flashing the hazard lights as final farewell.

"Our turn now, darling," I say. "Ring me when you get back."

"Come home soon, Mike. I'm sorry about last night. It didn't seem right, somehow."

"I know. As soon as the house is cleared, I'm on my way."

We hug and kiss, and I whisper, "Love you, Lu-Lu," in her ear before pressing my lips on the delicate convolutions. My other lovelies just get the hugs and kisses. "Keep up the texting," I say, before we move to the cars.

"Are you OK for the main road?" I ask Lou.

"I think so."

"I know, Dad," chimes in Hannah.

"Right. I'll check my messages before I leave."

They settle in as the interior lights fade, and then the headlamps flood the tarmac and the tail lamps red-eye to the rear. I wave as Lou steers this second sample of Japanese high-tech past me, with no more hum than from Mum's coffin this morning.

But it's not a good analogy when your loved ones are driving 200 miles on a windy winter evening. I used statistics to convince Omega's European bosses that our next fatality would be on the roads and not in the refineries when I pushed through the new vehicle safety policy. I've an agitated mix of emotions watching the Toyota go: I'm sad and I'm worried, which is understandable; but I also feel like an explorer on a precipitous edge, fearful about the descent and the hazards below. I can't explain that.

THREE

I'm back at Kilvert Road by 4 o'clock and sprawl on the sofa. I'm glad my evening's spoken for. I wasn't looking forward to yet another one here on my own, especially tonight.

Mum lived in this house for forty years. It's imbued with her – the evidence all around, and the dossier in my head. The smoking: the giveaway smell, her stock of Embassy stacked by the TV, all the ashtrays, the burn marks, the white surfaces turned buff; and the sound of her cough and the emphysema-sufferer's wheeze. And the depression: the doctor's pills and over-the-counter remedies, the clutter and grime, the shabby furnishings, the unchanged décor; and the sight of her sitting hunched and distant until you spoke and dragged out a response. And the hoarding: the women's magazines and free papers, the tinned stuff and tea and sugar, the chock-a-block freezer; and her pathetic pleasure at buying and stashing even more of it. She made the place her fortress, and I can't help feeling uneasy, as if I might be locked back in after being free for twenty years.

Anyway, I've got that slot for some serious memory download if I can get the technology to work. I'll start with that day going to the cemetery, when Mum's blouse matched the masses of red berries we saw in The Rowan Way. We often used to visit then, but that must've been in August. I'm sure something happened and Mum started to recover. She just takes the flowers off me but it feels like a huge relief after the atmosphere when we started out...

* * *

We're all dressed up so we could've got a flipping taxi there. It's two buses, otherwise; and this number 15's like a ruddy oven. The window's stuck and the seat's plastic and all sticky. It's stickier where you sit, under your legs and bottom. I were testing; but Mum said stop fidgeting. She's feeling a bit off-colour, she said. It's off-colour today; but she's always feeling something: 'really down' or 'too tired' or 'all headachy' or 'under the weather', and things like that. And then she gets shirty with me. I wonder if she'll ever be like she used to be before Dad died.

Now we're going past the Rovers stadium. I haven't been for a year. I wonder when I'll go again. Mum didn't want me going alone with Dad's friend Keith, and Wayne's dad doesn't like football – and neither does Ian's.

I hope the other bus is waiting, because that bus station stinks like the lavatories at my school. And someone'd done a sick in the waiting room the only time we went in there. Ulcethorpe's a smelly old place – not just the pong from the steelworks.

Hooray! I can see it, another Lindsey RoadCar one. I wait for the brakes to go pssh before getting off. Mum's walking the wrong way. "There's the Bardby bus, Mum, that number nine."

She turns and points to the exit. "Michael, I know. We're going to the florist's first. Why don't you listen?"

I did, but I forgot. I do my puffing noise to show I'm annoyed. It's like the sound of them brakes, but I don't think she can hear. We didn't get the flowers at the greengrocer's today. It's a poor selection, Mum said. Where do they get them from, anyway? It can't be from people's gardens… Everard Park? I don't know.

We go to the flower shop and then have to stand waiting for another number nine. It's got better seats; they're covered with that carpet stuff. I offer to hold the flowers to be a help to Mum. She lets me, and I keep them pointed straight up like when they grow. Bardby's a better part of town than where we live. The houses are bigger and there's a lot more trees in all the roads to keep off the flipping sun. Dad used to live here with Grandma Paine when he were a boy.

We get off the bus by the Corner Cafe and walk round into The Rowan Way. The trees are loaded with them little red berries. They're called mountain ash, Mum said, but there's no mountains anywhere round here. There must be millions, so it's a pity you can't eat them. The colour's the same as Mum's new blouse.

There's a lot of ace cars to see in this road – Jags and Rovers and that. I look in at every gateway, and then I see one what's really rare, so do my emergency stop – eek!

"Look at that, Mum. It's in my Observer book: Austin A-ninety Atlantic Convertible." It's easy to spot because it's got an extra light in the middle, like the eye on a Dalek. Dad gave me the book. He had it on his birthday when he were eleven. Grandma Paine's written in it, and then he wrote in it underneath for me: *this is yours now, Laddo; spot on; love from Dad.* It's my best book.

"Mm, that's snazzy. Just right for a day like today." Mum's come back to look. I didn't expect it. I thought she'd say, 'Come on, we haven't time,' or something. And she likes it too, really likes it. I can tell by her voice. "And that's a lovely house, too." She sounds cheerful for once.

"When are we going to get another car, Mum?" It seems like a good time to ask again and not get my head bitten off.

"I don't know." And then she says, "Soon," as if she means it. Then she asks me, "Shall I hold the flowers now to give you a rest? I'm feeling a lot brighter. The sun on all those berries has clicked a switch."

"What do you mean, Mum?" I ask, as I pass them over.

"I just feel I've changed – like a butterfly when it comes out of its chrysalis and gets ready to fly. I can't really explain, but it feels good."

"Oh." I still don't understand, but I'm glad.

* * *

Yes, she started her transformation then, I'm sure. And I had a different feeling after it. I glanced sideways at her as we walked on to the

31

cemetery, like an admirer thinking how good she looked. I was proud that she was my mum.

Inside the gates I remember we coincided with a cortège. I don't think I'd been up close to one before. It gave me a chance to look at some rather different cars, but I'm more interested in who's inside...

* * *

"Look, Mum, a Daimler... and an Austin Princess... and another."

She looks up from filling the jug. The Daimler's the one with the coffin in it and men with bowler hats. The others are stuffed with people wearing dark clothes. They look like dummies in a shop, staring out like that. Maybe Mum and everybody looked the same when they came with Dad.

We follow the cars. They're all black and shiny like Grandma Paine's piano. I like trying to play it when we go there. She said I could have lessons on it, but Mum said it's too far to go every week and then in between for a practice. I think she meant it's too often. It's a pity we haven't got room for a piano at home.

The cars are going very slow with hardly any sound, but we still can't keep up. There used to be a lot of black cars in the olden days, but they died out – like the people coming here to be buried. Now they only use them for going to cemeteries. They're making a reflection in the road called a mirage. People see them in deserts when they're thirsty – like I am now. The tombstones along this bit have got angels and vases and things on top. I don't know why – the people underneath won't care. They're so white they dazzle my eyes so I have to squint. I need some flipping sunglasses.

When we get to Dad's grave I hold the water and the flowers again while Mum gets the dead ones out of the urn. The water's making my arm ache. A pint of water weighs a pound and a quarter, Dad used to say. There must be a gallon in here, so that's ten pounds. Mum's in my way but I know the words off by heart.

32

IN LOVING MEMORY

of

ALAN MICHAEL PAINE

BORN APRIL 14TH 1943
DIED AUGUST 12TH 1974

Requiescat in pace

The last three are in Latin. Grandma Paine wanted them because she had the same on Granddad Paine's gravestone in France. It's a dead language, she said. It's what you can put on gravestones instead of *Rest in peace*.

"Pass me the jug and flowers, pet. You could put these in that wire basket for me."

We do a swap. The old bunch is crispy at the top but the stalks are still slimy. They should've lasted longer. Some of these graves have got plastic flowers what look really nice. Them relatives don't have to keep buying fresh ones at the flower shop – or even come here at all. Flipping heck, it's hot. I really need a drink. There should be a ruddy café in here. Someone should empty this basket; it's chock-a-block.

I look over at Mum pushing stalks through the holes in the holder. Her hair keeps falling forward and getting in the way. It's like two brown curtains. She should tie them back.

It's a pity Mum said I weren't old enough to see Dad's coffin put in the ground under there. I wonder if they wrapped him up like a mummy, so if the coffin's dug up and opened and that stuff taken off, Dad would be like he were. Only I can't remember what he looked like. It's a good job we've got the photos to look at. Them pictures are what's in my head now.

It's waking up in the night and Mum looking frightened, I can remember; and all that black smoke in the sky next morning, and her crying and saying he wouldn't be coming home. I'd rather forget all that.

Mum stands and looks at the flowers, and then looks round for me. I'm feeling fed up and kicking the grass by the basket where the mower's missed. I can hear it cutting somewhere else now.

She calls over. "We'll go into that little café by the bus stop for an ice cream or a fizzy on the way home."

Good. They do ice cream sodas so I can have both.

"Now come and think of Dad for a minute or two," she says.

She keeps smiling as I walk towards her, and makes her eyebrows go up high. It makes me smile too. Yes, she's a lot more cheerful now, so she's cheering me up. She puts her arm on my shoulder and we stand in front of the grave.

It's like a two minutes silence to remember the war. Usually when we come I think of Dad and me doing things together, but today's special because it's a year since he died. At first I don't know what to think of what's different; but then I have a feeling I might do a job like Dad's one day. He'd be pleased. It's like he told me what to think. But how can people make things happen when they're dead?

* * *

I remember the phone ringing almost as soon as we got home – when I had sweat leaking from my armpits on to my shirt, felt conspicuous, and was relieved to get indoors.

Mum answered and then told me to go up and wash and change back into my scruffy clothes. I went out to the staircase, but sat on the bottom step to listen. It was one of my two listening steps – the other was one down from the top so there was a backrest. I'd got into the habit of listening to Mum on the phone to Aunty Pam and Grandma Searle as compensation for her not telling me anything. Fortunately we kept the doors open downstairs because she thought it made the house seem bigger – like they're open now. I think that was when I first heard mention of Ivor Hughes in amongst Mum's broadcast of good news.

I can feel the stair nosing against my back, and a cooling draught coming down from above; and can smell the fibres of the carpet – springy and clean and nearly new then...

* * *

"No, Agnes is going this afternoon – with a wreath, she said... Yes, I thought that too; but widowed mother, only son. And that's me now. I ought to understand. I hope I don't get so possessive. I must ask her to tea before we go away... Yes, Dadda's driving down on Friday to collect us. Listen Pam, I'm going to learn to drive, and buy a car. Decided on the way, today – had really good vibes about the future..."

Hooray! Mum did mean it when she said.

"Yes, I know you have, but I wasn't ready then. Michael can help me choose it..."

That's ace – a lot better than going into Zodiac for a Dinky. But how do you choose a real car? It's not like they're all in one shop.

"Yes, and so would Dadda, but I'm going to do it myself, and spend some of the money that's left... I won't be, because that's another thing I've decided. I'm going back to work... Yes, Brown and Beasley or somewhere else... I'd thought of that. I can get my speeds back up at the College... Well, hours to suit, I hope, till he's eleven..."

Hours to suit who? Me, I suppose. I go to a new school then. I hope I pass that exam.

"Yes, I think it will – the new me... Yes, just about. I've a few bits still to iron. Going to clear out Alan's clothes and things this afternoon. Wish me luck..."

I could help with Dad's things too – but I'm not supposed to be listening, so I can't say anything.

"Yes, they rang yesterday. A reporter's coming tomorrow morning – an Ivor Hughes... You're always hoping, aren't you?... Well, I suppose I am, in a way – there must be someone who'll turn me on... No. I'm sure I told you... Yes, I want to, but can't feel it – well, not with anyone I know. It's just in my head. I'm a sexual anorexic.

35

Anyway, how are things your end?…"

What does she mean: 'I'm for sex or Anna wrecks it'? Mum's too old for sex now. And who's Anna, anyway?

"Oh, is it next week too? I'd forgotten… Oh, two weeks… I bet they are. Well, send us a card and have a lovely time… No, I wasn't; but we were just going to have something to eat. I'll ring you after six for a proper chinwag… Yes; and thanks again for ringing… Bye."

I climb up our twelve stairs on my hands and feet so Mum can't hear me. After putting my other shorts and a tee shirt on I go back down to the kitchen the dining room way, because last time I went through the sitting room. I like to take it in turns. Our house has got a really titchy hall with one door on either side and only the stairs straight ahead. Mum says she always wanted a proper hall, so I don't know why we still live here.

"That was Aunty Pam. They'll be in Spain while we're in Scarborough. They're going in an aeroplane. Becky and Robin and Helen are getting all excited. It's their first time."

I'm not bothered about aeroplanes. "If I had a car like Uncle Brian's I'd go in that, I would." He's got a new Volvo 264.

"Spain's a long way, pet. There, you can take your Sandwich Spread sandwich and lemon barley through now."

I lead the way to our round table and Mum sits opposite me. I can't have another fizzy because of her rules.

"What car should we have?" she asks, before I can have a bite.

It's a silly question. There's so many. "Not so big: just two doors – but fast. Brm, brm!"

"Yes, but what? You're the expert."

"We could have a Ford Escort GT, like Wayne's dad." That's quite fast.

"We don't have to have the same."

She asks me and then doesn't like what I say. "I know: you could get a magazine. Wayne's dad gets *Autocar*. They test a different car every week."

"Do you have to keep saying 'Wayne's dad' all the time? It's really irritating. I don't want to hear about Mr Baldry."

What have I done wrong now? I make my puffing noise. Mum being nice didn't last long. "Well, I haven't got a dad, have I?"

"No... No, of course you haven't. I'm sorry, pet," she says, and then gives me a nice smile, which makes me feel better. "Anyway, I'll have a look in Smiths. Maybe there's a mag with all the cars in."

That'd be ace. I eat my dinner thinking about all the cars I like and the ones I don't. Mum eats her salad sandwich and reads one of her magazines. I don't know which one, but they're all the same – *Women's This* or *Women's That*.

"Mum."

"Yes."

"You said I could go round to Wayne's when we came home."

"Well, if you've finished. Have you got that 5p from yesterday?"

I start nodding my head.

Mum carries on talking. "Come back to tell me if you're going to the park, won't you. And thank Mrs Baldry for having you. Don't keep nodding. You're not eating now; you're allowed to speak."

"Yeah, I know." I stop nodding. "I'll go, then. Bye-bye, Mum."

Mum just shakes her head and smiles.

* * *

We went next door that evening to Mr and Mrs Furr's – the one and only time, I think. I played with their twin toddlers, Dan and Ben, before they were put to bed. You could only tell them apart because Rose Furr had sewn their names on their clothes. Then and afterwards they made me puzzle over the pros and cons of having a twin: always having someone to play with, but someone with identical thoughts and ideas. I decided I'd rather keep my world private.

Afterwards, Mum unlocked our front door in the twilight, her bangle sliding down her bare arm. And I'm feeling bloated with a full bladder and distended stomach, wanting to pee and fart...

* * *

"You can be getting ready for bed, pet. I need to phone Aunty Pam. I said I would after six and now it's nearly nine."

I'm full up. I shouldn't have had seconds of that blackberry and apple pie. I can hardly climb the stairs.

"Guess who... Yes, I know. Sorry. We got an invitation to the Furrs' for tea. They thought I might need cheering up, with it being the anniversary... Yes, wasn't it? Dennis came round when I was clearing Alan's things, and by then I was feeling a bit edgy... No, not sorting the clothes; but there were one or two things I found... Well, it started with stuff hidden in an old jacket: a plastic hair slide, but not one of mine, and a photo of a girl just like me at thirteen or so. That gave me quite a turn..."

I can't listen any more. I need to do a wee. It must be all that fizzy I've had – but Mum didn't stop me. I do it as quick as I can and don't wash my hands, but by the time I can sit down and listen again I've missed quite a bit.

"I might be silly, but it all made me think I didn't really know Alan. And it got worse when I read one of his poems. It was in a little book I found with his nineteen-sixty diary... A girl. I don't know who – maybe the one in the photo. It started off: *She who I adore, I also abhor, for she is a whore...*"

Flipping heck, what does that mean? It might rhyme but it's just nonsense.

"Yes, very. I only read it because it followed on from one of his school mag poems. I'd flipped through to see if I could find any. I remember Agnes reciting some to me when we were courting... To boost Alan's image, I suppose – or to put me down. I bet she didn't know about that one..."

Why wouldn't Grandma know it if she read out his others? I like inventing poems too, but I don't write them down. I save them in my head.

"Yes, I don't see why not. I thought I'd read the diary next week. There might be some answers. Do you think Brian's got secrets too: things he's hidden from you?... Well, these may not be serious either... Controlling? Do you think he was? When we met, I think I did all the controlling... Yes... Yes... Yes... Yes, I suppose so, when you put together a list like that..."

Now Aunty Pam's doing all the talking, so it's not so interesting. So Dad had secrets like I do, but we can't find out about them now. It's funny I've got a secret photo too. I've put it in the box with my E-type Jag jigsaw. I haven't got a jacket to hide it in.

FOUR

So if Mum had started to rally before Ivor Hughes came into her life, why couldn't she pick up the pieces after he left? Theirs wasn't a passionate love affair – well, not in my perception. They just went out together twice, and the second time it was with me.

Anyway, by the next morning I'm sure I'd forgotten all about him when I was sitting on this sofa after breakfast reading a comic and the telephone rang. I heard her confirm some arrangements about someone's visit; and I watched her put the receiver down with an odd expression. And then she stares out of the window with a dreamy face…

* * *

"Who's coming, Mum?"

"A reporter. He writes for the newspaper."

"Why don't we have a newspaper?"

"We don't need one. I don't want to read about trouble in Northern Ireland every day. Anyway, there's news on the telly."

"Dad had a newspaper, and Wayne's dad does." It's men what buy papers. I've seen them in Smiths reading them first. And you get much more news in a paper.

"Dad liked to follow the sport."

"I'd like to follow the sport. Can I?" I could follow Dad's Ironsides and see how Rovers are doing.

"We'll see."

She always says that when she doesn't want to say no and have me moaning – or 'when you're older, maybe'. Anyway, why should a reporter be coming? "Is he going to write something about us?"

"Yes."

"Why?"

Mum comes over to sit next to me, moving my *Beano*. "Because he wants to tell people about how the Boroughcliff accident hurt the families whose menfolk were lost or injured there."

I look up into her face. "Does he want to see me?"

"I'm not sure. I hadn't thought. Would you like to tell him anything?"

Mum just smiles and doesn't give me any clues. I'd like to tell him about Dad – but where would I start? "I don't know," I say.

"That's all right, pet. You don't have to." She ruffles my hair, which I don't like. "I'd better get the coffee ready and smarten up." Her knees do their funny click when she gets up, and I pick up my comic and turn over for Biffo the bear.

When Mum comes back through she asks, "Are you going round to Wayne's?"

"His dad's taking them all out today." He didn't ask me. Maybe there weren't room in the car.

"What about Ian?"

"They've gone on holiday."

"Oh. Well, when Mr Hughes comes I think you'd better go up to your room. Is that all right?"

"Can't I stay down here and listen to you? Then I might think of what I could say."

"OK. We'll see how things go. But you'll have to keep quiet and not interrupt."

She goes into the dining room and brings back a photo album and then goes upstairs. I carry on reading.

* * *

She went up to shave her legs and underarms – I heard the familiar sound of her razor buzzing. She had a thing about hair then, and as

41

well as shaving pulled it out between her eyebrows – and removed it from elsewhere, for all I know. And it was the reason I couldn't have a pet – her aversion to its hairs and fur.

I looked up when she came back into the sitting room and saw a transformation: bare legs, arms, shoulders, and a seductive décolletage. She'd changed out of her jeans and top into her stripy sundress. I'm surprised. It doesn't seem right...

* * *

That's Mum's dress for getting herself brown – but it's not sunny today.

"He should be here soon," she says.

"I'll look out the window." I want to see what car he's got.

He's quite a long time coming, and Mum goes to the lavatory twice and mooches about, but then a Mini Cooper stops at the kerb. It's green with a white roof. British racing green, it's called – Dad told me.

"Here he is, Mum." Cor, he's got a really thick beard – nothing like Desperate Dan's. And it's ever so black. It's like a woolly scarf round his face, with a hole bitten through for his mouth. Mum won't like him. She doesn't like beards.

She goes out to open the door when he rings the bell.

"I'm very sorry I'm late, Mrs Paine," he says. He sounds like Jones the Steam in *Ivor the Engine*.

"Please go through," says Mum, shutting the door. "This is my boy, Michael. He wanted to stay and listen, and maybe say something. Is that OK?"

"Yes, of course. Hallo, Michael."

"Would you like to sit there, Mr Hughes?" says Mum, pointing to the swivel chair – Dad's chair.

"It's Ivor, actually."

And his name's Ivor, too.

"Would you like some coffee?" Mum asks him.

"Yes, please..." And he sort of waits for Mum to say something.

"It's Marlene," Mum says, before turning to me. "You can sit on the sofa next to me, pet. Do you want a drink?"

"No, thanks. I'll sit in the sag bag," I say.

Mum shakes her head and goes into the kitchen, and the man says, "You're nine, aren't you, Michael?" He looks like Cutthroat Jake when he smiles.

"Yeah. What's the Mini Cooper you've got?"

"It's a Mini Cooper S."

"What's the engine?"

"Ten-seventy-one cc. You sound like you know about cars."

"Yeah."

Now Mum's coming back in with a tray. "It won't be long," she says, putting it on the coffee table.

I can hear the percolator blub-blubbing. I haven't seen that for a long time. She doesn't make proper coffee any more. She's got some chocolate biscuits on that plate. Maybe I should've said yes to a drink so I could've had one. Mum sits on the sofa. He's already swivelled the chair round so he can look at her.

"It was brave of you to say yes to Mr Elkington," he says. "The features editor, he is."

"Yes, he said. I don't know why I did – or what I've let myself in for."

"Nothing too painful, I hope; but it's the human close-ups that make tragedies come alive. Focusing on the hurt people have suffered makes the readers concerned, see; makes them into a force for change – to change industry, to make it safer for workers. That's what I'm always hoping, anyhow… Sorry. I'll get off my soap box."

He sounds a bit like Mr Tilley at school when he says something important in assembly. He's getting a notebook out of his jacket pocket now.

"Well, I hope I can do my bit," says Mum. "Am I the first?"

"Yes, but I did a feature on the explosion itself. Did you see it?"

"No. I don't have a paper any more."

I said we should get a paper. We've missed that now.

"I'll send it to you, if you like."

"OK. Thanks."

That's good. I can read it. Mum didn't sound very keen, though. She's been talking like when she says she feels low.

"That was Boroughcliff from the air, so to speak. Now I want to swoop down and talk to people on the ground."

He's got a pencil out now. He must be going to write what Mum says. But you can't write as quick as people talk – she'll have to slow down.

"Where do I start?" she asks.

"Would you like to tell me about when the explosion occurred – what you were doing; what happened next."

"OK... Well, I was on this sofa listening to Sinatra. I never slept well when Alan was on nights, so I was still up. The house seemed to shudder and things rattled – and the stylus scraped across the record."

"And you wondered what it was?" he says.

Mum didn't talk slow and he's not doing proper writing. I think he's putting little squiggles in his book.

"I thought it might've been an earthquake. I don't remember hearing any boom, but I might've drifted off. I ran upstairs to calm Michael – he'd called out – and then I think I went outside. I saw a glow in the sky and thought something had happened at National Steel. I came back in and then realised it was in the wrong direction and different, somehow."

"How do you mean?"

"Brighter, and not as red as when they tip slag. Soon after, Agnes telephoned – that's Alan's mum. Her neighbour's into CB radio. He'd told her there'd been an incident at Performance Intermediates at Boroughcliff. I rang them but couldn't get through. I went out again and people were in the street and talking about an explosion. I could hear sirens. I think I nearly fainted. I came back, checked that Michael was asleep, made a cup of tea and just sat here praying that Alan would phone or I'd get a message. The phone did ring once, but it was Agnes worrying. I asked her not to do it again, raising my hopes and then dashing them – and stopping Alan getting through if he rang."

"And when did you get some definite news?"

"I had the radio on waiting for the first bulletin – at five o'clock before Simon Bates. When the newsreader said 'many fatalities', I feared the worst. I just froze – a sort of shock, I suppose."

Mum looks down and covers her face with her hands. He moves his hand out as if he's going to touch her, but stops and moves it back.

Then Mum looks up and uncovers her face. "And then it got light and I saw the huge cloud of smoke in the sky and I just knew – just knew Alan was dead. I think the coffee's ready now."

Mum goes out in a rush. I think she were going to cry.

* * *

I sat in the sag bag trying not to let my own eyes water with my memories in front of Ivor Hughes – but he was busy looking in his reporter's notebook and didn't notice me.

I've never forgotten that gigantic billow of smoke when I pulled back my curtains in the morning and what came next. I could see a police car outside and a policewoman getting in – and Dad's car wasn't on the drive. I was apprehensive already as I went downstairs in my pyjamas and heard Mum crying, and then transfixed with panic when I stood in the doorway unnoticed. She was hunched forward on this sofa trembling, with her face cupped by her hands. Then she told me he'd died, and I cried, and she hugged me until I stopped. But I couldn't stop shaking for ages, and then I lay here exhausted and Mum covered me with my quilt and I went to sleep.

Anyway, after he'd finished reading what he'd written he turned his head towards me and smiled, and I feel recovered enough to want to know what he's been doing in his book…

* * *

45

"What sort of writing is that?" I ask.

"It's called shorthand, Michael," he says, turning his chair round. "Lots of reporters use it – and typists as well. It's like a new language you have to learn. It makes the sound of the words – see."

I get up to have a skeg. "Yeah, it's funny. It's like a secret code." Mum must've done it; she were a shorthand typist. I thought it meant the way she typed. I turn round to sit down and see his car again. "Your car's dirty."

"Yes, just like Ulcethorpe. I live near the works, see, so I'm in their line of fire."

"Where's that?"

"In Coke Street."

"There's a funny little house there."

"That's the one, Michael. It used to be joined to others, but they've all been knocked down. I'm looking for a better place before they knock mine down too."

"I'd like to see it knocked down. I've only seen buildings knocked down on the telly – chimneys and factories and things."

"Here's the coffee," says Mum, coming back in with the percolator. She's not crying now.

He swivels round again away from me. It's like Mum's a magnet. "Do you want to carry on? Say if you'd rather not."

"Yes… Yes, I'll be OK. Let me pour the coffee."

I watch Mum sit on the sofa and fill the cups. It gives him another chance to look at her while she's looking down. Her dress shows off her knees.

"Yes, I want to tell my story even more now," says Mum. "I was thinking in the kitchen. Before, I thought I should without knowing why – maybe to help other people struggling after a sudden death. But what you said about changing things has made me see a more important reason." She sounds more cheerful now.

"I said you were brave, Marlene."

"Thanks."

He puts some milk and sugar in his coffee and has a drink. Mum just has the milk. She's worried she'll put on weight like Aunty Pam has.

"Let's go back to before you met your husband and how you met him," he says. "May I call him Alan?"

"Yes, of course."

Now Mum's having her coffee, but they haven't had a biscuit. I could ask for one. I think they've forgotten I'm here. Well, he has.

"I don't know where to begin," says Mum, when she puts her cup back down.

"It might be easier if I ask questions, Marlene. Did you grow up here in Ulcethorpe?"

"No, in Goole – with my elder sister and brother. My dad worked in a shipping office there. He's lovely – and so is my mum. It was all very much Happy Families. I've barely a bad memory. I came here when I got my City & Guilds – you know, shorthand and typing. I fancied myself as a bit of a hip raver, but was too timid to venture very far."

"Like London?"

"No. I think Sheffield or Leeds was the extent of my horizon; but Ulcethorpe had a reputation as a lively place. I stayed in digs and then found a bedsit in Froderby Street."

"And was Alan local?"

"Yes, he was born here, and then the following year his dad was killed in the Normandy landings, so he had a lonely childhood – especially when his mum went back to work at Bardby library."

"And how did you meet?"

"I was working at Brown and Beasley, the solicitors. They were having central heating installed. Alan arrived as the plumber's mate."

Maybe that's where Dad learnt about central heating, so he could fit it in here.

"And it was love at first sight, as they say?"

"Well, he couldn't keep his eyes off me, and I thought he looked gorgeous. I've got some photos of him for you to look at."

Mum opens the album on the sofa and passes it for him to have a skeg.

"I see what you mean, Marlene; and blonde hair – real film star looks."

I wish I looked like Dad. Grandma Paine says Mum and I look Spanish, our hair's so dark. I don't think she likes it. It's not as black as his, though. At least Grandma says I'm like Dad in lots of other ways.

"Yes, I've always fancied fair-haired men – attraction of opposites, I suppose. But he never said anything – you know, asked me out. I had to make the running. And he wasn't like I expected. He was clever and into classical music and always reading."

"Oh…" He sounds surprised. "Unusual for a plumber's mate."

"Yes. He'd been to Bardby Grammar School, but left in the upper sixth – suffering from an allergy to a surfeit of science, he always said, silly man. By the time we got married – that was in nineteen-sixty-four at St John's – he'd been taken on as a process operator at Boroughcliff when they built the new ammonia plant."

"And when was he appointed a shift supervisor?"

"In nineteen-seventy-two when Mainz Chemische took over and expanded the works to make P6."

"He'd risen up very fast."

"Yes, I said he was clever."

They're both drinking more coffee now. He keeps looking at Mum when he's not doing his special writing, but she's mostly looking down. And he says Mum's name a lot. He must like it. She were called Marlene after a film star during the war.

"How long is it you've lived here?" he asks.

"We bought the house when we got married. It needed a lot doing to it, but Alan thought it was too good a bargain to miss. He did everything: electrics, plumbing, carpentry – do-it-yourself became a hobby. He was the practical one, but let me decide on furnishings and décor. I've had to learn practical things myself in the last year: wiring plugs, reading the meters, replacing fuses – things like that. And whenever there's a problem with something I always think what he would've done."

"Does it work?"

"I've managed so far. I've surprised myself."

"And did he have other hobbies?"

"Yes, the usual man things: football, cricket, motor racing."

"Nothing you shared?"

"No… I suppose we shared our interest in the house and Michael." Mum looks over to me and smiles, and does a little wave to make me smile back. "It doesn't seem much, does it?" she says, turning back to him.

They have another break for a drink before he says some more.

"Shall we move on to the aftermath – how you've coped since the accident; how it's affected you."

Mum's hardly told him anything about Dad. I need to think of something to tell him, too.

"Yes, OK." Then Mum goes quiet and looks at me again. "I think you'll be bored, pet. Would you like to go up to your room?"

"I won't be, Mum. Do I have to?"

"Yes, please. You've heard what I've said about Dad. I'll call you before Mr Hughes goes, so you can tell him anything you want to say."

* * *

I didn't want to go and probably made my puffing noise to let her know, but Mum bribed me with two chocolate biscuits and permission to eat them upstairs. I took a plate to catch the crumbs – a memorable moment, invited to break one of the top five in her book of rules.

After opening and closing my door – a little subterfuge I'd worked out – I sat on my top listening step eating my biscuits to hear a two-sided conversation for once instead of just Mum's voice on the phone…

* * *

Mum's talking already so I've missed some…

"Yes, like that first morning, feeling numb and lost. It stayed like that for a long time – doing things on auto without thinking. But some days I was angry and cried – shouted even, if I was on my own. I suppose that's why it's called anguish: a sort of squishy anger. I tried to keep up a pretence of being normal for Michael, but sometimes I thought him a bloody nuisance, poor lamb – but please don't print that. I had to take tranquillisers and sleeping pills. Maybe they helped, or just the passage of time."

Why did she say I were a bloody nuisance? And she shouldn't swear. She blames me for everything. These biscuits are all right, but they're Cadbury's milk and I like the plain.

"So you feel a lot better now?"

"Yes – and quite suddenly. Looking back, I can see I was selfish and immature. It's Michael that was hurt the most. I might meet someone else and marry again, but he can never find another father. Alan can never be replaced for him."

"Yes, losing the genetic link; that's quite profound, Marlene."

I don't know what he means, but Mum's right; it is worse for me. I hope she doesn't meet anyone else. That would make it worse still.

"Did you get any support from Performance Intermediates after the accident?" he asks.

"No... Well, no counselling or anything like that. They just arranged for a solicitor to look after my interests with their insurance company who paid out the compensation. Alan had left the T and G union when he was promoted to staff. The help came from understanding things there better. He never used to talk much about work, other than about the people, and at first I didn't want to think about the horrible place. I suppose I worried he might've been at fault somehow."

How could she think it were Dad's fault? That's stupid.

"He hadn't mentioned any safety concerns about the temporary pipe replacing the reactor?"

"No – but as I said, he didn't talk about technical things. He probably thought I wouldn't understand them. But after a time I did want to understand them – every last detail. Henry Hallam, one of the other shift supervisors, helped me. He told me Alan had worried about that pipe when it was fitted. If only he'd spoken out. I really used the third degree on Henry to try and get a picture of what it must've been like for Alan near the end. And that helped me be less selfish, and so the grief lessened. I think grief's mainly selfish indulgence."

"And how about Michael? You mentioned him affecting your grieving, but how's he managed without his dad?"

"He seems to have taken it in his stride. He's behaved quite normally, anyway – but then he's always been grown-up for his years. Maybe underneath he was suffering, but didn't say – or, with me wrapped in grief, I didn't notice."

No, I didn't say. I don't think you should let people know what you feel because it's private. Maybe I should've made more of a fuss – like her.

"You mentioned being close to your parents. They must've been a comfort, living quite near."

"Well, yes and no. They moved to Scarborough when my dad retired. We talked on the phone, but it would've been better if we'd seen them more – especially for Michael, I think."

"And Alan's mother – did you see her a lot?"

"We're not that close."

No, she's two bus rides away.

"That's a pity."

"No, it was my sister Pam I relied on. I rang her every night. She lives in Sheffield, so my phone bill went stratospheric. She's my best friend. I was friendly with Gill and Joan, two other mums I'd met when Michael started school – it was like a club at the gate there. But after it happened they drifted off, made excuses. It was obvious why: I was either moody or wanted to talk about Alan all the time. They couldn't cope with me."

"Did you know any of the other wives widowed by the disaster – or meet them afterwards?"

"No, we never socialised with anyone from work, other than the Hallams. Three of Alan's Sunday football team were killed in the explosion, and they were married, but I'd never met them, let alone their wives. And I wasn't in a fit state to make new friends. I cope by retreating inwards. Group therapy wouldn't be my thing, if that's what you meant."

I'll go back down now. I've thought what I could say.

"It was more mutual support I was thinking of, but I understand. What about church or chapel – do they play a part for you?"

"No. I'm one of those three-times-a-life Christians – you know: baptism, wedding, and funeral. My mum and dad go to chapel, but I'm not convinced."

"Mum, can I talk about Dad? I want to now," I say, in the doorway.

"Yes, pet. It's 'may I?' remember. Come and sit down next to me this time. Give me your plate."

Flipping heck, the phone's bring-bringing – just as I were going to tell him. Mum gets up to answer it.

"Hallo... Yes. Who's that?... Yes, he is... I don't know. You'll have to ask him... Well, you can't. I'm going to pass the phone over." Mum turns round and holds the phone out. "It's Dave Fletcher at the *Argus*."

The reporter gets up to take it and Mum comes back to the sofa. I hope he's not long or I'll forget what I were going to say.

"Hallo... Dave, you never stop, do you? How did you know where I was... Did I?... Right, one-thirty. Can you tell her I'll be there... I will. Thanks."

He puts the phone back and sits in the swivel chair again.

"Sorry about that, Marlene," he says. "An interview with the Old Man – the editor, that is. It could be to confirm my appointment. I've been on probation for the last six months."

"That Dave's a bit odd," Mum says. "'Is 'e havin' a good time with thee, lass?', he said. I can't quite do his Yorkshire."

They're talking again. It were going to be my turn.

"I won't tell you what he said to me. He puts that accent on for effect. He's the *Argus* ladykiller. I have to share an office with him, although he covers sport. Sorry, Marlene."

"It's not your fault." Mum puts her arm round me to squeeze my shoulder. "Would you like to say your piece now, pet."

Hooray! "Yeah. Are you ready?" I ask the man.

"Yes, Michael. Fire away."

"Dad liked the things I like: football and cars. And he played for The Ironsides – proper football with goalposts and nets. Mum let me go with him to watch when it weren't raining. He were their right back. Once they won five-nil, and Dad scored with a header; but I missed that game." It's sadder saying it than thinking it. I won't ever see Dad score a goal now. "And he took me to watch the Rovers with his friend Keith."

"And did he like rugby?"

"He watched rugby league on the telly, and cricket. He said we'd go to Leeds to see England play Australia this year – in a Test Match." My eyes are watering, but I haven't finished yet. "He were a good driver. We had a Ford Cortina sixteen hundred GT. It were metallic silver, K reg." But where's it gone? Why didn't someone drive it home for Mum to use? Why do I feel like this? "And we went to Cadwell Park to see the racing… And…"

I run upstairs to my bedroom making an awful row. But I've told him. I press my head into the pillow hugging old Teddo.

After a bit Mum comes up and sits on the edge of the bed and strokes me till I stop crying.

"Mum, has that reporter gone?"

"Yes, poppet."

"He won't write about me crying, will he?"

"No, of course not."

"What will he write?"

"I don't know exactly. We'll see when we read it. There's no need to worry. He's a nice man."

I hope Mum's right. I wish I hadn't gone back downstairs now. And how long have we got to wait to find out? When somebody writes things the words don't disappear like when you're talking. They stay forever, for anyone to read.

FIVE

I probably thought I'd seen the last of Ivor Hughes, with only the worry of how he'd publicise my crybaby exhibition to come. But he made another visit the following day – or tried to – obviously enthralled by what he'd seen. It kicked off my obsession with Boroughcliff and how Dad had died.

Mum had invited Grandma Paine to afternoon tea before we went away – an occasional event in between our regular treks to Gainsborough Avenue for her five-star feasts. We'd just sat at the dining room table for Mum's two-star apology when she saw him through the window, said something about a journalist, and went to the front door.

I can see Grandma's head swivelling at breakneck speed to get a glimpse of him, and hear the inquisition in her voice…

* * *

"What journalist?"

I watch Mum open the front door just as the bell rings.

"There's a surprise. Caught me in the act you have, Marlene."

"I saw you on the drive."

"I've brought you my article, like I promised."

"About me?"

"No, the one about the disaster – *Lest We Forget*. I said I'd send it, but I've brought it round, see."

"Did you? I don't remember. But thanks, anyway. I can't ask you in; we're entertaining Alan's mum. It was good of you to take the trouble. Thanks again… Ivor. Goodbye."

Mum puts the newspaper on the windowsill in the sitting room and comes back looking like she's thinking of the answer in a quiz. That reporter didn't see so much of Mum today. It's sunny, but Grandma's here so she's got a dress on with sleeves what buttons right up to her neck.

"What journalist?" Grandma says it again – just the same, like playing back a tape.

"Ivor Hughes, from the *Argus*. He interviewed me yesterday about being widowed. They're doing a series."

"Yes, I know. You didn't tell me you were appearing." Grandma sounds annoyed.

"I told him about Dad, I did," I say.

"Did you, darling? Then I'm looking forward to reading it." She's not annoyed with me.

Mum pours their tea and my fizzy, because it's my time for it, and serves the cake. She only makes one when Grandma comes. It's a sponge today with raspberry jam and cream.

I'm the first to finish. "Can I have another piece, Mum?"

"It's 'may I' and 'please'; and the answer's no. You've had a big slice."

"Oh, let him, Marlene – a thin sliver at least."

Mum cuts more than a thin bit with one of her looks. It's not my fault; I only asked.

"It's lovely and light," Grandma says, trying to be nice.

"I used soft margarine. Here you are, poppet. You can thank Grandma for that."

Mum's OK again now. I give them both a big smile to say thank you before picking up my cake fork, which is another thing we don't usually have.

Mum finishes second and puts her fork down on her plate. She could've squashed up them last crumbs like I did. "I cleared out Alan's clothes and things on Tuesday," she says. "I kept a few bits and pieces back for Michael – and that Spitfire jacket as well."

"That's ace, Mum." But I'll have to grow a bit to wear it. "What else

55

is there?" I've only had things from Grandma so far.

"Shush. Don't talk with your mouth full. I'll show you later." Mum turns towards Grandma again. "There was a little badge, military I think, like a bugle. Was it Granddad's?"

"Oh yes. I gave that to Alan when he started asking about his father and the war. It's a King's Own Yorkshire Light Infantry badge. You'd like that, wouldn't you, darling?"

I nod. Wayne likes the war. He's got some badges from off uniforms.

"And a silver penknife and pencil, and a little silver box?" Mum asks.

"Yes. They were Leonard's too, or perhaps even his father's."

Good. I haven't got a penknife, but Wayne has. It's really useful. You can carve sticks and sharpen pencils. It should be called a pencil knife. You couldn't sharpen a silver pencil, though.

"I wanted to be sure. And I found something else: a photo of a girl I didn't recognise. I'll get it. I put it in the drawer."

Mum looks for the photo, lifting up the albums to see underneath. "This is it."

Grandma has to pick up her handbag to get her glasses. It's like a little sausage dog that's always next to her feet. "No, I don't know her. And yet... I've seen the face before – somewhere. Something about it is familiar."

"Because it reminds you of me?"

"Oh no. Her face is more delicate, Marlene, if you don't mind my saying. Even though the picture could be sharper, you can see that."

"Can I have a skeg?" I ask.

"Not now; when we've finished. And it's 'look', not 'skeg'. Where do you pick up these words?" Mum sounds annoyed.

"I don't think he's got the right friends, Marlene – that Wayne, for instance."

But I didn't learn it from Wayne. Deano Haynes says it at school when he wants to see my sums.

"Well, I can't help it," says Mum. "Anyway, might she be another girlfriend?"

56

"Alan had just the one girlfriend before you – Linda Saxby: such a nice girl; a doctor's daughter. She came to the house one evening with her friend Pat, or Patricia as I called her. It's not Linda, I can assure you."

"No, I know. He pointed her out once, parading with a pushchair in the market – thin and fair, like him. This one will have to stay his secret."

Grandma makes her mouth go very small, as if she's trying to stop any words coming out. I don't think she liked Mum saying that.

* * *

After Grandma had bestowed her usual hugs and kisses I watched her go to catch her bus, looking through the sitting room window to see her grey frizzle bobbing above the Furrs' front fence. Then I saw the *Argus* on the sill – with a headline about Ulster, I suppose. But that didn't interest me.

In the top right corner of the page is a notice: *Boroughcliff anniversary feature inside*. I pick the paper up...

* * *

"Mum, can I read what that reporter wrote about the explosion?" I call. She's in the kitchen stacking the tea things on the draining board.

"It's 'may I?'. I suppose so, if you really want to."

"Yeah, I do."

"All right; but you might find it hard to understand."

I sit on the sofa and look in the paper to find it. There's a picture of the fire and all the smoke. It's been taken from up in the air – from a helicopter or aeroplane. Underneath it says:

BOROUGHCLIFF 1974 – LEST WE FORGET

Forget? How could we? I can hear you say it. Sixteen men killed and eleven more injured. And many more spared by it striking at night. We'll never forget.

And we all know where we were at 11.44 p.m. on Monday 12th August 1974 too: in bed; in the bath; on the loo; in front of the TV; exercising the dog; at the club; in the pub; going home; at the works; at the wheel; on duty; on break; on a promise; or even walking alone under the stars. We'll never forget.

He's right. Well, I haven't forgot. I never will. I were in bed, and the bang woke me up. I wonder what 'on a promise' means. I'll have to ask Mum.

But scarcely anyone knew what went on at Boroughcliff – or what went in, or what came out.

Witches' brew

Cyclohexane, sulphuric acid, ammonia, oleum, hydrogen: they all poured into the witches' brew. "Double, double toil and trouble; fire burn and cauldron bubble". And from this stew they distilled and condensed and solidified a product so refined it kept its name private: P6. P for Polymer? Pastille? Panacea? Prophylactic?

Mum's right; it is a bit difficult. I think those are the names of chemicals going in, but what's the thing coming out? The only word I know is pastille, and that's a sort of cough sweet. It can't be that. If I'm going to do a job like Dad's I'll need to know.

Whatever, it's good for you, we'd have been told if we asked. It went to make something we all needed. In fact it was used to make nylon 6.

So at 11.44 that night in our ignorance we feared an earthquake or a plane crash or a nuclear strike or a wartime bomb or a meteor or molten steel. The words 'unconfined vapour cloud explosion' would have been double Dutch to us.

New elixir

Let me tell you a story. Once upon a time there lived a German prince with a passion for chemistry experiments – but a lonely prince. His father sought a bride for him with a similar interest. He sent envoys out to other countries. One came to England and discovered a perfect match. The modest lady had a large estate and a fine dowry. Her laboratory contained nearly all the chemicals the prince required for his new elixir. The envoy returned. Although the lady's portrait did not excite the prince, her list of property won his heart. The bride's father eagerly made over all her possessions and gave the prince a handsome bounty to bless the union. He, in gratitude, determined on England as their marital home. They built a splendid new laboratory on the estate. But they did not live happily ever after.

Perhaps you've already guessed. The prince was Mainz Chemische Fabrik Gmbh, and his father Dechemuga Gmbh. The lady was Trentbank Fertilisers Ltd, and her father Midland and Trent Chemical Company Ltd. They solemnized their marriage four years ago. The estate spread its acres at Boroughcliff. They chose Performance Intermediates UK Ltd as their married name. But their union remained unequal. The orders were given in German.

That's written like a fairy story, but I don't see what it's got to do with the explosion. It's just stupid.

Explosive mixture

Are you ready for some chemical engineering? Mainz Chemische transformed an obscure wartime fertiliser works by building two giant plants, bright with lights each night beneath the fiery tongue of the new flare stack. Mainz Chemische also brought cyclohexane to Boroughcliff.

This chemical fumes and catches fire and explodes in air like petrol. Over 120 tons had to be heated until it was half as hot again as boiling water and even further above its own boiling temperature.

Pumped round and round and round through six reactors, it would slowly change into other chemicals. Imagine six giant steel pressure cookers, the size of petrol tankers stood on end, and you have a picture of these reactors. Inside them the cyclohexane stayed a liquid. But if it all got out it could make enough explosive vapour to fill the inside of York Minster – enough to explode with the force of 40 tons of TNT.

York Minster; we've been there. That would be a lot of stuff exploding. It's ginormous inside. But what's TNT? Grandma Searle says TTFN when she means 'Ta-ta for now', but TNT can't mean 'Ta now ta'. Six petrol tankers would hold a lot of petrol – enough for thousands and thousands of cars.

Temporary repair

And here's some mechanical engineering. About two months before the date we'll never forget, one of the reactors did let some cyclohexane out through a crack in its side. The plant was shut down and the reactor removed. It left a large gap in the loop which would have to be spanned for production of P6 to resume. The proud and resourceful workers at Performance Intermediates grasped the opportunity to show their mettle to their German superiors, undeterred that their engineering manager had left the company. In two days they designed and built a 20-inch diameter 20-feet long bridging pipe with a concertinaed section at each end to allow for its expansion.

I've heard about the pipe, but I didn't think it were so big. You could crawl inside – like them pipes in the adventure playground in Everard Park.

But matters were not straightforward. The pipe needed a bend in it to join up with the reactors at either side, which were at different levels. This crookedness would stress the pipe and its concertinaed parts beyond their limits, and initiate a fatal flaw.

A few minutes before the time we'll never forget the cyclohexane was nearly at its hottest. And the pressure in the pipe pushed four

times as hard as the air in the tyres of your car. And then without
warning the pipe burst – catastrophically. And the vapour billowed
out as the liquid boiled up.

Panic stations

The operators at the scene were powerless to intervene. The shift
supervisor ordered the whole site to be shut down.

That's Dad, that is. Why doesn't it say his name? He were in charge,
but it weren't his fault. He did all he could. I can feel my eyes watering,
but I'm not going to cry.

They hoped the cloud would blow away without igniting. But the
tonnage of fuel to boil – and the volume of vapour to boil off – was
huge. We can hardly imagine their terror, denied the salvation of
"abandon ship". Did they pray? Did they panic? Did they relive their
entire lives in those few minutes? And then their torment ended – at
11.44 p.m. on Monday August 12th 1974.

I wonder what Dad did. Maybe he thought about Mum – or about
me, or Grandma Paine. He wouldn't panic – not like that Corporal
Jones. Dad were more like Sergeant Wilson. My eyes are watering
more now, but I'm not going to make a noise.

This is where we came in, as we used to say in the cinema. We
know what happened next – for us. Phone calls, neighbourliness,
the sound of sirens, the guesses and rumours, waiting for news
bulletins – and for some, a chilling dread. And for the fire crews
and police and hospital staff it was pre-planned disaster response.
And in the morning the ferocious fire, its enormous sooty plume a
smoke signal of doom: Boroughcliff put on the map and Ulcethorpe
hosting the world's press.

Disaster inquiry

But what happened next on the larger scale, in the longer term? The
Employment Secretary, Michael Foot, ordered a formal investigation

- a Court of Inquiry. It took evidence from witnesses, viewed the debris, consulted with experts, commissioned investigations, studied the outcomes, deliberated and deliberated. And finally it issued a lengthy report - fifty times as long as this article you're reading.

When I'm grown up I might like to read that. It might say something more about Dad; say how brave he were and how he died. But where would you get it? Maybe they'd have it in a library. Grandma Paine would know; she used to work in one.

It explains the obvious: the pipe that burst, the vapour that billowed, the explosion that wrecked and the fire that incinerated. It quite rightly exonerates the men who perished or those who took orders and made the pipe. The company and its managers are criticised, but mildly. But that was in the past. What of the future?

What does 'exonerates' mean? It sounds like they did something wrong, but that can't be right. I know it weren't Dad's fault.

The report gives many "lessons to be learned" by the chemical industry - too many to mention here, other than the most far-reaching. This is for the Government "to identify all those installations which present extreme hazards, and make sure controls are in place to prevent a disaster so far as is possible and to minimise its consequences should one occur".

I've read all that three times, but still don't know what it means. Maybe it's double Dutch.

So after the immediate fallout of soot and ammonium sulphate fertiliser comes this overdue fallout of prospective legislation for the control of potential disaster sites.
So if we did forget it wouldn't matter then? I hear you say. The new Health and Safety Executive will be looking after things for the Government, won't they? We can leave it to them, can't we?

I'm not so confident. The process for converting cyclohexane seems inherently dangerous to me (and to others more technically qualified) – so much of it sloshing round and round so very hot. Will this be the recipe in the new plant that's under construction or is something else being considered? This is not discussed in the report.

And how much autonomy did the new works manager have in making his decisions about the bridging pipe? I've been told that he was under intense pressure from business directors in Frankfurt to get the plant restarted very quickly. Remote and unaccountable, they weren't interested in technical details. How can we make them be? This is not discussed in the report.

And what about the neighbours? Don't the people living in Boroughcliff and further afield have a right to be told about hazardous activities on their doorstep? And have the right to express their concerns? And have the right to be consulted about changes? This is not discussed in the report.

So don't forget. Don't leave it to others. Stay just as concerned about Phoenix Intermediates (as Performance Intermediates has become) and Boroughcliff as you were in those days following August 12th 1974 – please! If we forget the past we're condemned to repeat it.

Ivor Hughes

This is the first of several features to commemorate the first anniversary of the Boroughcliff disaster. The others will focus on the bereaved, the survivors and the rescuers.

I think it's good – what I could understand of it. Mum did say. My eyes are dry now, so she won't know I were crying. Who's supposed to answer all those questions in the end bit? The people reading it won't know. Who else is there?

I fold up the paper and put it down. "I've read it, Mum," I say, going into the kitchen. She's washing up.

"When I've done in here we'll read it together – then you can ask about what you didn't understand. I might be able to explain."

I don't think she will – not like Dad could've.

Through the dining room door I see the photo's still on the table. I can have a look now. It's only black-and-white. The girl's on a coach. She's got her school blazer on, so maybe it's a school trip. She looks a bit surprised at having her picture taken. Mum had her picture taken this morning by the newspaper. She asked the photographer if they wanted one of me, but he said I weren't on his schedule, whatever that means.

The phone's bring-bringing now. Mum has to get her rubber gloves off before she answers it. I hear her say, "Ruddy things," as she slaps them down.

"Hallo... About my story?... We're going on holiday tomorrow – a week in Scarborough with my mum and dad – so the answer's no, I'm afraid. Sorry... Er... Well, you could. I'm not sure... All right... Thanks."

Mum comes back into the kitchen and picks up her gloves.

"Who were that, Mum?"

"The journalist: Mr Hughes – Ivor."

"What did he want?"

"Don't be nosey. You don't need to know."

I hate it when she says I'm nosey. I like to know things. If you don't ask how do you find out? Grandma Paine and my teacher don't say it when I ask them. Anyway, he must've asked her for something. Maybe he wants to come here again. I hope not.

SIX

Ivor Hughes hadn't written his article for nine-year-olds, but after reading it again with Mum it became imprinted in my mind as a sort of holy testament to my dad. But while elevating him to a tragic hero, it also started my fixation with his demise (the exact mechanism, I mean). I suppose in a circuitous way it also led to where I am now – or where I was: Senior Consultant, Central Safety Services, Omega Oil, Fenchurch Tower, EC3.

When we went to Scarborough that Friday – the last happy holiday I ever had as a boy – I asked for a detour via Boroughcliff to feed my burgeoning interest in the disaster. My other worry – the possible advent of Ivor Hughes into our lives – surfaced before we even set off.

I waited at the sitting room window, anxious for Granddad to arrive so we'd have a car on the drive again – even his, and if only for an hour or so. I felt we were second-class without. I'm filling in time driving Corgis and Dinkys on the sill. Then I look up and see him reversing over the pavement and through the gap in the hedge, the slanting pale blue rear of the Renault framing its number plate: MBT 448M…

* * *

"Granddad's arrived, Mum," I shout.

"Oh. You open the door, pet. I won't be a mo." She's emptying the pedal bin. It's on her list of jobs. She makes lists because Dad told her she should. It were after we had to come all the way back from Lincoln for her hairdryer that time we went to Skegness for a week. I think the liner's split. I heard her say, "Ruddy thing."

I park my cars and go out to see Granddad parking his. It's a Renault 12. I don't like the shape or the colour or the inside, but Granddad said it were recommended in his *Which?* magazine. Well, whoever wrote it hasn't got a flipping clue.

"Hallo, Granddad."

"Hallo, young sir. Ready for your holiday?" he says, through the open window.

"Yeah."

He's stiff getting out, as if he needs oiling. My Chopper bike needs oiling. I'll have to do it myself now – the hubs and the chain and all that. I'll just do the same as what Dad did. Granddad smiles and ruffles my hair. Why do grownups do that? It's like they think we're pets. He's rubbing his back now.

"Dadda!"

Mum's jumped over the doorstep like Zebedee. Now she's giving Granddad a hug and a kiss.

"Hey up, lass. I need lessons in self defence," he says, when she lets go. She used to do that with me.

"Sorry. But we've been so looking forward to you coming, haven't we, Michael?"

I nod.

"You especially, lass, by the feel of it."

"It's been a hard week, Dadda – the anniversary, the interview, tea with Agnes. I'm ready for some seaside," says Mum. And then she sort of sings, "I'm going to be, the first to see the sea," before saying, "and now you see it all the time."

"Aye, that brings back the old days. And you were never first because Pam and Graham always cheated, with their x-ray eyes."

Granddad's kissing Mum now, but just a little peck on her cheek while his arm's on her shoulder.

"Had a letter from Saudi. The project's still on time, so he should be due a nice bonus," he says. I think he's talking about Uncle Graham.

He goes to foreign countries to work. "And he's got a new boyfriend – Rupert."

"Oh." Mum doesn't sound very interested. Yes, Granddad were talking about Uncle Graham, because he has boyfriends, not girlfriends. I don't know why.

"You're looking good – all that tan." Mum's changed the subject.

"A face like a walnut shell, more like."

She leads the way indoors and we go into the sitting room.

"I expect you're thirsty. Cold drink or a cuppa?" she asks Granddad.

"Aye, it's a grand spell of weather. I wouldn't say no to some tea, though."

I go back to the window and my cars. She didn't ask if I were thirsty because it's not my time to have a drink. We have far too many rules.

"How was the newspaper chap?" asks Granddad.

"Nice; sympathetic. He was a Welshman," says Mum.

"And when do we read all about it?"

"I'm not sure. Next week, I think."

"How will you get a copy, then?"

"Don't worry. He'll look after it."

"How?"

"I don't know, but he will."

"Aye, aye. I reckon he's smitten."

"Sit down and I'll switch the kettle on." Mum sounds a bit annoyed, and goes into the kitchen.

Granddad sits on the swivel chair and turns it round so he can see her through the kitchen door. "Well, is he, then?"

"Is he what?"

"Smitten."

Mum comes back to the doorway and leans against the frame. "You always know. Yes, he asked me out to the theatre."

So that's what he wanted on the phone.

"And?"

"It was this Saturday."

"So?"

"He's phoning again when we get back. Oh, Dadda, I don't know. He's really interesting – what he says and what he writes about industry and safety. I can just see him preaching in one of those Welsh chapels. The trouble is, I don't fancy him, if you know what I mean. He's small with a black beard."

"And you want him tall and fair and clean shaven."

"Yes. Well, no, not exactly. Oh, I don't know what I want."

"You can't bring Alan back, lass. And there's no need to be single forever. You still look a treat. You're wasting yourself as a widow. Give the lad a chance, I'd say."

The kettle cut out clicks, and she turns round without saying anything.

"Granddad, can I drive your car?" I ask.

"Why? Are you practising for your driving test?"

"No, not yet." Granddad's always making little jokes.

"Well, don't touch the handbrake or horn."

"No, I won't. Thanks."

I go back outside and get in. It's ace. The wheel won't turn much, but the gear lever moves all over. Brm-brm, brm-brm. And I can move this stalk. Tick-tuck, tick-tuck. And if I slide forward I can reach the brake pedal. Eek.

I hope Mum doesn't do what Granddad says. I don't want Mum having a man to take her out – and Dad wouldn't like it. He used to get annoyed if other men just looked at her – like on the beach and places. We'll be on the beach tomorrow – or even today. Hooray!

At last we're ready and Granddad's putting our cases in the car. I get out to watch. Mum must've ticked off on all her lists. I packed my own case this time. I had a list in my head – but Mum would go round my room afterwards to see if I'd left anything out.

"Can I sit in the front?" I ask.

"It's 'may I?'. Is he big enough for the seatbelt, Dadda?"

"Aye, I reckon so. It'll stop him from fidgeting from side to side in the back."

"I'm a car-spotter, Granddad," I tell him. You get a better view at the front.

"I guessed as much."

"Dad were a locospotter." Spotting things is what boys do, in case he's forgotten.

"Was he?"

"Yeah. I've got his book. Did you know a lot of steam engines had names?"

"Get in then and clunk-click, or I'll sit there. Phew!" Mum makes it sound as if it's my fault she's in a sweat. "I think I need the holiday to recover. What time's Mum expecting us?"

"Not too early. She's a deal of scrubbing and hoovering and polishing to get through yet – you know how it is. I thought we'd stop on the way for a bite. I can rest my back."

"That's a nice idea," Mum says, getting in behind me.

"Granddad, can we go past where Dad worked?" I've been thinking I want to see it since we read what that reporter wrote.

"Aye, I reckon so, if Mum says it's all right. It's not much of a detour."

"Yes, let's. We've not been since. You should've said, pet."

Good. Hurry up, Granddad, and put the key in. At last. Brm-brm. And now the gear lever to the left and forward, and then the brake lever down. We're off.

We've only gone as far as Ettisham Road when Mum says, "Dadda, can we go back? I've forgotten the diary. Silly me; I didn't put it on my list."

"What diary?" says Granddad.

"Alan's, from when he was at school – when he was seventeen. I found it on Tuesday when I was clearing out his things. Decided to read it on holiday."

"I'll turn round at the Earl Haig."

"Can I read it?" I ask.

"We'll see – when you're older, maybe." I might've known.

We have to go all the way round the roundabout, and a green

Hillman Imp goes beep-beep-beep because I don't think Granddad signalled properly. I hear him say, "Stupid blighter." He parks at the kerb this time instead of driving in.

"Won't be a mo," says Mum, and her sandals go slap-slap as she runs back to the door.

"Why do people have diaries, Granddad?" I ask.

"Well, it varies. Sometimes they put birthdays and appointments in them. Some people write about what they did each day – like Samuel Pepys."

"Who's he, Granddad?" There must be a lot of people I haven't heard of. I've been learning facts.

"Pepys Road over there is named after him. He wrote a diary two or three hundred years ago. It's famous now. It's been published."

"Will Dad's ever be famous?"

"I don't reckon so. Most diaries stay private because most folk don't do anything special."

"I might write one," I tell him. I might do something special. Pepys Road is a funny name for a road. I thought it were made up. "Granddad, is our road named after anyone?"

"No, I don't reckon it is."

And then there's Boswell Road and Woodforde Road. If they're not people they might be places. Grandma Paine's road is named after a place.

The front door slams. Mum's holding a little brown book up and looking pleased with herself – like when she won those soaps and things at the raffle at my school.

It doesn't take long to get there. The road goes out of town past the bowling alley we went to once, and then that Texas store Dad were always going to for his DIY. When he said he were going the first time I thought he meant to America.

You have to go through a little wood before you can see anything. The factory's down the hill. I came with Dad once when he called in about something. That big flame's not on now. He called it the flare. It burns all the gases they don't want, he told me.

70

"Is it working, Granddad?"

"No, lad, not yet. They're rebuilding it."

"It looks finished already."

"Aye, but that's the old part that's been repaired. I reckon there's a lot more to be put in yet."

"In the fire, were Dad burnt?" I didn't think about it before reading that paper. Mum said he were blown over and knocked his head.

He waits for Mum to answer. She leans forward to hold my arm. "Yes, pet." That's what I worked out. Mum told me wrong.

"Where?"

"All over," she whispers.

I meant where down there in the factory – but it doesn't matter. Burnt all over, like Guy Fawkes. That's why Mum couldn't see him afterwards. They didn't let her in case she got too upset.

But Guy Fawkes were a bad man. He deserved to be burnt, but Dad didn't. I feel like crying again, but I won't. I'm going to be brave for Dad. I wonder if the man in charge let Dad be burnt. If he did I'd like to burn him.

SEVEN

On the way to Scarborough I focused on pictures of Dad burning instead of the other cars on the road, imaginings fuelled by Bonfire Nights and helpless flaming Guys. The holiday's only a faded mural of sandcastles, paddling, boating, dodgems, arcades, playing Newmarket, eating chips and writing a diary now, but those images are still as sharp as Banksy graffiti. They started my nightmares, but I tried not to let them spoil things.

We played Newmarket after high tea, betting with 1p coins. Grandma Searle called the game Pennies On, and we still call it that now at home. I ate chips on the promenade in the evening with Mum – we were like two kids on a first date. It was a new experience, fun – even exciting. And inspired by Mum reading Dad's diary I started one of my own.

Mum bought me an exercise book to write it in – a red Silvine with that sheen. I've still got it, stored with the diaries from my teens. The weather was wet on the Tuesday and I'm sitting opposite Granddad at the dining room table recording our days in Scarborough so far...

* * *

Granddad says, "Ouch!" getting up from the table and stops me writing. He's been choosing his stamps out of a titchy album someone sends. He bought me a bigger album and some foreign stamps, but his are English from the olden days. All stamps are boring, but his haven't even got any pictures on.

He goes through the arch to the lounge – it's not called the sitting room here. And the lavatory's the toilet, and the spare room's the guest room. I sleep in there; I'm the guest.

"It's looking a deal brighter, and rain's slackening off," I hear him say. "I think I'll go to post office with these approvals. I can stretch my back as well as my legs. I don't reckon I'll drown. Oh, did I interrupt?"

Mum's in there reading Dad's diary.

"Yes, Dadda."

"Sorry, lass."

"It doesn't matter. Can you post these cards for me?"

He comes back and goes into the kitchen and out of the back door. Then I carry on with my diary to finish yesterday.

"I've done it, Mum," I call out, and get down from the table. I can see she's reading again now, but she looks up with a nice smile.

"What, including today?"

"No, not today: Friday, Saturday, Sunday and Monday. Today's not finished yet." I bounce into the other soft chair opposite her.

"Are you going to read it out?"

"Isn't a diary private?"

"It doesn't have to be."

I'm not sure. It's difficult. I feel my face creasing up as I try to decide. "Just to you, then." I have to go back to the dining room to get it. "*Friday. Today we went to Scarbrough for our holiday and I sat in the front. My granma made high tea. After that we looked at the fishing boats and played the waterfall game but only with 2p coins. We had some chips on the way home in the dark. At night I had a very bad dream about Dad.*"

"That's lovely, pet. Am I going to get some more?"

"Yeah. *Saturday. Today we went to Peashome Park and I were in a boat with my mum. My grandad were better at rowing. We had a picknick and went on the beach. I paddled in the sea and built a castle with my grandad like on top of the hill, and then we went to the castle and looked at the views. After high tea we played a game called new market which you bet on and my granma won. I had a bad dream again.*"

"Very good. I expect the dreams will stop when you stop thinking about Dad."

"But I can't." He keeps coming into my mind – how he died. How do I stop it? "Mum, when you burn do you die first or after?"

"You die first, I'm sure. Why?"

"I just wanted to know." So it couldn't have been like that.

"Shall we talk about something else – my rowing? It wasn't so bad, was it?"

"No, but we kept going crooked, didn't we?" I suppose it weren't so crooked.

"Shall we go again to see if I've got better?"

"I could try it."

"When you're bigger, you can." It were worth asking. "Can I hear Sunday's now?" I think she should've said 'may I?'.

"All right. *Sunday. This morning my grandad and granma went to chapel and then we had roast beef and yorkshire pudding. We went to hear the brass band but it were boring so my mum took me to the dodgem cars. They were very good but a fat man kept crashing into us and making signs and my mum were annoyed. We had tea in a café with waitresses. After we came home I helped my grandad water his tomatoes and all his flowers. He's got a lot more than us. I don't remember any bad dreams.*"

"That's good as well."

"What's good as well?" Grandma's come in with her apron on.

"Michael's diary."

"Oh, have I missed it?"

"Not exactly. It's for my ears only."

"It's private, Grandma," I say.

"I'd better go out again then." Grandma sounds a bit annoyed and has a funny look on her face.

"Don't be silly, Mum. I can hear the rest later."

"Anyroad, Michael, talking about missing things, can you try and aim straighter when you go to the toilet?"

I turn round so she can't see my face. Now I'm annoyed. I were having a skeg at their cistern and the chain. It's like in the lavatories at my school. I think the water flushes the poo better when it comes

74

from higher up. It must be going faster.

"He's usually good at home."

"Well, not here, he isn't. That's the second time. Where's Father?"

"He's gone to the post office," says Mum.

"To post some stamps, Grandma." It's a good joke, but I don't think she gets it.

"Look at me. Aren't I a silly? I've still got my pinny on." She's looking in the mirror above the fireplace. Now she's spinning round like a dancer. It makes her dress spread out. She'll get giddy. Then she stops and says, "TTFN," and goes out.

"Grandma's funny sometimes, but you don't know when," I say.

"Yes, pet. It's to do with getting old, I think."

"Is she old?"

"Sixty-eight."

Mum starts reading Dad's diary again. She's got her head in it all the time. She's forgotten about mine.

Sixty-eight: that's too old to spin round – or to zoom about all the time cleaning. She's like a ball zigzagging in one of them pinball machines. She'd score five hundred thousand at least.

I get up to watch for Granddad through the window. It's a bay window like at Grandma Paine's. You get a better view sideways with them. The weather's better now. We were going to Robin Hood's Bay, but it started to rain. I don't know why it's called that. Robin Hood lived in Sherwood Forest, and that's nowhere near here.

"Mum."

It takes a time before she hears. "Yes."

"How far have you got with Dad's diary?"

"Not as far as I would've without being interrupted."

"Sorry."

"It's not just you, pet. I'm on the seventeenth of March. Dad's put his name down for a school trip to see a ballet, and in the dinner hour he's played over the records for a talk he's giving after school with a boy called Andy about twentieth century music."

"Is that the music Dad sometimes played at home?"

"Yes."

"What you didn't like?"

"Yes." Mum looks a bit annoyed.

"What did he do next?"

"He had practical physics. That's studying things like heat and sound and electricity."

"I'd like to learn about that, I would." Then I'd know how everything worked.

"Well, you will at secondary school."

"Can I have a skeg?"

"You 'may' have a 'look'."

I go over and stand next to Mum's chair. Flipping heck, it's written ever so small. "It's hard to read." I lean closer and have to screw up my eyes to see.

MARCH 1960

17 THUR

Walked to school with some records for evng. PS in library first two lessons. Celia sitting at next table, so hard to concentrate. Theory of quadratics with Mr. Summers after break. After putting names down for 'The Rite of Spring' ballet visit next month Andy and I in Room X all dinner hr. We played over the records for our talk on 20th C music in Music Club. Practical Physics all afternoon. Worked with Rich on coefficient of thermal conductivity. Over to X at 3.50. Audience of 15 and talk was successful. Celia came in late, beautiful and breathless at 4.10. Home on bus. Usual evening, some Physics work, TV and radio, including funny 'Does the team think' with Ted Ray, Jimmie Edwards, and Tommy Trinder.

"I don't think I'll bother with any more. It's too titchy," I say.

"No, pet. I didn't think you'd want to."

"Who's Celia?"

"I don't know; just a girl at school."

Mum sounds a bit shirty so I go back to the window. Dad didn't have many for his talk, but he had that Celia. She were beautiful and breathless. Maybe she's the girl in the photo. I think she were beautiful. And maybe she'd been running because she were late and didn't want to disappoint Dad.

After a bit I see Granddad. "Mum, Granddad's back."

"Oh, is he?"

"Yeah." I wave as he goes to the kitchen door. He'll have to wipe his feet on the outside doormat and then on the inside one. Grandma's got two mats at the front door for us as well. "Mum, can we go out after tea like on Friday?"

"I don't see why not. And if Granddad and Grandma don't want to, we could go on our own."

She's in a good mood. "To the amusements?"

"Yes, and then the chippy."

"Hooray!" I suddenly want to kiss her, and so I run over to put my arms round her neck; and then she pulls me on to her lap and kisses me and hugs me ever so tight. It's ages since we've done it – not since Dad died. But I pull away and go to the other chair when I hear someone coming in. It's Granddad.

"Job done."

"How much for my stamps?"

"Forty-one pence including Graham's, but I'll treat you – just like we've been treated."

"Mm? How?"

"Jim Lumb's wife's poorly. They were going to Library Theatre Wednesday night. He's given me the tickets."

"That's nice. You and Mum never go to the theatre."

"And we won't be going Wednesday neither. I've asked her before. If it's not music hall she'll have none of it. It's you and me I thought of."

"Well, only if she's happy for us to go. What's on?"

"*Bedroom Farce*. Sounds a bit saucy. It's by that Alan Ayckbourn, the local genius. They get good write-ups and go to London after."

"What's a farce, Mum?" It sounds interesting. It might be funny, if it's saucy like them postcards.

She has to think before she answers. "It's a funny play where people do silly things and everyone gets confused."

"I might like it, then."

"You might, young sir; but I've only been given the two tickets. You stay and keep Grandma company. She'll enjoy having you all to herself."

"We could play Newmarket again."

"Two's not enough for that, pet," says Mum.

"Oh." Two's not enough for a lot of things.

"It's time for the one o'clock news," says Granddad, and switches on the telly. It's got a bigger screen than ours, and fits on a stand in the bay window. He sits on the sofa to watch. I'm looking at my diary and Mum's looking at Dad's. It's only when we hear what the man says that we look up and Mum twists round.

"The lunchtime headlines today: three men killed at an industrial explosion in Lincolnshire; and sabotage of the pitch during the test match against Australia in Leeds. First, an explosion and fire have rocked the town of Ulcethorpe in Lincolnshire only a year after the catastrophic explosion at Boroughcliff, just four miles away."

"I don't believe it," says Mum. "It hasn't started up yet."

"Shush, listen," says Granddad.

"The blast happened at five minutes past three this morning at National Steel's Ulcethorpe works. There have been three fatalities and a number of men have been taken to hospital with severe burns. We're going over to our regional correspondent Jane Devereux, who is outside the works gates now."

"Thank you, Robert. Yes, this is a major disaster for the town. Details are sketchy at the moment, but there's to be a press briefing this afternoon. I understand a cast was in progress on the Wellington furnace – that's one of the four blast furnaces here (I think you can see two of them behind me) – and molten metal was flowing into a torpedo ladle. That's an insulated container almost as large as a railway carriage. There were problems

78

with the furnace and some cooling water got into the ladle too. When the shunting locomotive moved the ladle there was an explosion. Over two hundred tons of molten iron showered out everywhere."

"Jane, that sounds horrific; and presumably people were exposed to the hot metal."

"Yes, operators were burnt and plant and equipment caught fire. The iron temperature is over a thousand degrees centigrade. But all fires have been extinguished now. As well as the three men pronounced dead there are ten casualties in Ulcethorpe General Hospital, with six of them in a critical condition."

"Jane, thank you for that. We'll come back to you before the end of the bulletin for an update. And now the other main story: protesters campaigning for the release of George Davis have dug up the wicket at Headingley before the last day's play in the third test match against Australia..."

But Granddad doesn't want the rest of the news. He's got up and turned off the telly. I think that were the match Dad were going to take me to.

"And they say lightning doesn't strike twice in same place," Granddad says.

"Yes. When it started I thought they meant Boroughcliff, but it couldn't be much closer," says Mum. "It's dreadful. How many widows will there be this time? I'm glad we weren't there."

"So am I," I say. I would've been thinking about those men burning. I hope I don't think about them here. A thousand degrees, she said – and it all showered out. Dad told me water boils at a hundred degrees, so that iron were ten times hotter. I wonder what happened when it fell on them?

"What could've caused it?" asks Mum.

"It'll all come out in the wash, lass. Anyroad, it's given your newshound friend something to get his teeth into. He'll be at that briefing, no doubt, gnawing to get all the meat off the bone."

"He's not my friend, Dadda." Mum shakes her head.

79

"Not yet."

Mum laughs. "I wonder if he came to Ulcethorpe because of Boroughcliff. He's only been with the *Argus* six months. This'll drive him to despair; but it's fallen right into his lap."

"Aye, like you have."

"Dadda! I haven't."

And I hope she doesn't.

EIGHT

Mum had discovered retail therapy a few weeks before our holiday and devised a new Saturday routine. She'd deposit me at the Baldrys', go shopping in the town centre, and collect me in the afternoon. I had a Ruth Baldry cheese doorstep for lunch; she snacked daintily with the blue rinse widows at Heatons in their restaurant on the top floor. It must've been the Saturday after we came back from Scarborough when she agreed to go out with Ivor Hughes.

I'd been waiting for her to get ready and looking at the Fine Fare carriers piled on the swivel chair. They were filled with Dad's clothes and destined for Oxfam or wherever, and I was trying to guess the contents by remembering what he used to wear. I give up when it makes me sad, and wonder what else I can do…

* * *

Mum's a long time titivating – that's what she calls it. She likes looking nice to go shopping. It makes her feel good, she says. She doesn't always buy anything, but today she's going to buy a car magazine.

I could have another skeg at what that reporter wrote about us. I read it yesterday after getting back from telling Wayne what I did on my holiday. It's a bit soppy, like the stories in Mum's magazines – like this bit: *Marlene lowers her head as she stares into her memory for images of Alan, so savagely taken from his beautiful young wife.* And there's some more like that; but he's put in some of what I told him about Dad, and about me helping Mum by being brave. He said I struggled not to cry, but didn't say I did cry.

81

Now the phone's bring-bringing. I'd better pick it up. "Hallo."

"Hallo, Michael. Is your mam there?"

"Yeah, she's upstairs."

"Can you call her? It's Ivor, say."

"Yeah, all right." I knew it were him; I recognised his voice. I go into the hall calling, "Phone, Mum," but not saying his name. She must've heard it ring because she's already at the top of the stairs. I can see up inside her dress.

"I'm coming, pet."

I sit on the sofa again and Mum zooms to the phone. I can hear her breathing.

"Hallo... Yes... Relaxing: I had a big dose of my mum's looking after – just what I needed... You went home to your mum as well?... to fill the vacuum?..."

Mum used to fill the vacuum with coffee when we went out for the day with Dad. Maybe he needed a drink when he went home.

"Don't say that; you're being silly. Oh, and my dad took me to the theatre: *Bedroom Farce*... Yes, he lives there. It's where they're put on first... So you're an actor?... I'm sure it was more than that, but I can understand why she did... OK... Yes... Are you still there?... Silly man... Well, calm down. I've said yes. What sort of do is it? I need to know what to wear... Sounds fab. And what time?... Fine. See you then. Bye."

Mum looks happy when she puts the phone down and her eyes are shiny. I'm pretending to read the paper and don't say anything. It's obvious: she's going out with that man.

"Are you ready?" Mum says. "We can go early. I might need longer in town now."

"Yeah." I'm annoyed, and don't ask why.

"You can carry one of the bags for me as far as the Baldrys'."

"All right."

I pick up one and she takes the rest.

"Hell!" she says, stepping out of the front door. I think she nearly twisted her ankle. It's her own fault. She shouldn't wear shoes with heels like that. They're too thin to balance on.

*　*　*

I saw the red dress in the afternoon. Mum modelled it for Mrs B, who loved it, but it shocked me – although if a lookalike of Mum that day stood in front of me now wearing it I'd be thinking 'Phwoar!' But a worse shock came later when a second gruesome fact about Dad's death emerged. I'd had a horror comic in my mind from imagining him burning. To be told he'd been crushed as well added even grislier strips.

Ruth's trademark bellow summoned me downstairs to hear that word 'bobby-dazzler'. I'm relieved at being rescued from the discomforting attentions of precocious Jayne...

*　*　*

"Michael, your mum's here." Wayne's mum is shouting ever so loud, like she's always doing: Wayne!... Jayne!... Elaine! They rhyme, so you can't always tell who it is she's calling.

Wayne didn't have enough Lego for what I were building, so I played with Jayne's kitten in her bedroom. Well, it's Elaine's bedroom as well, but she's gone out. I think Jayne likes me. She keeps saying she wishes she were in my class, and getting up close to me. And she's given me that photo of her, and says she wants two of me, one for her and one for her friend Sarah Rivers. She's prettier – I'd rather have had a picture of her. Anyway, I'm not going to ask Mum.

Wayne's mum's so big she fills the doorway, but I can hear Mum saying, "And I bought some shoes to match."

"That looks gorgeous," says Wayne's mum. "Silk, isn't it? A real bobby-dazzler, as my ma would say."

"What's a bobby-dazzler?" I ask when I get downstairs. It's an interesting word.

"Your mum's new dress."

She moves out of the way for me to get past. I can't see a dress. Mum must've put it back in that black carrier bag.

"I know, Marlene. Why don't you model it for us? Go on. You can change up in our bedroom. You won't be disturbed. Colin's working overtime this afternoon."

"No, Ruth, I'd better not..." Wayne's mum looks sad. "Oh, all right. I got a bit flustered in the shop. Maybe I ought to try it on again and you can tell me what you think."

"Come on in. Our bedroom's on the right."

"The same one as mine," says Mum. Their house is just like ours.

We go into the sitting room to wait while Mum goes upstairs. Wayne's mum's been watching wrestling on the telly. I don't like it, but have to watch. The men are like Wayne's dad. Well, maybe he's not quite so fat. With the sound up high we don't hear Mum come back down.

"Here I am," she says, from the doorway.

So that's a bobby-dazzler. I don't know what to say.

"You look fantastic, Marlene. You should be on a catwalk. It fits like a glove. Hang on; let me turn down the volume."

Mum stands in front of the fireplace so we can see her better. It's a bright red dress with a bit of a shine. It's got sleeves, but there's a long split up the side. Mum's like someone on the telly – in a variety show, when they sing and dance and all that.

"What do you think, pet?"

"It's not like you, Mum."

She laughs. "No, it's a new me. But do you like it?"

It's been a shock. She looks nice, but... It's not right, somehow. "No, not much," I say.

"Well, I love it, Marlene – that slit makes it. I wish I had your figure. You've got smashing legs."

"You can only see the one, and not all of that," says Mum.

"Yes, but... You know... It's obvious."

"And I'll be worried about my creaking knees."

"The men won't. They'll be looking, not listening. Couldn't you get shoes with more of a heel?"

"I didn't want to. He's not as tall as me."

"You are thoughtful. I hope he realises what a prize he's getting."

"Yes, I think he does."

How can Mum be a prize? She might win a prize though – in one of them beauty contests on the telly. Why is she getting so dressed up for that reporter? Maybe she thinks that then he'll shave his beard off if she asks.

I have to watch more wrestling while Mum changes back into her normal dress, but at least the sound's still down low.

"I think your mum deserves a night out, don't you, Michael?" says Wayne's mum, when the adverts start.

"We went out twice at night at Scarborough." She doesn't need to do it again. "We had some chips in a shelter on the promenade. I had twenty-three in my bag and Mum only had twenty-one."

"Yes, but this is special."

"That were special. I learnt a new word – some older boys and girls were in the shelter on the other side."

"What was it?"

"I mustn't say. Mum told me what it meant but said it were very rude."

Now Mum's come back down so I get up ready to go.

"What do you say to Mrs Baldry?" she says.

"Oh. Thank you for having me."

"Bye, love."

"Goodbye, Ruth – and thanks again."

We go past two cars on the way out. One's a Morris Minor Wayne's dad is doing up. He's a car mechanic and works at the garage where they sell Fiats. I wonder why he doesn't have one of them. The other car's under a cover like Grandma Paine's tea cosy. It's a Riley Pathfinder, he told me. I know what it looks like because it's in my book. When we're on the pavement Mum sees me looking at her shopping bags.

"Yes, I got a car mag: *What Car?* It seems good. It's got them all in.

We'll look after tea. I bought us a Danish each."

"That's nice." I hope it's the sort with currants and icing.

"What did you do at Wayne's?"

"Nothing much. Mum, where are you going in that dress?"

"To a party next Saturday."

"Where?"

"At Ravenby Manor: it's a house out in the country."

"Who lives there?"

"A friend of the journalist who wrote about us – you know, Ivor Hughes. He's taking me."

She tells me who's taking her as if she thinks I don't know. "I'm not going, am I?"

"No, pet. I'm going to ask Grandma Paine to come and look after you. I think she'll like that."

That's good. Mum and that reporter will have to put up with people staring at her. I won't be there. It'll be her own fault. She should look like all the other mums. "That'll be nice," I say.

After we turn the corner into our road, what Wayne told me comes back into my mind. "Mum."

"Yes."

"When Dad were burnt were he squashed as well?"

"Why should you think that?"

"Wayne said."

"How would he know?"

"He heard his dad telling his mum when she were reading about you in the paper."

Mum doesn't say anything at first. "Do you really want to know? I've never said because I didn't want to upset you."

"But I'm upset already."

"Yes." She takes hold of my hand. "Yes, pet. Wayne's right. Dad was crushed. The building he was in collapsed in the explosion and then everything was burnt."

Crushed and burnt. Poor Dad. I manage not to cry till we're indoors.

Then Mum cuddles me till I stop.

"Come on, pet. You'll feel better when you've had your fizzy and Danish," she says, trying to cheer me up. "And then we're going to look at that mag."

* * *

I don't think the lemonade and Danish pastry cheered me, but after sitting up close to Mum on this sofa with my head against her shoulder to watch Michael Crawford's *Some Mothers Do 'Ave 'Em* antics I felt much better. And then came the delights of *What Car?*...

* * *

It had everything in – even Aston Martins, Lamborghinis and Maseratis. Mum didn't want to look at those and kept turning over too soon. And I didn't want to look at some of the cars she liked. One page got torn, but she only laughed. She's in a good mood, like on holiday.

"Do you want to write a list, so we don't forget?" she asks.

"Yeah. I'll put it at the back of my diary, shall I? I'll go up and get it. It'll be easier writing in the dining room, though."

"Right."

When I come back down with the book and a biro she's already at the table with the magazine.

At the top of the page I write: *Possible cars for Mrs. M. Paine and Master M. Paine.* And then I write the list.

Ford Escort GT. I wanted that, and Mum didn't mind too much.

Alfasud. Mum chose that. It's snazzy, she said. And I like it too – it's got a good shape.

Austin Maxi. Mum said it's practical, but I don't like it.

Citroen GS. It's interesting and unusual. We both agreed.

Mini 1275GT. Mum said the Mini were for her and the 1275GT were for me.

"That's quite neat," says Mum. "I think writing your diary has helped you."

"Yeah."

"I must get the brochures now. But I did something else this afternoon: I booked some driving lessons, starting the week after next when you're back at school."

"That's ace, Mum." And I get down and go round to her chair and give her a hug and kiss.

"Is that cupboard love?" she says, smiling.

"What's that?"

"Showing love because you've got what you want."

"No. I love you all the time." And it's true. But I have got what I want. Well, if she passes the test and buys one. Most of the mums I know haven't got a flipping clue about cars and can't drive.

NINE

On the Sunday we took our two buses to one of Grandma Paine's teas – occasions, I suppose, Mum suffered in the interests of peace and harmony, but which soon afterwards ceased. The house is above the road like a castle on a motte and must've seemed as forbidding to her as was its owner. Anyway, that day she came away with what she wanted: Grandma's promise to stay the night at Kilvert Road and look after me.

I remember we were still outside when she had an excuse to relieve some tension. It showed her new persona was as fragile as the butterfly she'd imagined herself to be. She's pushing at the gate and it's scraping on the flagstones because of a broken hinge…

* * *

"Grandma should get her flipping gate mended," I say.

"Don't you dare say 'flipping'."

Flipping heck, she sounds like the wicked witch. She always gets shirty when we come here. "Why? Wayne does."

"Well, he shouldn't."

"They say it at school." It's not one of them bad words – like that one in Scarborough: cunt. It's not fair. I pout and make my puffing noise.

"Well, I'm sorry, but I don't like it. Please don't say it."

I nod. "I won't say it to you." That's fair.

After running up the sixteen steps I twist the key of the funny bell. It doesn't sound so good as ours. I can see Grandma coming through the coloured glass in the door. "Your gate's broken, Grandma," I tell her, when she opens it. Her dress is very coloured too.

"Yes, darling. I've a man coming to cut the hedge and he's going to mend it for me."

"I like your dress, Agnes," says Mum, as if she wants something. "Magenta, isn't it?"

"Thank you, Marlene. I saw it in Heatons and thought I deserved a fillip. I've bought a Teasmaid as well." We follow her into the sitting room. "I thought we'd have tea in here this time."

I can't see any tea. Maybe it's on the Teasmaid. We usually have it in the dining room sitting up at the table.

"I've bought a new dress, too – for a party next Saturday." Mum says it really quick.

"It's a bobby-dazzler, Grandma," I tell her. "And it's got a slit up the side."

"And why not? I'm sure Mummy deserves it and will do it justice." She looks back to Mum. "And who's the lucky man? I assume you're being taken."

"Ivor Hughes – the journalist. Agnes, would you like to come and look after Michael and stay the night?"

"Yes, of course. I'm pleased you've asked."

"Thanks ever so, Agnes." Mum's not shirty now – just the opposite.

"I could see he'd taken a fancy to you, Marlene, when I read his piece in the *Argus*. It wasn't difficult to read between the lines. But it was quite unbalanced: a paean to you, and yet not a mention of a mother's grief for her son."

"But he didn't interview you," says Mum.

"No, but he could've used his imagination; he seems to have plenty. Anyway, don't let's fall out about it. I'm sure Michael and I will have as much enjoyment together as you will with him – won't we, darling?"

"Yeah. Can we play cards when you come, Grandma? We played Newmarket on holiday, but that's for more than two."

"I'll teach you a new game – one I used to play with Daddy when he was a boy. It's called Bezique. Now sit down, both of you. Are you ready for tea?"

I nod. I feel hungry. "We had high tea on holiday." It's titchy sandwiches with no crusts here.

"I expect that's a Yorkshire custom. Afternoon tea and dinner is more correct, I believe."

"Shall I help?" says Mum.

"Yes, dear. You can get out the Royal Worcester."

They go out and I sit on the big chair beside the bookcase to have a closer look. Some of Dad's are still here: the orange and white ones, and some others. They're so flipping squashed in I can't get hold of one. Lots have got a little penguin on them. Some of mine have got a puffin. I might be able to read them. They could be for older boys. I haven't heard of any, though: *Sons and Lovers*, *The Collector*, *Term of Trial*, *Lolita* – that's by somebody foreign. Lolita's a nice name, if it is a name, a girl's name. Lolita. I make up a little poem: "Lolita might be neater, but she couldn't be sweeter."

"Are you talking to yourself, pet?" Mum's come back.

I twist round to give a smile. "No. It were a poem. It just came into my head."

Now Grandma's wheeling in a trolley with everything on. "Is that your Teasmaid?" I ask.

They both laugh at me. "No, darling," says Grandma. "You've seen this before in the dining room. The Teasmaid is up in my bedroom. It makes me a cup of tea in the morning."

I feel a bit stupid – but how were I supposed to know? I wonder what it's like. "Can I have a look at it?"

"Yes, later on. It's a wonderful thing. We'll switch it on so you can see it in action."

Grandma pours the tea and hands it out, and gives me a plate to put my cucumber sandwich on. She always likes to be in charge.

It's difficult having tea sitting like this. I've got my cup and saucer balanced on the arm of the chair while I eat. I have to hold the sandwich tight and bite hard or the slices come sliding out. One just did but

I caught it on the plate. I don't like milky tea much, but Grandma doesn't have fizzy or squash. They're not good for you, she says.

"It's Assam today," Grandma tells us, drinking her tea. She has different types but they all taste the same. "Did you have a lovely holiday, darling?"

"Yeah. I wrote it all down in my diary. I'll read it to you when you come."

"You've started a diary? Daddy used to keep one."

"Yeah, I know. Mum's been reading it."

"But they're still in his bedroom – two or three of them, I think." She turns to Mum. "Marlene?" She says it like she thinks Mum's pinched one.

"Well, this was in our bedroom. I found it when I was clearing out before we went on holiday. It's for nineteen-sixty."

"And you've read it?" Grandma sounds surprised.

"Not all of it yet. I don't see why I shouldn't."

"Oh, well; but I don't think I would've – out of respect. If he took it with him it was because it was private and he didn't want anyone else to read it." Grandma's mouth goes as thin as a slice of cucumber.

"I didn't know," says Mum, looking a bit red in the face.

"Can I have another sandwich, Grandma – a different one?" Mum's too busy feeling told off to say 'may I'.

"Yes, there's red salmon or Brussels pate."

Brussels pate is a new one; but I don't like Brussels sprouts so I have the salmon. "I read a bit of the diary too, Grandma. Dad liked a girl called Celia. She might be the girl in that photo."

"Celia? I'm sure he never mentioned the name."

"Yes, she is. He took the photo on a school trip to see a ballet – *The Rite of Spring*," says Mum. She sounds pleased to know more than Grandma.

"Yes, I remember the visit," says Grandma. "I wasn't sure it was suitable for the younger ones. They went to Sheffield. But he didn't have a camera then."

"No, he borrowed one: a little Minolta, from Keith's dad. He was very keen on her, Agnes – always looking out for her, anyway. She was in the third form. He mentions her so much I've got quite intrigued. It was a real obsession."

"Really?"

"Yes, and there're a lot of other things he never told me. I didn't know he was a leading light in the film society, for example. They used the school projector to show films after school. He mentions hiring *The Ladykillers* and charging sixpence for admission, and having to show it twice it was so popular."

That man who phoned when the reporter came were a ladykiller. I wonder what it means.

"Yes, he was interested in films, Marlene, but not passionate – not like his love for music and literature. He seemed to give all that up after he met you."

"But not because of me, Agnes. He wouldn't use headphones, and then said listening knowing I didn't like classical music spoiled it for him. I couldn't make myself like it, but I never said he couldn't have it on. And he didn't read so much because he had less time – working and renovating the house."

I didn't like his music much either, but I could go up to my room. Mum didn't have anywhere else to go.

"Perhaps so," says Grandma.

"Definitely so," says Mum, with a louder voice.

"Anyway, it's academic now."

"And talking about things academic, there's something I don't understand. He did really well in the end-of-year exams: top in chemistry and second in applied maths, I think; and good marks in pure maths and physics too. And yet he always told me he'd made the wrong choice doing science and couldn't cope, and that's why he left school in the upper sixth."

"Well, I'm sorry I don't have an answer, Marlene. He was adamant he wanted to leave. He'd lost all interest – or perhaps the teaching was poor or the syllabus became a chore. We weren't discussing his schoolwork as much by then. I was very upset, as you can imagine, but he wouldn't listen to me. Anyway, you haven't had a sandwich yet."

"I'll try the pate, but only one. I don't want to put on any inches before I wear my new dress. Are you sure there wasn't some other reason, Agnes?"

"Yes, quite sure." Grandma twists her head quickly to look at me. "Another for you, darling?"

"Yeah. I'll have a salmon one again, please." I think I'll have four sandwiches altogether before going on to the cakes.

"Your dress is close fitting then?" Grandma asks Mum, after she's offered me the plate.

"Yes, rather."

"And where are you showing yourself off?"

"Ravenby Manor."

"Oh, at the Sanderson-Smiths."

"You know them, Agnes?"

"Not the present generation, but Father was friendly with George Sanderson-Smith before the war. They'd met because of Father's position as borough librarian; George was a borough councillor. My parents went to stay for a weekend house party once or twice. It's the son who owns it now – Richard. Is he a friend of your Ivor Hughes?"

"No, I don't think so. It's a Sylvia who's directing the play Ivor's rehearsing. She could be the wife. It's her party. Did you ever go there, Agnes?"

"I went once with Father. George was chairman of the Libraries and Arts Committee. He wanted to get opinions on improvements to our service, and Father offered me as the library assistant mouthpiece."

"What's the house like?"

"Imposing, as I remember. There's a long drive to one of those symmetrical Georgian facades with lots of tall windows, and that's attached to a much older wing at one side. I only saw the entrance hall and drawing room when we went in. I remember saying how grand it was and our host replying that he thought it quite a modest house. I suppose our perceptions defined our class: middle for me and upper for him."

So there's classes for people, not just at school. I wonder what class we are – the same as Grandma, or lower down? Anyway, Mum's going to the same big house. Grandma only went once. I hope Mum doesn't go again either.

"I guessed it might be like that, by the name. I hope I can live up to it – and them," says Mum.

"So do I, Marlene; but I think you might feel a little out of your depth."

I think we must be lower down.

TEN

We watched from the sitting room window as Ivor Hughes, dapper in a floral shirt with matching tie, escorted Mum, stunning in her sheath of red silk, to his car; and then Grandma taught me the basics of Bezique. I think the prepared pack, thronged with kings and queens, made that first game appeal – the first of hundreds more over the years Grandma's love helped to compensate for Mum's going AWOL. She made me feel special; she plugged and bailed out the leaks my frail craft suffered in the choppy waters then; and as she and Mum severed their connections, I took the role of go-between and 25 Gainsborough Avenue became my second home. For her, I think I became Dad. But for me, she could never be my mum.

I tried to stay awake in bed until Mum came home, to ask about the party if she came in to tuck me up, but failed; and at breakfast the topic seemed sub judice, so I waited to find out something when we were alone.

But I had a compensation: the *Playfair Football Annual 1955-56*, and another of the series of Dad's boyhood possessions Grandma had started bestowing on me like retainers to moderate my attachment to Mum. I still have it, with its split spine, browning paper and tiny print…

* * *

There's loads of numbers in this football book: results and scorers and tables and crowds and records and everything. It were Dad's. Grandma brought it yesterday afternoon. Oh, the phone's bring-bringing. Flipping

96

heck, Mum's in from the kitchen like she's in a race.

"Hallo... Pam! You're home. I rang you yesterday... Oh, I see. Thanks for the card... No, only the one so far – from Granada, the day you hired a car. How was it?... Well, it would be. Oh, I can hear Agnes on the stairs. She's going for her bus. I'll have to ring off in a sec... She was babysitting last night... Yes, I went to a smashing party... Who do you think? A man... No, not now... Calm down. You'll have to be patient for a few minutes. I'll ring you back... Bye."

Grandma's come in now. "That was Pam," Mum tells her. "They've been in Spain for a fortnight."

"They're welcome to it. I don't hold with all this European business. I voted against. We speak different languages for a reason. Study them, by all means; but fraternisation, most definitely no. No good will come of it, mark my words, Marlene."

"Michael, don't just sit there. Grandma's going. Get up." Flipping heck, Grandma says something and Mum gets shirty with me.

I do as I'm told. "Bye-bye, Grandma. I were reading that book of my dad's."

"Do I get my kiss then, darling?" Grandma says that. I hear Mum say, "Was reading," as well.

"Yeah."

She puts down her handbag and the one she calls her Gladstone to hold on to me. She smells very flowery when she kisses. "There. That should last me for a while. We'll play Bezique again."

"Yeah, it's good." But you need two packs of cards so I can't play it with Teddo. Grandma brought some new cards but she's taking them back home so we can play when I'm there.

"Are you sure you won't stop for lunch, Agnes? I've catered for you – a shoulder of lamb," says Mum.

"No thank you, dear. I won't outstay my welcome."

Now she's buttoning up her raincoat – but it's sunny outside. Oh, I remember: it were raining when she came. She had a plastic cover over her hair. It folded into a strip on its own when she took if off so she could put it in her bag. Ooh, hurry up, Grandma; I need to do a poo. I were putting it off because of that book.

Mum stands in the doorway to watch Grandma go, and I look from the window. Then I take the book up to obey another rule before going to the lavatory. When I come out I can hear Mum back on the phone, so I sit on my top listening step. I want to know what she did at that party.

"Yes, and he rang the day after. I hemmed and hawed and then he asked again when we came home from Dadda and Mum's... Well, with a beard and being small I didn't – you know... Yes, I suppose he would... Pam! You're awful. I don't fancy him like that... No. It's his mind I like, his conversation... Yes, it is. He's really passionate about workers' safety, but quite sweet underneath… Well, obviously… Oh, younger than me, and he's married but separated now, I think… By about four or five years, I worked out. He told me how he was only in his teens when the Aberfan disaster changed his life – made him care about people – and that was nineteen-sixty-six…"

I don't know about that disaster. I wonder what sort of factory it were.

"Because he was a junior reporter on the *Merthyr Post* and went there straight after it happened. He's had this vision of a higgledy-piggledy heap of bodies dying and being trampled on by company directors after every disaster since…"

I wish I hadn't heard that: a heap of bodies. It's horrible. I'll be dreaming about it now as well as Dad dying and those men at the steelworks.

"No, it isn't. Anyway, I understand what he means. I've never thought about politics and campaigning before. Alan never talked about anything like that – well, not to me. Ivor's so different. He's working on a scoop about National Steel at the moment and how the managers are cheating on safety. The men of steel and their feet of clay, he calls them… Yes, I am; and so would you be if you heard him. There was a nasty accident there while you were away: several men were burnt to death. And with them ignoring a new safety law and having lots of other problems the story could make his name... Sorry, if I'm boring you..."

Mum's boring me a bit. She's going on about that reporter like a telly advert what tells you how good something is when it isn't.

"Yes, of course you do... No, I bought something new. I decided to make a big splash... No, not there. Do you remember those boutiques we went in last summer?... Yes. I looked in Angelina first, but got it in That Frock. Thirty-nine ninety it cost me, and nine ninety-five for some shoes to match..."

Flipping heck, that's almost £50. I didn't know we were so rich. Well, not so rich now.

"Yes, I know. I was bonkers, but I don't care. Oh, and I did get an evening bag thrown in... It's full length with long sleeves and a slash neck; and – wait for it – a slit up the side... Yes, that's the piece de resistance... Didn't I say? It's red. I was the scarlet woman..."

When Grandma saw it she opened her mouth but no words came out.

"Ravenby Manor. It's a big old house out on the edge of the Wolds... Well, Ivor's in GODS, one of the amateur theatre groups... GODS – Gunterton Operatic and Drama Society – G,O,D,S. They're doing an Alan Ayckbourn at the Arts soon – *Absurd Person Singular*. The director's a Sylvia Sanderson-Smith, and it's her house... No, she's got a husband, but she wears the trousers – a turquoise pyjama suit last night, in fact. She's super, Pam. She's persuaded me to join the group... No, I know; but neither had Ivor. She just has that effect: convinces you you can do anything. She saw me dancing and said she was going to put me on the stage..."

It's getting worse. Mum's going to do acting and things and have people pay to look at her. Dad wouldn't have let her.

"No, they had a disco – mostly sixties stuff. But there was a free bar and a scrumptious buffet. I had champagne, Pam – and Ivor did. It was our first time ever... No, never – not the proper stuff. It was Moët et Chandon... I know. The whole do made me realise I've spent my life under a stone... Well, I have. You were only saying the other day how Alan was so controlling..."

I think she means Dad were always in charge. Well, he were. He went out to work; he drove our car; he did up our house; he took me to football; he knew everything. You need somebody like that in charge. But Mum made all the rules. Now she's in charge as well and there's no one on my side.

"They were mostly people in GODS... Well, I only talked to a few. I was too busy twisting the night away... Yes, I think so, but you know what I'm like afterwards, wondering if I got it right... Yes. Anyway, Babs Divine was amusing. She runs a hair salon in town, and is Ivor's wife in the play. I think she feels she has to look after him because of that. Her husband Tom's in it too, but I didn't like him much. He's an estate agent. They all seem such clever dicks... Well, you know what I mean, then. And there was Kay Wilson. She works at the *Argus* offices and pushed Ivor into GODS. I met her fiancé, too. She's really nice. And Ivor spent some time with Sylvia's daughter Sarah. She works for a publisher in London, and he wants to write a book about Boroughcliff. It turned out she's in fiction, but she promised to help if she could... I know, but I'm excited for him. He deserves to do well..."

That's a book I'd like to read one day – if he writes it. A book's better than a paper. You keep it on a shelf or it's in the library, but a paper's just chucked away.

"I hope so. Oh, and I met another of the cast: Janet Smith. She's a games teacher, quite petite and really fit – like that gymnast Olga Korbut. She had a strapless dress on, so you could see... Well, the muscles in her arms and shoulders. She was there with a reporter called Dave Fletcher who works with Ivor. It was all a bit odd, really – Ivor told me about it afterwards. It seems this Dave had seen Janet with Ivor and the rest of the cast in the pub they go to after rehearsals, and taken a fancy. Then he tricked Ivor into telling him where she lived, saying he wanted to write about school sports facilities – he's a proper ladykiller, it seems. She's married, but to someone who's not into partying – a bit like Alan, by the sound of it. And then she turns up at this do with Dave in tow... Yes, really devious, I should think – well, both of them.

Ivor reckons he's met his match: she's stringing him along in revenge, and he won't be getting a bite at the cherry..."

What cherry? They put a cherry in Babycham. Maybe she had one in her champagne. I forgot to ask Mum what a ladykiller is. It must be a man who likes ladies a lot.

"Yes, weird isn't it. I liked her, but she's got a hard streak. God help the next woman who takes his fancy, though, and doesn't play ball. I had a dance with him while Ivor was talking to Sarah. It was the only way of getting rid of him... No, he's very good-looking and rather droll. Think of a rugby player – the ones in the scrum or maul or whatever it is – with blonde hair who reckons he's every woman's dream. And of course by then the music's smoochy. You can imagine what it was like..."

Moochy: that's a funny word. Mum tells me to stop mooching about when I'm bored. Maybe the music were boring.

"Yes. I could've been in a maul myself. I'm glad Ivor didn't see... No, I didn't have to with Agnes still up. I'd said on purpose I needed to leave at midnight like Cinderella... No, but I gave him a peck when I got out of the car. I was too quick for him. Anyway, he's phoning to suggest an outing next weekend – all three of us. I thought it was him when you rang... I don't know; I'm leaving it to him... That's good of you, but stop matchmaking. I don't need Michael out of the house. It's not like that. I said... No, it isn't. Look, I'll have to ring off. I need to put the joint in... Yes, I thought she'd stay. I never get it right with her. It'll be wasted on us. I'll ring you this evening and you can tell me all about Spain... Bye."

Why might Mum need me out of the house? She asked me to go up to my room when he came before. Maybe it's to make sure I don't listen to what they say – or see what they do.

* * *

Mum offered a trip to Everard Park after our roast lunch, but I favoured an afternoon with Ian Ivatt and his dad and their Hornby railway layout. They'd bought a new loco for it – 'Mallard' in LNER blue. When I came home I found her in the back garden, sunbathing on the canvas lounger (the same colour as the streak). I can see her now, face down in her striped dress with the hem pushed right up and her legs shiny. Dad's diary is open spine upwards on the patio next to a bottle of sun lotion and a glass of orange squash…

* * *

Mum's asleep. She's tucked her dress up in her knickers like the girls at school when they do handstands and things. She must want to get her legs brown. She's been reading Dad's diary. I'll see where she's got to. Oh, only August.

AUGUST 1960
4 THUR Tragedy!

The usual Carrs routine. The long morning dragged to its close. I continued transferring figures to slips from wages cards. Collected trousers in lunch hr. A great improvement. Suit will be smart, but doesn't matter much now (see below). The afternoon occupied as in morning. Home at 5.30. After heart searching I rang Alice's number (easy to find with her surname). Tragedy. She said no. She nice about it, but still no. Not allowed boyfriends till she's sixteen. Or perhaps an excuse? I couldn't help crying. After months of waiting it has come to this. Mum in and asked what was the matter. She annoyed when I didn't say. Just spaghetti on toast followed by choc. mousse. Went to bed early. Listened to Luxembourg heartbroken.

Dad cried when he were a boy – just because she couldn't be his girlfriend. So it's all right for me to cry when I think about Dad dying. Anyway, I thought the girl he liked were called Celia, but it's Alice he phoned… Alice… You can make Celia out of the letters of Alice. Maybe it were a code and it's the same girl.

Mum's waking up. I think my shadow must've cooled her down. "Hallo, pet."

"Hallo. You haven't finished the diary, Mum."

"No, not yet. Give it back."

I pass it over and she shuts it up. "When's tea time?"

"Not yet."

"Can I have the rest of that orange? And can I watch the telly?"

"You *may* have my squash if I *may* have a kiss."

She's in a good mood and bribing me. I kneel down as she rolls on to her side for the kiss.

"Don't I get a bigger one? That was only a peck," she says.

I finish her drink and bribe her too. "If I *may* watch the telly."

"Cheeky. What's on?"

"Cricket – you know, Sunday League on BBC2."

"Oh, yes. All right." This time it's longer and she does the kissing. "What's happened to your diary, poppet?"

"I don't do it any more. It's harder at home because everything's the same."

"Mm. I've never done one. When you're back at school it might be better."

"We'll see; or when I'm older, maybe." I stand up smiling. "Can I switch the telly on then?"

"OK." And then she gets my joke and laughs.

I run indoors. Everything's much better when Mum's like this. I hope her going out with that reporter again doesn't spoil it.

ELEVEN

I was included in Ivor Hughes' plans for the following Saturday, and the thought of my first ride in a Mini Cooper must've overcome any resistance to going out with Mum's new man. He collected us late in the morning and sped eastwards and up on to the Wolds. A pub lunch was first on his agenda. We ate alfresco, despite the cool breeze – because of me being under age, I suppose – and sat at a picnic table. Mum's opposite him and next to me...

* * *

We're outside the White Lion. I thought lions only came in brown. We're so high up we can see Lincoln Cathedral, even though it's miles and miles away. Maybe that's where we're going. A mystery trip, he said.

"You said you were married, Ivor, but are you divorced?" asks Mum. It stops him having another bite of his sandwich.

"Not yet. We have to separate for two years first. But it's all finished between us, like I said."

He must be married but live on his own. Deano Haynes' mum and dad live in different houses. I wonder if he's got any children. "So you can't be my dad, then?"

"I could never be your dad, Michael. Your dad's special to you. He can't ever be replaced."

No, he can't. He's right about that. They're both looking at me. "No. I meant you can't marry Mum?"

"No, but I can be her friend – and yours."

"Would you like that, poppet?"

She looks really happy, and wants me to say yes. He doesn't follow football, but he likes cricket and rugby. And he's got the Mini Cooper S – though it's only a G reg. Still, the exhaust sounds good. I nod and say, "Maybe," and eat the last inch of my sausage roll. Now I can drink the last inch of my lemonade. Mum's kissing the top of my head. She said I had to have my hair washed this morning. I hate it; the shampoo always stings my eyes.

"That's quite an honour, Ivor, Michael's 'maybe'."

"Can I go on the swings?"

"You may, if you've finished."

I climb up on to the seat to get out of the table and then do a big jump down. When I turn round to see if they're watching me Mum's staring at him with a soppy face.

When I sit on the swing I can still hear what they say. It's windy up here, and their voices are blowing my way.

"What went wrong with you and...? I don't even know her name," says Mum.

"Megan. She never... We were never suited – emotionally. We fancied each other, but even by nineteen-sixty-nine the swinging sixties hadn't sailed that far back up the Taff. So we got married – and I discovered she was manic."

"Mad?"

"No; manic depressive. I should've guessed before, but she was clever. And I wasn't watching out for thorns, just eager for the fruits. I had to make the best of it. I'd made my bed and had to lie on it, as they say – the only part of our marriage that worked, as it turned out."

"So she kept changing from being very happy to very sad?"

"When you put it like that it might not seem so difficult. Happiness and sadness I could've managed; but in the manic phase she went over the top talking, talking, spending, spending; and when she was down she sucked all the sympathy out of me till I lost my temper, and then blamed me for the moods."

"So you argued a lot?"

"Hell, did we argue. In the early days I even hit her once or twice – just slaps. I felt so cheated and frustrated. I know it was bad, but I think she provoked me on purpose. She wanted it: to be my victim, to make me responsible. I've not told anyone before, but I want to be totally honest with you – no secrets, nothing hidden."

He shouldn't have hit her. He might hit Mum. Maybe she won't like him so much now.

"Thanks. But isn't there any treatment – Valium and things? That's what I took."

"Pills might've helped if she'd taken them. I thought she was; but she fooled us both, the doctor and me. And there's no cure. Even film stars with their private psychiatrists suffer. I moved back home, but she blackmailed me to come back – threats to cut her wrists, or coming round and making disturbances at night. And that's just two of I don't know how many tricks she had. So I came here. Anywhere would've done – but I'm glad it was here."

Mum whispers something. I think it were, "So am I."

"Do you want something more? You've only had those biscuits," he says.

Mum's had a coffee as well. She drinks left handed when we're out because Grandma Searle says there's fewer germs on the cup that side. I had a glass so it didn't have sides.

"No, I'm fine. You finish your sarnie and we can be off. Where to next?"

He eats the last of his sandwich and then turns round to point.

"Lincoln," says Mum. "I've not been properly for ages. It was always on the way to somewhere else. Good thinking, Ivor Hughes."

"I went two weeks ago, but didn't see everything. That was the night I stopped outside your house on the way back."

"Why? Did you ring the doorbell?"

"No. It was too late; and I just needed to look at where you were."

It were his Mini I saw. That were the night I couldn't sleep, thinking about the cars we might have. When I looked out of my window it drove off.

106

"Funny man. Well, you don't have to act like a stalker now; we're friends. You can phone or call round. Anyway, if you've finished I'll take these back."

Mum gets out of the table and walks over to the pub holding the tray. The wind lifts up her dress, so I can see her legs. I think Wayne's mum were right. If Mum does do any acting she could be in a pantomime and play the prince. He's always a woman what shows her legs. But Mum's not very good at singing. And what's a stalker? I'll put a dictionary on my birthday list so I won't have to keep asking about the words I don't know. Now she's coming out, so I get off the swing and walk back to the table to meet her.

When she's closer he says, "I thought we'd have tea and cakes in Lincoln, and then finish up in Ulcethorpe and see my new flat. I've got something in I can cook for us."

"Can you cook?" I ask. "You're a man." I didn't think they did it. Dad never did.

"I had to learn, or I'd have gone very hungry. There's spaghetti Bolognese, but if you don't like eating foreign I can turn it into a cottage pie."

"We'd like the spaghetti, wouldn't we, pet?" says Mum, taking hold of my hand.

I'm not sure – but she's already decided. Now he's holding her other hand, and she's swinging our arms and skipping between us on the way to the car.

* * *

Lincoln always puts on a good show, but for me at nine the castle's battlements and dungeons were the star attractions. My strongest memory in the cathedral is Mum and Ivor Hughes staring at the Rose Window, hand in hand, and me waiting and wondering how they could look up at it for so long without getting aching necks. They held hands the whole day, and I don't think I minded. After a lavish spread at a Steep Hill teashop Ivor gave another demo of vroom-vroom driving and sleight of hand with the gears along Ermine Street and now on the A18…

* * *

We're back in smelly old Ulcethorpe. I don't know why we've turned off to go past the steelworks; it's not the quickest way. There's these great long sheds you can see through the wire fence. They go on for miles.

"What goes on in there, Ivor?" I ask.

"Those are the rod and plate mills, Michael," he says. "In short, there's an awful lot of crash, bang and wallop. It gets the steel into shape." Mum laughs. "Well, I don't know all the details yet. I'm still mugging up."

"So, Monday's the big day now for your story," she says.

"That's what the Old Man said. There was a legal quibble, see, and he wants it to be spot on. At least from the stony silences I know he's pleased with it. I think I'll call into the office for my copy and the file. I meant to bring it home yesterday for a last look through."

"And then you've the book to begin."

"Yes, thanks to you. Next week I'm seeing Henry. I've made a start on a proposal already. I just knew he'd help if you asked him – like I would. And now he's retired, I think he was quite keen."

Mum goes quiet and turns her head to look at him. Then she says, "When's your birthday, Ivor?"

"I've just had it – on the first of August. Twenty-eight, I was."

Mum's quiet again. She's thirty-three. I think Ivor's too young for her – or she's too old for him. It's the same thing, either way.

"Why did you ask?" he says.

"Oh, I was just thinking about something."

"What?"

"Something I might buy you; but don't ask me to say what. You're a Leo, aren't you? I'm Pisces."

108

"What am I, Mum?" I ask. I can't remember.

"Libra – the scales. You're going to be a judge or a politician."

"Am I?"

"No, not really. It's all made up by astrologers. It's not serious."

"What's Ivor?"

"Leo is the lion; and I'm the fish."

"He might eat you. Cats eat fish, and lions are big cats."

"Silly."

Now we're at the big roundabout what joins up five roads. It's a bit like the dodgems, but with the cars whizzing round a lot faster – and you've got to avoid having a bump. But I'm not worried – not like with Granddad. Ivor's driving is almost as good as Dad's.

"I had my driving lesson on Thursday. Mid morning in Ettisham Park was a bit quieter," says Mum.

"Mum had an Austin Allegro. That's got a quartic steering wheel. It's sort of square with round corners," I say.

"Did it? I never noticed."

Flipping heck. Why can't mums understand cars? "And it had dual control, in case she got it wrong."

"But I didn't, Mr Clever. Mr Still said he wished all his pupils were like me. Lots of times he said 'beautiful' when I changed gear or turned a corner." She turns round to face me. "Wait till you learn. It's not as easy as it seems."

"No, Michael. It might seem second nature for me now, but I remember when I was learning I dreaded every time I had to make a gear change. It sounds as if your mam's a natural."

"Dad were a natural."

"Yes, and so can I be."

"Here we are," says Ivor. He's parked in a one-way street with buildings on one side and wooden boards on the other. "Are you coming in?"

"No, we'll sit here and mind the car," says Mum.

"But, Mum, I want to see where Ivor works. Can't we?"

"Oh, all right."

We don't go in through the front. Ivor says it's locked because the receptionist doesn't work Saturday afternoon. It looks a bit like a cinema entrance with big glass doors. He's got a key to the side door. When we get in I ask, "Is this where they make the papers?" I can't hear anything going on.

"No, Michael, not any more. We've got a new print shop on Trentholme Road. This is just offices now."

It's a pity. I wanted to see how they did it – the machines and things. We go up two lots of stairs and along a corridor. We don't meet anyone, but I hear people talking and typewriters clattering. Then Ivor opens a door right at the end.

"Dave! I didn't think you'd be in. Don't you phone your copy through?" he says.

"I'm checking it, Taff. I don't want to read that Rovers scored with an explosive shit just inside the post two weeks on the trot, do I? How about you?"

Now I can see who's talking. He's the other side of a desk as big as a bed, and leaning back in his chair with his feet up. He's big as well – much wider than Dad. He's got more hair than Dad, too, but it's the same colour. Dad were starting to go bald. He said 'shit', but I think he meant 'shot'.

"Just picking something up, I am," says Ivor.

"Aye. And brung thi new family with thee an' all," says the man. He's seen me in the doorway and Mum behind. His voice is different now – as if he's making fun of how Granddad talks.

"Yes, very funny, Dave," says Ivor, opening a drawer on our side of the desk.

"Come reet in, lad. Don't be shy," the man says to me. He's got a friendly smile.

I go over to the window to look over at what's going on behind them boards. I can see big squares of concrete where they might be going to build something. I hear the man say, "'Ow do, Marlene. Today's me lucky day."

"Why's that?" Mum asks.

"Seeing thee again. I'm reet med up. Absence meks t'eart grow fonder, folks say."

"Does it?" Then I hear Mum take a deep breath before saying, "Ivor, I need the Ladies. Then I'll see you downstairs."

"Yes, right. It's back down the corridor and the last door on the left."

"Mm, tasty," I hear the man say to himself. I don't know why – he's not eating anything. Maybe he's thinking about Mum because he's a ladykiller. Then he asks me, "Do you like football, lad?" He's talking normally again now.

"Yeah. I used to watch Rovers with my dad."

"I was at Ettisham Road this afternoon. It's my job."

"What were the score?"

"Rovers won two-nil."

"Hooray! Did Trevor Stubbs score – Stubbsie?"

"One of them."

"He used to be my favourite player."

"Don't you go now?"

"No."

"You should ask Ivor to take you – or I could. I'll ask your mum."

"Yeah."

"Right, Michael. We can go now; I've got everything," says Ivor. He's holding a folder full of papers. "See you Monday, Dave."

"Aye. Enjoy thissen, Taff. 'Appen toneet's t'neet fer it. I'm reet jealous thinkin' on what thee might ger up to. 'Ast 'a remembered what I've telled thee?"

It's difficult understanding what he's saying – and what he means.

* * *

Ivor Hughes had moved to a spacious top flat in a converted Edwardian villa on Bardby Road – a flat with a balcony and furnished with a variety of things I haven't seen before…

"Is that real, Mum, that rug like a zebra?" I ask.

"Yes, I think so."

"This looks like an elephant's foot, this thing with all the sticks in."

"Yes, that's real as well."

I sit in one of the soft chairs. It's really comfy; you sink right in.

"It's very *Ideal Home*, Ivor. I don't think I could've left it if it were mine," says Mum.

"She's on some assignment in Sweden. With the rent so cheap in Coke Street I could afford to treat myself. I had to give references, mind. It felt like I was being chosen to look after a stately home."

"There're some lovely ornaments. They're real objets d'art, aren't they? And I like how they're in clusters."

Ivor looks pleased and just smiles; and then they go out into the hall. I feel a bit tired and lean back in my chair.

"I like the chaise longue in here, and the drapes, but are you going to make it a bit more macho?" I hear Mum say; and then a bit later, "Ooh, what a huge bath. You could almost swim in it." She sounds very keen on everything – as if she wants to move in as well.

They come back into the sitting room. "I think I'll start on our meal, if you want to make yourselves comfortable. Oh, Michael is, already."

"I could be cook's boy, if you like," says Mum. "Have you got an apron?"

"I haven't, but she's left several."

"I'll take my cardie off to show I'm stopping."

"Can I – may I go on the balcony, Ivor?" I ask.

"Yes. You test it for me. I've not had the chance to go out on it yet. Come on then, Marlene."

I open one of the French windows to get out. Both Grandma Paine and Grandma Searle have got them on their houses, but downstairs. I look over the handrail. But it's cold in the wind, and I'm missing what's going on, so I go back inside.

"This is where you learn your lines, then," I hear Mum say.

"This is where I do everything at present. I'm not used to the sitting room yet. It's a bit grand. But we'll eat at the table in there tonight."

"Is this your part underlined – Geoffrey?"

"Yes."

"There's a lot of it. And you've never acted before."

"Have this Babycham apron – it matches your dress."

"Thanks."

"I acted at school, and I've sung on stage."

"It's still brave. I'll ask for a tiny part, if I start."

"*If* you start?"

"All right, when I start."

I wonder what part Mum could have in a play. She could be a teacher; she's a bit bossy like Mrs Watson at my school. She could be a cook; she's good at that. She could be a typist in an office. She could be a nurse – they only have to look nice and give people medicine and pills. She could be the wife of a man in the play. What other parts are there?

"What do you want me to do?" asks Mum.

"Would you like to mince the steak while I get on with the vegetables? There's a mincer in that drawer you can fit on the table."

"Sirloin. Nothing but the best."

"I'd use ready minced for cottage pie, but for this it's worth it."

"Where did you learn to cook, Ivor?"

I hear Mum sliding a drawer what's a bit stuck.

"I got the basics from my mam; but when I saw I couldn't rely on Megan I enrolled at the tech for evening classes."

"Ivor Hughes, you're a man of many talents."

She's right; he is.

"Marlene Paine, you're a woman of discernment."

I wonder what discernment means. I think it must be something nice.

* * *

113

Mum asked Ivor Hughes to bring us home early because I went to sleep after our meal. She invited him in for coffee to tie more strings between them, like they'd been doing throughout the day. Even I could see she was falling in love; and as I lie in bed thinking about all the new experiences I'm feeling glad...

* * *

I'm not sleepy now. I think I went to sleep at Ivor's because I had a taste of that wine. Frascati, it were called. Or maybe it were because the things they were talking about were boring: how Mum won prizes at school for sewing and cookery, and what dolls she had; and how he took his eleven-plus exam twice and who his first girl friend were. I think they forgot I were there. Maybe I could take my exam twice if I have to.

He did a good meal. That cassata were a lot better than the ice cream Mum buys. They've had one of her soppy records on, and then I heard them talking but it's gone all quiet. Maybe they're asleep now.

I need to wee. I forgot to do one when I came to bed. I switch on my lamp and open my door softly so as not to wake them up. Oh, they're not asleep; they're kissing by the front door. Well, it looks more like they're biting each other. And Mum's got her hands in his hair, like when she shampoos mine. Ivor's got his hands on her bottom – he's sort of lifting it up... Now he's pulling up the back of her dress and tucking it into her knickers... I'd better not watch any more in case he sees me and gets annoyed – like Dad got annoyed when I came home early from Ian's party and he were kissing Mum on the swivel chair and her dress were undone.

I do my wee but don't flush the lavatory so they won't know I'm up. Oh, they're not there now. Ivor must've gone home. I can't hear them talking. I shut my door and get into bed. After a bit I hear Mum's music again. Then I feel like I'm going to sleep.

TWELVE

Other than at Barcelona (and as a stranger) I never saw Ivor Hughes again until today. But just as his reappearance put on that video, playing it has triggered memories of what came next. They focus on Mum's relapse: her decline from elation to despair. It started next morning – or a morning soon after – when she got into my bed. I'd woken early and I'm reading aloud when she opens my door…

* * *

"You're awake, poppet." Mum's got her nightie on.

"Yeah." I had another of those dreams about Dad dying. I can wake myself up now before they get too bad.

"I thought I could hear you. What are you doing?"

"Reading to Teddo."

"Can you see? You've not got your light on."

"It's *Winnie the Pooh*. I can remember it, can't I Teddo?" I do his voice. "Oh yes, you're a very clever boy."

Mum breathes some big sighs. "I'll open the curtains, and you can read some to me as well. It's light now."

"Would you like that, Teddo?" And again I do his voice like those ventriloquist people on the telly. "Yes, please. I'd like some more, too."

Mum comes to sit on my bed and gives me a kiss. "Shall I get in with you?"

I nod. It's a surprise. Dad got in once – after that flipping Deano bashed my mouth with his Dinky in the playground; but Mum hasn't ever. I'm all right now – but maybe she isn't.

"Move over then."

I prop Teddo up against my lamp. Mum slides in and puts her head on my pillow and pulls my quilt up to our chins. It would be nice lying close like this, only she keeps twitching and shaking and spoils it. I hold my book above my head and start reading, because I can't remember all the words. It's the bit about the expedition, only Pooh thinks it's called an expotition.

"Mum, are we going on another expotition with Ivor?"

"No... No, we won't be seeing him again. He's... He's got to go away."

I don't understand. It were good going out with him, and then they were kissing and things by the front door. I thought we'd have a lot more trips out, like with Dad. Maybe she didn't like him feeling her bottom – or him being a stalker and hitting his wife. It's a pity, but I don't ask why. Something tells me not to, so I carry on reading. And it doesn't matter; we can still be happy together, just the two of us. I don't think Mum's listening now. I've stopped, and she hasn't said anything. She's sniffling and shaking even more. I put my book down and pick up Teddo and give him a cuddle.

* * *

I accepted Mum's explanation of Ivor having to go away, and by doing so he disappeared from my mind as well. Mum reverted to her morose and moody state as if her renaissance had never happened. But I'd seen it, and so thought it could happen again. I looked for possible signs, and one morning when she's washing my hair I remember getting optimistic about our future. But it's a hope that something stamps out and it never ever recurs...

* * *

"Do I have to, Mum?" I don't usually have my hair washed just to go to school.

"Yes, pet, you do. I want you looking your best for the photo. It

116

makes your hair all glossy. And I've done your best shirt for you to wear. Take that tee shirt off and come into the bathroom."

A photographer visits every year after the summer holidays. I don't know why Mum wants another photo of me, though. She's already got one from last time. I don't think I've changed that much. I kneel at the side of the bath while she unhooks the shower.

"Can I have something to stop the shampoo getting in my eyes?" I ask.

"Just keep them closed."

"I like to watch the water running out round and round."

"OK, if you must."

"Yeah, I must."

She folds a towel so I can press it on my forehead, and I lean over and wait for her to start. I feel like that king must've before he had his head chopped off.

After she's finished and rubbed my hair a bit with the towel, she says, "I think I'll blow it dry. Follow me."

She sits on her bed with the hair dryer, and because she's got jeans on I can stand between her legs. I like this bit: the hot air blowing and her combing.

"There, that should do," she says.

"Is it dry?"

"Yes, and if you have any more you'll be asleep. I saw you closing your eyes."

"It were nice, Mum." And I put my hands on her arms and give her a kiss. It's the first time we've done it since she got into my bed.

It doesn't last long but it's something. "We haven't time for more now. Wayne'll be here soon. Move out of the way." She lifts the lid of her dressing table to put the hair dryer in, and takes my blue shirt from a pile of clothes she's ironed. "Here, you can be putting it on while I get your cereal out. Weetabix or cornflakes?"

She goes downstairs and I'm left hoping she might be getting better. Maybe she'll feel like a butterfly again.

I finish my breakfast before Wayne calls and we start walking to school. We see Mr Furr on his drive with a green Austin Maxi, P reg. He has a company car, because of his job travelling about selling clothes, and gets a new one every year. He did have a Vauxhall Victor estate. The Maxi's one of those on our list, but I don't think Mum's done anything about that yet – she hasn't said. School in the morning is normal and boring, but after dinner we have the photos taken and it's good fun. Mr Tilley lets us out a bit early when they're all done.

Wayne's knocking at his gran's now, like he often does on the way home. If she's in he'll get one of her fairy cakes or jam tarts, and sometimes a 5p. Yes, she is, so I wave bye-bye over the fence. It's a pity Grandma doesn't live close to us – although I don't think Mum would like it. I could call in to see her before I went home. But then I'd have to have a sandwich first before any cake.

I go round to our back door, but it's locked. I don't know why. It never is when I come home from school. It makes me feel upset – as if I'm not wanted. But then I think Mum might've had to go out somewhere. I get the key from under the brick. It's hard to get it in the lock, but I jiggle it and then I hear the other key drop on the floor. When I open the door I can hear water running into the bath because it's above the kitchen.

I put my key back and then go inside and put the other one in the lock. "Mum, I'm home," I call out. There's no answer. She must be in the bathroom and can't hear me. It's a funny time to have a bath. She always has it in the evening or at night.

I'm thirsty, so I have a drink of water. I see Mum's got a coffee sponge for tea. I don't like them as much as chocolate. She'll say there weren't much choice in the shop. If we had a car she could go to Fine Fare more. They have better things. I go into the sitting room and sit on the sofa. I could see what's on ITV, but I have to ask before I switch the telly on. They have things on in the afternoon. There's *Blue Peter* on BBC1 at a quarter to five and I want to see *The Wombles*. It started again last week instead of that stupid *Hector's House*. Mum's *Woman's Own* is next to me so I have a skeg at that. It's all about cooking and knitting or there's the soppy stories. There ought to be a *Boy's Own* magazine.

Mum's not long. She usually takes ages. I hear the bath water running out, and then her going into her bedroom. After a while she comes downstairs.

"Michael! Why are you home? What time is it?"

Flipping heck, why's she so shirty. I haven't done anything. It's like she thinks I've caught her out. And she's smoking a cigarette; and she's got her grey flares on now, not her jeans.

"Mr Tilley let us out early after the photos."

"Well, he shouldn't have. I hope you smiled. How did you get in? The door was locked."

"I used the key under the brick."

"Well, never mind. Do you want your cake and fizzy now or later?"

"Can I have it now?"

"It's 'may' I have it now. Will you ever learn?"

I make my puffing noise. "Sorry. May I have it now?"

"I wish you wouldn't do that."

She goes through to the kitchen and I get up and follow. I watch her suck her cigarette very hard and then get a saucer out of a cupboard to rest it on. I remember her smoking after Dad died, but I haven't seen her do it for a long time. She said she smoked before she married Dad, but he asked her to stop. She sees me looking but doesn't say anything.

"You're smoking again, Mum."

"Yes, that's right."

"Why?"

"Because I want to, that's why."

She slides the cake out of its box and unwraps it. Then she cuts out a slice and gets a plate to put it on. "Here you are. Take it into the dining room."

"Aren't you having any, Mum?"

"No. I don't feel like it. It's too early. Go on; I'll bring your drink."

I do what she says. She's still in a bad mood. She's pouring my lemonade – I can hear it fizzing in the glass. She comes in and puts it on the table.

"Has Mr Furr got a new car?" I ask.

"I don't think so. Why?"

"He had an Austin Maxi on the drive this morning. It's one of those on our list."

"What list?"

"The list of cars we could have."

"Oh, that. I'm not sure about a car now."

"Why, Mum?"

"It's all too much hassle: learning to drive; choosing it."

"Why?"

"For God's sake, stop asking. Why do you need to know the far end of everything? I don't want to be bothered with driving lessons at the moment. I'm cancelling them. So there's no reason to think about cars. Do you understand?"

Flipping heck. She says it as if I'm stupid, or something. "Yeah."

She goes back into the kitchen and I hear the water running into the washing up bowl and her squirting in the Squezy. She starts talking to herself, but I can't hear what she's saying. Then she turns the taps off and runs upstairs the sitting room way. She's been odd and shirty for a bit now, but this morning I thought she were getting better. Now she's a hundred times worse. What's going on?

When I've finished I put my glass and plate on the draining board and go up to my room. At the top of the stairs I can hear Mum in her bedroom. She's not crying but making a sort of moaning noise what sounds even worse. I look out of my window but there's nothing interesting to see – there never is. What can I do? I know: I'll teach Teddo some more interesting things from out of my *Zebra Book of Facts*. That might stop me feeling sad. Facts are better than feelings; they stay the same. What you feel keeps changing and you never know when. I don't like what I'm feeling now. If I think about facts maybe it'll go away. I don't want to feel like this for long. Please, God, let Mum get better again soon.

THIRTEEN

After squeezing my brain for those last few drops of memory juice, I need a cuppa; and in Dad's once modish galley kitchen I reflect on the tragedy of Mum's decline while the kettle sings and bumps to the boil. Her butterfly period lasted no longer than a real butterfly's life. Ivor Hughes must've dumped her, but I can't see why. And neither can I understand the way she collapsed – as if rejection on top of bereavement overloaded her. It was like the pop of gas that found the flaw that destroyed the flats and killed the four and injured more at Ronan Point. Mum must've had her design flaw too: a sleeper gene coded for mental fragility awaiting the call. Grandma Searle's abnormal focus on cleaning degenerated into OCD before she died. The inheritance was in place.

And for me, was it a tragedy? I can't decide. Those years of desolation at home made me what I am, and I'm not ashamed of any of that. In fact, I'm proud of what I've achieved – and I'm not stopping yet.

I take my tea into the dining room and give my mind an easier ride in the present by making a dial-up connection to respond to e-mails from work. It's straightforward stuff apart from a query about burning velocities from an engineer at Wiremouth who doesn't seem to know I've left CSS.

After tapping out my answers I can click the laptop lid and shutter my shop for the day. Well, almost. In this job I'm never totally free: there's always the mobile and someone in Omega demonstrating their needs. I contemplate my various activities tomorrow while letting the six o'clock news depress me with more Sunni-Shia warfare in Baghdad.

121

Now that the house clearance guys are coming on Thursday I need to sort out what I'm taking home. I could begin this evening, before going out. It felt premature before the funeral; and yet by Friday the house will be flushed and scoured like a shipwreck pounded by the waves, with a lifetime's paraphernalia washed up as flotsam, for resale or reject, the shop or the skip. It's all down to price now. The value of everything only existed through Mum's eyes and collapsed when she died. I'll salvage what I can.

After zapping the box – one of the few new things Mum was forced to buy – I force myself up from the sofa to make a start with Mum's room. Lou stripped the bed this morning, but I haven't been in at all. I hope there's not a lot. I slide open drawers like a burglar might with someone sleeping in the next room; but for me it's the aura of Mum in this one. I don't want to disturb her. It's a very reverential search, delving beneath blouses and sweaters, nighties and slips, gloves and scarves, tights and underwear to see if there's anything that needs keeping. No – and there's not so much clothing either. She's not been hoarding that. She must've had a clear-out and filled some of those charity bags. She tried to make it easier for us.

Opening the Habitat dressing table top I see the dark face with the brown eyes and scarred lip in the mirror fixed under the lid. He's wearing a five o'clock shadow and a black tie. Yes, I need to shave and put on the patterned one for Owerston Hall. Again there's been an obvious clear-out, and it's the same story in the dove grey wardrobes, once his and hers. So unless there's anything in the bedside cabinets, it's just the rosewood jewel box in here. I lift the lid and inspect the sparkle of rings and things. Most were Grandma Paine's and part of my inheritance along with the box. I hadn't met Lou then so gave everything to Mum – although she wasn't keen because of whose they'd been.

There's not much stuff in her bedside cabinet drawer either: tissues, paracetamols, biros, a puzzle mag and some specs. But in the cupboard beneath sits a fat carrier from Knit It with knitting needles poking out.

I peer in to see navy blue. It's the Guernsey she started last Christmas for my birthday. She didn't get far; it's mainly balls of wool. My eyes are starting to water as I pull the bag out and sit on the bare mattress for a closer look.

After a few minutes the spring winds down or dries up and I stop the sobbing – my second paroxysm. I thought I'd finished after the first. But the room's used to it. I'm only replicating what Mum often did in here when I was growing up. I suppose the knitting was her way of showing love without touching; and I'm touched, sitting here with three-quarters of the back of her last demo. The model on the pattern has a satisfied smirk. Well, he would; he's wearing the end product. And I resolve to get even with him and make a success of Mum's failure and have my present. I'll take it all home and ask Lou to find someone to finish it. She could design knitwear but knitting's not her line.

I don't expect anything in the other cabinet, but I'm wrong. There's a diary and a little notebook in the drawer, side by side at the front as if not to be missed. They must be Dad's, and Mum must've placed them like that. The diary's for 1960 and just like the ones I've already got for 1958 and 1959, with the year in a rectangular border – although I think they're green and this is brown. They came with his things from Gainsborough Avenue when Grandma went into the care home. Why didn't Mum give me this one then? I flick and squint to confirm. Yes, the same timetabled minutiae – lessons, homework, sports, meals, books, radio, TV. I'm sure it's the diary Mum pored over in Scarborough when I started my own. I flick the larger maroon book too. It looks like a mixed bag of writing: poems and lists and bits of prose, and everything's less microscopic. I don't remember her reading this then. I'll give it a go when I get back home; it might fill in another page or two of Dad's sketchy bio. Anyway, it's time I got ready to go out.

* * *

I'm about to phone Lou when she rings me. Well, Hannah does. They'd normally be home by now, but there's been a snarl-up on the M25. It's a relief; I could feel anxiety's grip on my innards. They're on to the A12, so they've only another twenty minutes to go. Lou's driving is a lot better than her map reading, so I shouldn't really have worried.

"Tell Mum I'll probably be late back tonight, so I'll ring tomorrow morning." I picture my lovable Lu-Lu processing the message as she steers her defensive course with the customary frown.

"She says that's OK because we're all going to bed early. Where are you going, Dad?"

I explain.

"Oh. I hope he's nice. Dad, I've got a French test tomorrow. Wish me luck."

I make my own journey – out of Ettisham Park's maze of 1920s crescents and cul-de-sacs and on to Owerston – without my usual musical accompaniment. My mind's fully occupied by both looking and thinking ahead. He seemed as keen to invite me this evening as I'd been to get him to our lunch. I know my agenda, but what's his? What could I have that he wants?

After slotting the car between two rival thoroughbreds – a silver A6 and a bronze V70, and maybe from corporate stables without a visibility prescription – I hunch into the once baronial hall with my anticipation spiced with trepidation. I glance towards the desk, but the receptionist's ancestry is more in the Punjab than Poland. It's disappointing.

With my overcoat hung in the lobby we used at lunchtime, I walk through into the residents' bar. My American buddies loved it in here – the ambience, you understand. It's a gallery of Elizabethans: men in ruffs and doublets, women in hoods and jewelled bodices. OK, the period's wrong for Owerston Hall and they're repro, but with ornate frames and some old oak furniture it's an effective pastiche. The lighting's nicely muted too.

He jumps down off a high stool to greet me with more crematorium cordiality. It's more than avuncular; it's paternal. Well, I think it is, but not being an expert I can't be sure.

"Choose your poison, Michael. Then we'll sit in the comfy chairs."

I order a tonic water and examine the smart-suited couple murmuring tête-à-tête in the corner, while he asks for another Ardbeg and signs the chit. Ivor Hughes is still 'he' to me, not 'Ivor' yet. Tut-tut! Call me old-fashioned, but a gentleman shouldn't be massaging a lady's thigh in public. I can even hear his hand skidding on the nylon under her skirt.

We plump down opposite each other and raise our glasses. "How did she…?" "How did you…?" Our questions collide and stall.

"You were first," I concede.

"How did she die, Michael?"

"*Carcinoma, left lung* and *cachexia* were on the certificate. She smoked herself to death, in other words."

He looks puzzled. "Did she smoke?"

"Not when asleep. She started again when Dad died – sixty a day."

"But not with me, she didn't." He's almost indignant.

"Well, maybe she stopped and started again when you went."

He goes quiet and it's my turn. "How did you find out?"

He samples his drink before replying, prompting me to start sipping mine. "I saw the announcement in the *Argus*. Henry Hallam used to send me the Saturday one, but since it cut back to a weekly I've had it direct. I've always kept in touch with Ulcethorpe; it's special for me."

"Because of Boroughcliff?"

"Not only that." And he pairs a shake of the head with a wistful smile.

"Is that the Hallam of Hughes and Hallam, *Dissection of Disaster*?"

"Yes, the very same. He was a friend of your father – and one of the other shift supervisors. I went to see Grace in the nursing home this afternoon. She's his widow."

"Yes, Henry and Grace; they used to visit. I'd forgotten."

"It's a long time ago."

"Mm… Anyway, the book got a mention in Management of Safety at Imperial, but I only got hold of a copy three or four years ago on line – second hand and no dust jacket and no author bios. So I've a link to both the writers."

"Yes, indeed. You went to Imperial College then, Michael?"

"Yep, Chemical Engineering; graduated in eighty-eight."

"And afterwards?"

"Process engineer with Omega at Wiremouth and then a spell at their Houston office. I got a reputation on the safety design side and came back to work out of London for CSS – Central Safety Services."

"But not any more?"

I have a drink before replying, and see the amorous duo stand up like conjoined twins. She's a leggy piece, taller than him with her heels.

"No. I decided the staff job was a blind alley, even though I saw a lot of the world. I wanted to get back into refining or something similar. You need to be in the line to make it in Omega – and that's what I want to do."

He nods, but looks as if he'd rather be shaking his head – as if my ambition has let him down.

"You look disappointed," I add.

"Not for you, Michael, but… to make industry safer we need all the talent we can get." His words are unwelcome echoes of Lou's.

"Yes, but I've done my stint."

"Is that all it was?"

"No, I enjoyed it, and did some good stuff; but we can't all be on a crusade."

He looks pained and sips his malt. But what right has he to try and make me feel guilty? He's forgetting what our business is: to drill for crude oil and turn it into what's needed to feed his Mini Cooper and fuel his 737 to Spain. Safety's integral with every operation, but it's not the be-all and end-all – or paramount (the word too often bandied about). If it were, we wouldn't be doing any of our stuff. He needs to take off his blinkers once in a while and look how we identify hazards and manage risk.

"I suppose not," he concedes. "So what are you now?"

126

My answer's stalled as the lovers saunter out of the bar. I have to watch, seeming to be obsessed by totty today. Her jacket's short and no protection against his hand caressing her tailored bum. The barman's all agape at the sight. I don't see any confetti caught up in her dyed black hair, but they could be honeymooners, I suppose. No, they're on a business trip together – probably their first – and he can't wait to pull off her knickers before pulling off a deal.

I continue with my mini bio, and how proactivity and pushiness paid off with the distribution job and its extent.

"Brentfield's a COMAH site, then?" he suggests.

"Yep, and a top-tier one under the regulations."

"So what about the safety report?"

"It's been accepted."

I suppose I sounded smug. He shakes his head, and his smile's as wry as they come. Anyway, why is he quizzing me about all this?

"Not convinced?" I ask.

"In my old age I've become even more sceptical. Of course, I'm pleased you've been rubber-stamped, so to speak – though I'm sure HSE gave it a very thorough scrutiny. But it's only the blueprint, only the theory. It's what actually happens that counts."

"That's why we have our audit schedule."

"But it's scheduled, Michael. That's its weakness. It's not enough; you need spot checks too."

I nod. I don't disagree. There is a gap between what's written and what's read, between the instruction and the action. The challenge is to reduce it – from crevasse to crevice, at least. Total closure might never be possible. We've come a long way since Boroughcliff in managing safety and reducing risk. We've got the theory now; it's the practice letting us down. Maybe there is room for spot audits: the safety police swooping in secret in the middle of the night – even at Omega sites.

We sit with our drinks, too absorbed to speak, but I'm sure our thoughts are in harmony. An overweight man in an oversize cardigan at the bar is asking about cocktails; the ones I hear mentioned –

Honeymoon, White Lady, Between the Sheets, and Screwdriver – seem to tell a little story reflecting my strange obsession today.

"How old is the Brentfield site, Michael?"

We're getting into more and more detail, yet I'm sure he didn't ask me here to talk about my new job. It must be a smokescreen. He's not ready to show his private self to me yet.

"Built in sixty-six, but extended in the eighties. And the control system's a lot more recent. Why?"

"I was thinking about another variable in the equation: the life cycle. You know, obsolescence and decommissioning. It's an issue facing industry now – North Sea oil and nuclear power for instance."

"You don't think my empire's crumbling already?"

He smiles. "I hope not, although some of it is nearly forty years old. But a rig, or reactor – or a fuel depot – is like a human body, see. The birth, the start-up, may be traumatic, but then everything's pristine for a time with the bloom of youth. There is deterioration, but it's very subtle and scarcely noticed. But the rate increases, like those run charts in one-day cricket. It's inexorable is aging. Organs, components, decay or malfunction due to disease: corrosion, erosion, creep, fatigue, furring, hardening, cracking, loosening. Repairs become impossible, replacements uneconomic. And so in the end there's a death – but not a violent one hopefully – and burial, demolition."

I strike back. "Yes, but we know all that. It's why we have an inspection and testing set-up; why we do planned and preventative maintenance; why we measure thicknesses and search for cracks and use all the other techno-stuff."

"But do you know what you don't know? You can't test everything."

I'm feeling uncomfortable with my position impugned. It would've been worse but his put-downs are tempered by geniality. And I'm enduring a lecture when I was expecting to be questioning him. I look away to the bar.

He notices my reaction. "It's not you, Michael, that I'm aiming all this at – or Omega. Don't take it personally, please. And engineering codes and standards do make good armour. The chink is usually due to a cock-up."

I'm almost placated. "Yes. It's that gap between script and performance. You were talking about nuclear and North Sea. Well, Chernobyl and Piper Alpha were both down to human error."

"Yes, indeed – as was that Atogas explosion."

"What was the outcome? I don't see the reports any more." The CSS job might've been a dead end, but it gave a good view of the global petrochem world. I miss that now.

"It was a start-up cock-up: a distillation column overfilled and overheated. Procedures weren't followed, see, and then the pressure relieved to a blowdown system that couldn't cope. Forty tonnes of hot gasoline make a big bang. There were twelve men too close who lost their lives."

And how many boys lost their father, I wonder.

We've both finished our drinks, and he looks to the door as a woman in her forties comes in. He must have good peripheral vision, or maybe her highlighted hair was a beacon. But she's not a waitress, dressed like that: flowing purple sweater, loose grey trousers and 200 grams of beads. She takes her outsize woollen to join the man with the cocktail's cardigan at the bar. He raises his Screwdriver like a gentleman and bids her good evening. Maybe he thinks he can pull her.

"Du Pont's claim is that ninety-six per cent of accidents are caused by people – their unsafe acts," I continue. "It's not usually the conditions."

"I'd be quite happy with that if they meant people at all levels, not just those at the bottom of the pile. But they concentrate on shop floor observation. The bigger the splash the further the ripples travel, and for disasters you find they go a long way upstream. The causes can often be laid at the boardroom door. It all cascades down, Michael."

"I've always felt pretty comfortable with our safety culture. I couldn't have worked in CSS if not." If I sound pious, too bad; it's what I believe.

"Omega may be one of the best, but you know yourself they're not perfect. And chemical giants have been cutting and pasting themselves into new entities and losing corporate values they'd accumulated over perhaps a hundred years. At Atogas it was the site culture: a tissue of short cuts and quick fixes. One of my US buddies talked about Band-Aid and superglue maintenance."

"You don't lay the blame for that one at Board level, then? Chief Executive Sir Smart Alec Masters not guilty again."

"Masters? I expect he will be your bête noire, Michael, and that's quite understandable; but he'd thick enough skin and a sharp enough mind to live down Boroughcliff. Almost anyone else in his position would've sunk without trace. And now he's living it up, so to speak: a fat cat with a knighthood."

"I could never have worked for them."

"Of course not. But I'm loath to let him off just yet. See, I don't know what pressures were being put on the refinery manager – cost savings, for instance. Ever since Aberfan I've had this bee in my bonnet about corporate responsibility, although that wasn't a phrase bandied about then. I came here wanting to dig up the dirt on Boroughcliff as further evidence. And now thirty years later…"

But he doesn't finish. Karen, our smiling waitress from lunchtime, has glided up to us.

"Excuse me, Mr Hughes; your table's ready now, if you'd like to come through. Good evening, Mr Paine."

It's nice to be recognised again and exchange smiles as if we're old friends.

"Thank you," he says to her, before adding, "we'll carry on over dinner, Michael."

Yes, but not for too long about the management of safety, I hope. I need to get him to open up.

We're led out with my eyes on Karen's barely concealed black bridle of bra straps beneath her white blouse. I don't know what's the matter with me today. I feel I'd like to attach some reins so she can't escape.

FOURTEEN

The decorative theme in the restaurant is Victorian worthiness, achieved with yet more heads on walls. An assortment of men in business and trade, with not a smile between the oil-painted lot of them, stare down on the diners like the portraits in an Oxbridge college hall. It's not great art, but maybe the probity of the faces restrains any sharp practice in the wheeler-dealing that goes on in here.

We're guided between twenty or so tables, many already occupied by diners singing the praise of the food: a choir of contented gastronomes. Being the only *Good Food Guide* entry anywhere near Ulcethorpe, Owerston Hall requires even residents to book to get in at weekends. I refrain from inspecting anyone, content with Karen's lithe hip sway in front.

She seats us beside a hearth now no more than a stage for the Waltz of the Flowers – this evening proteas smooching with lilies – and provides menus as large as fire screens to ward off conversation while we're choosing. Once A5 was big enough, then A4, then A3 and now we've almost reached A2. And the size of plates and dishes has grown too. Yes, and in inverse proportion to portions. But he's keen to finish the interrupted sentence. My hiding behind the glossy invitation to gravlax, oyster soufflé and the rest doesn't deter.

"I was saying in the bar, we still don't have proper laws about corporate safety crimes. Do you remember that Law Commission draft bill covering corporate killing? In nineteen-ninety-six, it was."

I'd rather not be choosing my food under interrogation. I suppose I'm warming to him, but at close quarters he can overpower with his fervent anti-corporation stance. I drop a hint with, "These starters

131

look very good," but there's a silence, so I'm forced to reply. "Yes, but I'd lost track of how long ago."

"Nearly ten years. I had high hopes then. And it's a Labour government that's been sitting on it ever since. Now we've managed to progress as far as a second draft. The Home Secretary blew the trumpet in March: The Corporate Manslaughter Bill. How many more years to enact it, do you think, Michael? Sometimes, I despair."

He goes quiet and I settle on gravlax and pollo spago before laying my screen aside and offering some consolation. "At least you're no longer a lone campaigner, with all the victim support and corporate policing groups."

"That's true; but it's a pity they had to be brought about by even more disasters: Zeebrugge, King's Cross, the Marchioness and all the rest. Sometimes I feel a failure because of that. Still, I've done good work with some of them, so I suppose we're winning."

"And you've majored in the process industries. Our record's pretty good. Some of the credit for that's down to you."

"That's very kind, Michael, but I'm only an unqualified amateur: a little Welshman with a big mouth and the gift of the gab."

"And with an honorary chem eng degree from Swansea, as I remember. And you inspired me in Barcelona. I liked your catchphrase: 'a little fire is a large fire just beginning'. It says it all."

"Well, it was two way. I got a lot of encouragement myself, seeing your GPSC set-up in action: members hanging out their dirty linen for everyone to see the stains and learn something – companies that are deadly rivals being pally together for the common good."

I take the compliment like a proud son receiving his father's posthumous gong. The club was formed after Boroughcliff, and most major oil and chemical corporations have membership cards. Dad's horrific crushing and incineration was part of the price for its inception. The plant's long gone, its reconstructed version lasting only a few years, and the site's now a trading estate, so Wren's epitaph, si monumentum requiris, circumspice, doesn't apply to him. It sets off my familiar

132

pondering on what he'd have been like if he'd lived – and what I'd have been like, with a dad and a happy mum and no nightmares. I look away and see Karen wending her nubile way to us with pad and pen. After eight hours on duty she still appears as fresh and wholesome as at lunchtime.

"Are you ready to order, gentlemen?"

My mind is suddenly awash with a stream of orders I could give her, none culinary. What's got into me today with all this sexualisation? I'm seeing it everywhere: the priestess, Alicia, Karen – and even with Helen, to an extent. I don't usually do erotomania when I'm away from Lou. It must be part of my release to freedom, unless it's a reaction to her rare 'no, Mike' in the spare bedroom last night.

Karen writes down our choices with a deliberate roundness, steadied by a protruding tongue. I can't see the page but can visualise it as written by Emily. The sex slave fantasy fades. Our waitress reverts to a personable school leaver eager to please in her first job. He has time to scan the wine list and I'm happy to accept his choice of a Tavel rose.

"You told me how you found out about Mum, but why did you come – from wherever?" At last I've asked.

"From Finchley; I've lived in North London ever since leaving here – various places."

He stops to pour us some water and choose his words. I hope they're not about his progress on the property ladder.

"It's quite simple. I loved her. I fell in love with her at first sight – or at first absence, when I left your house after interviewing her – and never stopped loving her."

I've counted three 'loves' already. He really wants to convince me. He puts the jug down and looks up in time to see my wide-open eyes.

"You look surprised," he adds.

"Well, yes and no, I suppose. It's true Mum was a real looker, as I was reminded today. Did you notice Helen this morning – my cousin? She takes after her."

My question ploughs his brow with troubled furrows. "I couldn't not notice. I was flabbergasted when she walked up the aisle."

"Sorry, that was stupid. I wasn't thinking."

"I was seeing my Marlene at her funeral. I've been carrying her face around in my head for all these years: my private icon. I could conjure it up whenever I liked; and it never aged, like the real Marlene – like the woman in the coffin. It was my figment, my compensation – mine..." His voice fails and his head drops.

Yes, he did love her. "Ivor," I say, with all the sympathy I can compress into that one word. He's had no one commiserating. I scan the other diners to give him privacy to recover, and notice Karen bring in the cocktail-drinker and his new lady-friend. They look like a couple, smiling and chatting to each other; but then they're led to separate tables. Maybe one or the other has missed a trick.

After a deep breath Ivor raises his eyes with an abashed little smile. "My turn to say sorry; I'm better now. You know, saying her name, Marlene, it's still a thrill, even after so long. Perhaps you can't understand that."

"Then why did you dump her and never try to make up?"

"Is that what she said?"

"No. She never said anything about it, other than you'd had to go away. It's what I assumed, thinking back after this morning." In fact, I don't think she ever spoke about him again at all, but it'd be cruel to spear him with that.

"Why?"

"Because all the images I've managed to capture for that day out are the same. Not literally, but they all share something: Mum's happy. No, not just happy: ecstatic, radiant, loving. It was never ever the same again."

"But it was me that was dumped, as you put it. And I still don't know why."

"Well, I'm... staggered." But I believe him, even if it doesn't make sense.

"No more than I was then. I was hoping you could explain it all; solve the mystery."

Karen returns with a plate of dainty canapés and our wine already opened and sheathed in a vacuum flask.

"Would you like to taste the wine, Mr Hughes?"

"I'm sure it's excellent. And we can pour it ourselves."

He smilingly demonstrates, and she leaves with a little breath of relief. Good for Ivor. I've seen too many vino-swilling colleagues sniff, sip, contemplate and nod as if they were Masters of Wine.

"What actually happened?" I ask, before tasting the Tavel.

"She telephoned next morning to give me the brush-off, as I call it."

"Saying what?"

"I could tell you verbatim, but I don't think you'll want to hear. I've never forgotten her words. They were like acid etching into my memory. In essence, she'd seen the light and would never want a man again. Forget me and don't come round or phone, was the message."

"And did you – never see or phone her?"

"Yes." He sees my eyes betray my surprise again. "All right, it seems limp by today's standards. But I loved her, see, so obeying her gave me a sort of pleasure. A very masochistic compensation, I admit. Perhaps it was a mistake. I did write a letter – a love letter, you could say, repeating what I'd said on the phone. I'd been agonising all that Sunday. It gave me some relief, and she hadn't actually forbidden that – but there was no response."

He sips some wine and I savour a pastry boat crewed by truffle slivers. Yes, he was very limp, I think – a sail in the doldrums. Like that, I'd never have landed on Lou's shore. The cream of head office talent; we guys drooling moths to the flame in Publications; a date on the third attempt with my brainwave of lunch and the Tate exhibition; and two more tries to get a second – and what a second. How pester power pays.

"So overnight she had a revelation," I say. "It's weird."

"Or just second thoughts."

But now there's a revelation stabbing through my mind. "No, more than that: something more dramatic," I insist. That memory of being in bed next to Mum – with her sobbing and shuddering, and me clutching Teddo and not knowing what to do – now has a meaning. It was then, after she'd seen the light. "I think she made a discovery that set her against men in general, not just you. But I don't know what."

A flutter of suspicion skitters up my spine. But I think I know where. Might those little books in the drawer have the answer? Mum must've read something in them to derail her like that – maybe something bad about Dad: something he thought or something he did. I hope not, but what else could it be? "She was reading Dad's diary. I'll get in touch if I turn anything up."

"If you would, Michael. Here, have my card." He tries to be calm, but I can see he's as desperate for news as a relative after a disaster.

I give him my business card in exchange.

"So what happened after your rejection?" I ask.

"Life went on, though I had to force myself. I'd several other things on the go, which helped, though nothing could take my mind off my Marlene. I had this perpetual hope of a phone call. One thing was my acting. I sent her a ticket for the opening night – my debut, it was."

"But she didn't come."

"No. I didn't really expect it; but I was keeping in touch, see."

"So you acted, did you?" He seems an even less likely luvvy thespian than me.

"A raw amateur, and only the once: Geoffrey in *Absurd Person Singular* at the Arts. I saw it on the telly later. I don't think I was quite Michael Gambon, but the *Argus* was very complimentary. And don't go thinking it was because I was on the staff there."

"But you didn't want to do any more?"

"Too busy with my book, I was. Well, our book. No, I suppose it was mine: me at the coalface and Henry the overseer. Author and mentor, we were. By then we had a publisher and a contract and a deadline, see."

"Before you'd written it?"

"Oh, yes. I'd started to make my name as a sniffer out and digger up of secrets – the Welsh terrier, the *Argus* editor called me."

I smile. It's a good nickname: a small black-haired worrying barking champion of workers' rights.

"I'd been investigating National Steel, as it then was; how they were failing to implement the nineteen-seventy-four Health and Safety at Work Act, only providing safety clothing in accordance with old union agreements rather than up-to-date assessments of risk, and a good few other blemishes. Asbestos was one, I remember – they weren't identifying the blue variety that causes mesothelioma. My piece came out soon after the molten iron eruption that burnt nine poor blighters to death on the Wellington furnace, so it was topical and I had plenty of hard evidence."

I'm surprised. So Ulcethorpe had its very own disaster and I don't know a thing about it – or do I? I didn't just dream about Dad's crushing and burning; I had nightmares with other scenes of gore and horror, and men showered with glowing metal eating through their skin into their bones was one. I ask for details of the accident and Ivor serves them up while Karen serves up our mains.

"It made the front pages of the broadsheets but not the headlines. Contained within the works, it was; no blast damage off site, no plume of smoke and soot dispersing over the shires. But my expose got syndicated and dispersed to good effect: the general manager sacked and me noticed. And unlike Masters, he never got back on top."

I'm placing my vegetables to coop up the chicken, when my mobile demands attention. "It's probably a text from one of my girls. Do you mind?"

He shakes his head and attends to his tuna as I read the message: *Hi Dad Im in bed w lite out We had pizza&salad&iscream T w Daisy 2moro aft skool C U soon Luv E.*

"Yes, Emily," I tell him.

"Do you text a lot?" I can hear disapproval.

"To the girls, yes."

"High tech semaphore, I call it – unnatural, and open to misunderstandings."

"Well, they like it; and I like getting them when I'm away or working late. It's additive, Ivor. It doesn't replace anything. It's how we should use technology – integrate it, and then trim off any excesses from the old and the new."

"Mm. More addictive than additive. Anyhow, what did she have to say?"

"Nothing much, but it's nice to know she still loves me. Do you have any children, Ivor?" It's a question that pops out without any thought, and his pained look forces me to dredge up my self-justification: I'm sure he was married before meeting Mum.

"No. It's the second regret of my life."

I don't need to ask about the first. "But you were married, weren't you?"

"Unhappily, yes – before divorcing. But we had no issue. I never looked for another woman after Marlene because I wanted to be always available. I didn't pester her – just told her my address and phone number when I moved. I knew from the Hallams she'd stayed put."

"That's such a pity," is all I reply.

I start dissecting the chicken. It would be crass to say anything more; to express what I'm thinking: that he took root on a platform and didn't notice the train shunted off to the scrapyard, the tracks ripped up and the tunnel of love blocked off. Thirty years of life – or at least, his sex life – wasted in a delusion that his love would come to him. His Marlene died the day her rejection burnt into his head. The woman who gave up the ghost last week had become Miss Havisham for as long as he'd been imagining Estella. But he couldn't see it – or didn't want to, the contented voyeur with his idol. I doubt if Mum ever gave him another thought. It's not just a pity; it's another fucking tragedy.

Ivor leads our spasmodic talk as we give due attention to our food, and directs it on to my life with Lou and the girls. Mum doesn't get another mention. And it's not polite conversation. I mean, it is polite, but he seems to want to know everything about us. And it's not as if he's put his old hat on to write another feature for the *Argus* either. He really seems to care. I feed him a variety of titbits with his tuna – Lou's artistry (with watercolours, decor, cuisine and the rest), Hannah's mathematical mind, Emily's ballet lessons, Lou's flower power parents, Emily's impersonations, my duets with Hannah on our new Yamaha – and as I do, my eyes open to see his interest as part of the ensemble, with that handshake, his cordiality, this meal. And by the time I place my cutlery parallel on the empty plate I think I know his intentions: I'm to replace Mum in his affections – I don't say love – and those I love are to have a share.

It's a scary prospect – a sort of arrest warrant issued on the same day as my release – and something I'd be very happy without. Once I would've welcomed a surrogate father, but then I structured my life to be self-contained, self-reliant – to do without. I don't have anyone close to me who's male. OK, I'd be making atonement, and I can't say he doesn't deserve it, but... Anyway, I don't have to do anything yet. And it is just my suspicion; he hasn't said.

* * *

We opted for coffee in the residents' lounge. The walls in here are headless, adorned like in hotels the world over with framed botanical prints – or reprints of pricey Regency aquatints, as Lou has told me. It's another example of faking it: the surface upstaging the substance. It's all the rage now.

We're facing each other from opposite ends of a three-seater sofa well away from the embers of the log fire. He's been telling me about his current project to debunk the glib statements politicians make when public inquiries report – the ones about learning lessons so things don't happen again. How rafts of recommendations sink without trace after that overblown buoyancy of publicity bursts. There's truth in what he says about lack of funding and lack of auditing, but he's too dogmatic about it – like a ranting preacher discomforting his congregation into avoiding the message. He needs some of my pragmatism. We'd make a good pair.

"So what's it called?" I ask.

"*Will we ever learn?*" He sees that I'm not overly impressed, and adds, "It's a working title."

"Well, whatever, I'd like a copy," I say – and not for politeness, but because what he thinks and writes is challenging stuff.

"You'll have a signed one, Michael. Let me write your home address on the back of your card. And next time you're free in London I expect a phone call."

I smile and nod. Yes, he's taken another step in his scheme; but I don't know that I will. I'll see how I feel. He takes my dictation. He's already finished his Armagnac. I've deciphered Hannah's even more coded text. The long-case clock's struck eleven. It's time to go. It's been an exhausting day, I explain, before thanking him for his hospitality. Out in the corridor he waits sociably while I retrieve and put on my Crombie. I feel he's looking at me like a bespoke tailor confirming his tape measure has produced the goods. But will I measure up to what he expects? Anyway, my first task is to try and find out why Mum rejected him. I'll start directly I get in.

We walk together into the hall. Our parting handshake is conventional this time, so maybe he feels I'm already captured. I swap a 'goodnight' for a 'nos da' and there's another of his shoulder pressing demonstrations of connectivity. And then as he turns with reluctance to the staircase I turn eagerly to the front door. Out of the corner of my eye I've already noticed Alicia standing there. I can't stop myself. I'm being pushed along a diagonal of the chequered floor like a black bishop on a chessboard to take the white queen. It's the culminating move of my sex obsessed day. Thoughts of reading Dad's diary and notebook are left way behind.

FIFTEEN

Dressed for home (and funerals) in a black caped raincoat with a black woollen scarf tucked into the collar, Alicia's hair seems blanched even whiter by the contrast. That's all I can see of her. She's peering outside for somebody or something through the reflection of reception in the glass.

"Dobry wieczór," is my greeting as she turns. She must've seen my reflection too. The animation in her face takes my breath away. Now Pygmalion's statue is Galatea.

"Dobranoc, Mr Paine." It's a valediction for someone about to go out through the door – but I don't. She's switched off the fire in her eyes now, but not yet wiped the flush from her cheeks. Yes, she's trying to revert to calm and cool, and I'd better do the same.

"Do you have a problem? Can I help?"

"Bloody taxi is late… Excuse me."

"Then let me take you. I'm driving into town."

There's more than a grain of self-interest inside my Sir Galahad husk. She's falling into my lap. Or am I being a total prat? Nothing's going to happen. I don't even want it to, do I? I've been mixed up about women all day.

"Thank you, but it will come."

Having been rattled by Ivor's overtures, I should accept her declining mine; but it's a half-hearted refusal and I'm not deterred.

"Maybe; but if you've been on duty all day why should you wait? Come on, I insist." And I bribe her with what I hope is a charming smile.

"You are right. Dziękuję." She nods, but doesn't smile back.

"Proszę bardzo." I open the door for her, and she winces as the wind slashes.

141

"You are very kind, Mr Paine."

"It's no trouble. Where do you live?"

She waits for me to lead the way. "Ettisham Road. We have nice flat."

"It's on my route. So you share with someone?"

"Tak, Karol."

"Is she Polish?"

"Polish, tak; but he is boyfriend."

No, nothing's going to happen. I can breathe easily. "Yes, of course. He's a lucky man."

"Dziękuję. You are right."

Mm, she's got a conceited streak. I press the Beemer into its welcoming routine to show her where we're heading. "Karol, like Karol Szymanowski, the composer?"

"Tak."

In the car our synchronous seat belt clicking brings our heads together; and as she peers down at the clasp, my oblique close-up is like looking down on her. It's another few seconds of that sensation at reception this afternoon, but now vitalised by our intimacy in the cocoon of the car.

"You have heard music of Szymanowski?" she asks, as I start the engine and the interior lights dim.

"A violin concerto; the *Stabat Mater*, I think. He's not on my A list."

"That is pity. He is buried in Krakow. Who is on your A list, Mr Paine?"

"Chopin," I say, to please her. He is on it, but not at number one. "I've four of his pieces in my repertoire."

"So you play piano?"

I don't reply until we're out of the car park and gliding between the rhododendrons. "I'm just an amateur – grade three or four, but I don't take the exams. I used to play about on the piano at my grandma's but didn't start proper lessons until after I married."

"You play quite well, I think. There is no easy Chopin. I am musician."

At the narrow entrance another car's patiently waiting for our exit before turning in: a white Peugeot 406 broadside to my lights and proclaiming *TAXI* on its front door to the council's specification.

"My taxi," she says.

"No, I'm your taxi," I joke. At least it should be a sociable drive back to town. "A professional musician, you mean?"

"Tak, but not in Philharmonic. I play violin in quartet and for folk music, but there is not enough work, not enough money."

"So you earn more here?"

"Tak; and Karol also."

"What does Karol do?"

"He is electrician at steelworks. We work hard to save to buy flat at home, and send money for my sister. She has bad illness."

"I'm sorry... What will you have to pay in Krakow, if you don't mind my asking?"

"Nie. Fifty thousand euro for one bedroom. We have fifteen now. We go back at twenty-five and take loan. I want so much to go back."

"And what made you come to Ulcethorpe?" I ask, slowing for the tricky crossroads where safety conscious Owerston Parish Council have chosen to concentrate all four of their street lights.

"Because of Karol's aunt. She lives here. She is English. She helped us when we arrive."

"But Karol's Polish?"

"Tak. I said." It's a sharp retort but she instantly retracts. "I am sorry I snap. It is long day. You forgive me?" For the first time her voice is soft and appealing.

"Yes, don't worry. I understand."

"I explain. Karol's uncle came here in nineteen-forty in Polish Air Force. He flew in bombers. He met Doris then and they marry after. They had one... Oh, look! The deer! Slow down. You see their eyes. They are often here in this wood. I call them mine."

I was already braking in case a muntjac decided to dent my motor. But they've certainly pierced her immaculate bodywork deep enough to release some emotion. "There's a small herd near where we live."

"In Ulcethorpe?"

"No, in Essex, near London."

"But we have address in Ulcethorpe for you."

"That's my mother's house. It was her funeral today. I'm staying there until Thursday."

"With your family?"

"No, they've gone home."

She's quiet for a few seconds. "What is your business, Mr Paine?"

I tell her, but I sense her mind is elsewhere. It's only when I ask about her sister's ailment that her animation returns for a discourse about Irena and the tribulations of MS. She's still in full spate now, and we're already half way along Ettisham Road.

"We are here. Stop under this lamp."

I stop ten metres or more further on, not wishing to lock up the inertia reels or bother the ABS.

"Would you like to come in?" she asks.

It's unexpected. "It's rather late." I'm stalling. She probably wants to show Karol off. "May I park here?" The only other cars are a hundred metres away.

"At night it is OK."

"Then I will. Thank you." I deserve the treat: a chaperoned look at her from across a room for half-an-hour or so. Our proximity in the car has only provided a view of her knees.

We're blown up the path and steps to the front door by a wind like the blast from a tuyere. I can make out three bells and three labels. The top one says Kryszto-something – I don't take in the last few Ws and Zs. She uses a Yale key and leads onwards and upwards, giving Orpheus a lesson in not looking back. I hear music approaching on the first flight, but receding on the second. Mm. This time it's a deadlock. Yes, the door opens on to darkness and silence. She flicks on the light and turns the key.

"Is Karol in bed?" I ask.

"No. He is in work: the ten to six shift. Please come this way."

Corus feeds on shift workers, but somehow I'd thought of Karol on days. The correction comes with a frisson of… Expectation? Apprehension? A synergistic mix of both, I think. Whatever, I'm happy to let her take charge. I follow into a large yet cluttered room where posters, throws and rugs brighten the drab furnishings of the landlord. She clicks more switches and strikes matches to provide subdued lighting and gas heating.

"If you like to sit I take your coat." She's already removing hers, and I do the same. She hangs them out in the hall and sticks her head back round the door. "Would you like drink? Coffee?… Vodka?… Juice?"

I opt for the alcohol and she fetches a bottle and glass. It's Żubrówka, preserving its vertical stalk of grass. She puts them on the coffee table as an invitation for me to sit on a long sofa and help myself.

"I need coffee. Please be comfortable." And her first smile of the evening displays her teeth and more white perfection.

I pour the chilled vodka. I hear Alicia clinking in the kitchen. I survey the room, the music room: the violin case, the music stand, the accordion, the keyboard, the sheet music, the guitar; a room waiting to come alive, waiting for a performance. And I wonder how I've come to break into their world. Now I hear doors opened and closed and the loo flushed and refill. I sip my drink and flip through a magazine. She's clattering in the kitchen again. What's keeping her?

"I am sorry I take so long."

My eyes widen; she's dressed for bed. Well, undressed; I assume there's little or nothing under the short black kimono. She sits next to me, kicking off black mules to rest her feet on the table and show off the curves of her silky white legs. But I'm not salivating. My throat feels like it's been patch tested with silica gel. And I'm lost for words. I lean forward for more medication, which comes with a close-up of ten purple-varnished toes.

"Mm. It is nice to be out of uniform."

"How long were you on duty?" I'm glad to hear I'm still talking sense.

"Twelve hours. It is too much – and for seventy-eight pounds before takeaways."

I smile unseen. She's staring at the hissing gas jets and the glowing ceramic grilles. "That's not enough."

"Dziękuję. You are right." She pauses. "So how much do you like me, Mr Michael L Paine?"

I've no reason to pussyfoot. I inspect her shell cameo profile. "I think you're stunning… beautiful." Her lips move to suggest a smile.

"But how much?" And presumably for complete transparency and to put her offer in writing, as it were, she moves her feet to the floor, twists round, unties a bow and unwraps herself. "A hundred pounds-much?"

I swallow. She waits a few seconds for her meaning to crystallise before covering up, but I still see her breasts, as pert as any Bernini sculpted, their pearly nipples suckling my eyes. And I'm calculating – not about the money, but how we've got to this. She must see me as the wolf I felt at Owerston Hall. Inviting me in meant she was on her own, and my coming meant I was up for it. It's all about that flat in Krakow and Irena. And she might possibly have done it before. But now I am up for it – like the grass upstanding in the bottle – and with that urge I felt twenty years ago when Amanda yanked me into her bedroom for my initiation. And Alicia needs the money so I'd be rude to refuse. Well, that's how I sell it to myself: I'm doing her a service, a secret service. No one will ever know. It seems a fitting climax to a weird day.

"Well? I think it is not too much."

"No, no; but I don't have that much on me." I've never paid for sex and don't have a hooker's price list in my head, but it seems a bargain. I'm certainly not haggling.

"You have cheque book?" How does she stay so cool? Normally I wouldn't have, but for this trip with all its unknowns I've brought one. When I nod she adds, "For the balance, Mr Michael."

But I do know it's payment up front, very appropriately. I deal two £20 notes on to the table from my wallet; and it's not just my hand that's stiff as I write Alicia Wajsowski to her dictation on the cheque.

She slips into her mules, picks up her proceeds and goes out to stow them away. And with her gone, second thoughts come to offer rescue. I'm being unfaithful to Lou; I'd be stacking up another secret; and even, can I perform with a stranger? But I dismiss them all in the interests of business: I've made a contract and need to see it through. I gulp the last of my drink to put the fire back in my belly. By the time she returns I've convinced myself I'm doing the right thing, and not a selfish dude eager for a taste of hedonism as a nightcap.

"Something for you to put on," she says, placing the little packet on the coffee table before crouching to adjust the fire.

"Right... Where?..." I was expecting our coupling to be on their bed.

"In here, on settee – or this rug; it is clean. You can take off your clothes in bedroom. It is across hall. The door is open."

I don't ask why, but do opt to undress in private, as it's obvious she's not planning to assist. I leave her moving cushions from the sofa in preparation for our performance. The room will be coming alive after all, but not with the sound of music. I'm quite calm folding my stuff and piling it on to a chair (the bed's occupied by her jacket and skirt). I could be getting ready for a medical – only the room wouldn't be so chill. Maybe that's why we're not doing it in here. It's all so clinical I'm starting to lose my appetite. I haven't even touched her yet. There's been this rift of formality between us: the supplier and the client. But when I think about bridging the gap with Polish foreplay for starters I'm soon hungry again. Naked and eager I pad across the hall's varnished floorboards and back into the gas fired fug of the living room. Alicia has taken off her kimono, briefs and mules, and is flat on her back on the sofa staring up at the ceiling. She's like a body on a mortuary slab. I know this is a first for me and so I'm no expert, but something doesn't seem right.

SIXTEEN

After getting back to Kilvert Road shagged out but wide awake, I pour a glass of semi-skimmed and flop on the swivel chair with it. I should've said no in the car, and then once she flashed I felt I had to go on. Now I've a guilty conscience and post-coital tristesse – and a scorched buttock from our fuck on the flokati in front of the fire. Our fuck, did I say? No, just mine; I was trying to melt an ice cap with a blowlamp. She didn't lift a finger – or any other part of herself. She should give lessons in necrophilia. I've anatomised the most perfect milky-white corpse. But what did I expect; that my hundred pounds could buy reciprocated passion? So after being the little boy grabbing a new toy and forgetting the better one at home I became the little boy indulging in the other use for his penis. And what was it like for Alicia, moonlighting on the game to collect money for her sister? I can't complain if she's got an on/off switch hidden away.

Anyway, I feel cheap and ashamed. I've spent the first day of my new freedom eyeing up women like a lifer out on parole, or a celibate priest who's renounced his vows – or, cutting the euphemistic similes, because I fancied shagging them all. My DIY job with Alicia was my punishment – and it's going to be my cure. I know Mum's departure is a weight off my shoulders, but I need to get my feet back on the ground. Lu-Lu, I'm sorry, I'm sorry. Your Mr Perfect is a fraud: he's selfish, he's pathetic, he's let you down. After more verbal self-flagellation while I drink my milk, I force myself out of the swivel and into some positive action. I'll have a look at Dad's little books to see if Ivor's answer is there.

I fetch them down, turn on *Through the Night* for some music to accompany the wind machine running at full tilt outside and slump on to the sofa this time. Mum must've read most if not all the diary before that Saturday outing, but I decide to give the last three or four months a glance in my hunt for the needle that pricked her into thirty years' paralysis. As I turn the pages forward looking to start with his autumn term a heading *Tragedy!* stops me, and I read about Dad trying to date a girl called Alice, and her turning him down. And as I decipher the tiny blue biro writing I realise this is a page I've read before – in Scarborough or maybe in the garden that time.

I carry on turning, looking for any other page with a title to invite me into an eventful day. A month later I find one. Dad's making it easy for me.

SEPTEMBER 1960
6 TUES Good and bad!
Up at 7.15 and resumed the going-to-school routine. Cycled there at 9. Most of the lads arrived by 10. We now in Room N. Assembly 10.15. New position for prefects at back of hall. Then break and usual settling in. In Form Room lunch hr as drizzly weather. PS all p.m. like Tues last yr. Started large batch of chem. notes on Sulphur. Saw Mr. Haddon re being one of the lab assists. (5 hrs/wk, pay just under £1). More money for my box, but can't spend it on her now. So ended first day of what will be a hard year of work. Alice not in school. Disappointing. Home at 4. Tea. Then more chemistry notes to background of records. Mum home to do steaklets and chips meal. Cleaned soccer boots. Some TV and 'pops' on radio before bed.

A hard year: yes, this is the year Dad dropped out. But he hadn't dropped his amorous sights, by the sound of it. Alice was still his target. I turn forward, and on the following Monday there's another heading: *A bitter blow.* I soon get to the gist: *Had to see Mrs. Pope in the office to sign the employment form. Took a risk and asked about Alice. She's gone for good. Her parents have sent her to boarding school. Another bitter blow. Must wait till half-term.*

Now I know where to look – somewhere near the end of October – because I've had a sudden hunch that whatever Mum found to shock her has something to do with Dad's fixation with this girl. I'm getting warmer, hunt-the-thimble-wise, but I can't stop a little shiver. Is it fear that it's going to knock me off my comfortable perch too? No. I realise the central heating's been off for three hours. I go into the kitchen to press the advance button on the boiler timer before pressing on with my search. I soon find the pages I want.

OCTOBER 1960

29 SAT Hackby

Up at 7.30. Raining. Breakfast. Bus to bus station to meet team. Baz turned up in the new Velox and I went with him to Trentholme in car via school for his kit. A cup of tea before the rest arrived. A hard match which we lost 2-4 after 2-1 up. They improved when rain stopped. Home with Baz at 12.30. After lunch Mum out shopping and I cycled out to Hackby and Alice. Found 'Two Elms' at last. I should've looked for the trees. Large bungalow just out of village. A wood almost opposite with gloomy fir trees. Hung about in there but didn't see anybody. Home after Mum. Said I'd been at K's, so missed tea. TV included 'Strange World of Gurney Slade' fantasy. Mum wanted it turned off! Cheese and biscuits before bed.

OCTOBER 1960

30 SUN At last!

Up at 9.45 called by Mum. Boiled egg as usual Sunday breakfast. Cleared bathroom and started painting the walls 'warm white'. Small brush so slow work. Listened to radio as I did it, music and Family Favourites. Lunch at 1.30, casserole stew with wine. Needed break and fresh air so said I'd go for bike ride as weather nice. To Hackby. Rover on the drive. In position for ages, but then Alice came out with small dog. Looked marvellous in black stockings and wears her hair up now. Home after seeing her return. Late, so said I'd had puncture. Finished the paint but not the walls after tea. Did some pure maths and spent 2 hrs on a poem, untitled as yet. Bed at 11 satisfied.

So, Dad became a teenage stalker; creepy maybe, but not enough to turn Mum off him in retrospect and tar another man with the same brush. There's nothing more during half-term, so I flick through the pages to get to the Christmas hols. It wasn't until after the festivities – about as festive for them as mine were with Mum (apart from the couple of times we went to Pam and Brian's) – that he was back on the trail.

DECEMBER 1960
29 THUR Alice again
Up for breakfast with Mum and then more bed till 10. Got coal in and lit fire. Then settled down to read some of 'Tales of the Unexpected' by H.G. Wells. Absorbing. Early lunch of beans on toast. Biked to Hackby. Waited in the wood. Alice came out with dog at 3 and walked up lane. Difficult following through trees. There's a track into wood further along. She went in for dog to poo. It's called Gem. Some trouble with her hair and she dropped something. Didn't try to follow her back but found her slide. Home just before dark. Had to relight fire. Played new Simpson symphony record after tea. Mum in late after a library do and we had cold turkey and fried potatoes. 'Ask me another' on TV before more of the Wells stories. Cornflakes before bed.

Dad must've been besotted with Alice to fight his way through a forest just for a sight of her – he didn't know he'd be taking home that little trophy. On the Friday he went again. *Out to Hackby the other way and waited just off the track in the wood. No Alice. Waited till nearly dark. Back past 'Two Elms' but no lights etc. Thwarted.* Maybe he'd planned to do something bolder this time. The last day of his year was a damp squib: no Hackby, no Alice, no celebrations. He didn't even wait up until midnight: *Then radio 10.30-11.20 – 1960 pops. Bed.* But that's not quite all. He's written a little epilogue on the opposite page.

> Thus the year has ended. The main event, I suppose, was doing something about Alice though nothing has come of it yet. There was also the six weeks working at Carrs. A cursory glance at these pages of close packed script gives the impression that every day was packed with "adventure". It was not! There will be no more chronicles of the routine, but instead a record of any special things that happen.

And in the maroon book, I'm sure. I do a swap and open it. He starts with lists of stuff: the books he's read, the music he's listened to and the records he's got. I can see where my being so meticulous comes from. Now I'm skimming his poetry – the collected works of Alan Paine. It's mostly not bad enough to embarrass me, but there're two that could well have upset Mum. At least the first is short and has a hint of jokiness.

Dilemma

She whom I adore,
I also abhor;
For she is a whore.

Not ostensibly, but in fact.
It is with lowered eyelids
She coquettes, performs her act.

But when she's made her mark,
She bites with the teeth of a shark.
Now nothing is reserved – it is stark.

Objectionable, you see.
But I wish that her teeth were gripping me.

But the next is a turgid admission of his obsession with Alice. I'm sure she's the:

She who is pictured within

Clear her from your mind;
Dispel your passion and banish your thought.
So speaks my conscience,
But weak-minded, I cannot do as I ought.

For a while I comply;
But when I see her, resolve is burnt in her fire.
She regards me not directly.
She knows me not. Yet does she sense my desire?

She has the seducer's look:
The cold compelling gleam of silver.
She could rule me if she wished.
This I concede, and for this I hate her.

Her body is firm and unblemished,
Though some other might sample it soon I fear.
Thus wisdom says: Love her now,
While she is fourteen, lithe, without smear.

Yet I know not how to begin.
What sparks off that passionate chain?
My desires will have no satiation.
She is cold, while my mind is a boiling pain.

But I know how to finish it all,
My life of heartache and empty frustration:

End hers of haughty disdain.
Yes, I have the final solution: consummation.

And yes, it could've given Mum a sick feeling, but it's not enough even to make her vomit. After a few blank pages there's more poetry, but this isn't Dad's. He's copied out some of the proper stuff – and the theme's obvious: sex. Alex Comfort's *The Postures of Love* is an eerie reminder of Alicia – haven't I just been riding her thighs' white horses? It's the same Alex Comfort who found fame by collecting postures of love into *The Joy of Sex*, I'm sure. Next I'm on to Julia, Robert Herrick's paramour, and the admiration she inspired: *Upon the Nipples of Julia's Breast* and *Upon Julia's Unlacing Herself.* Dad then moves to the Metaphysicals, inscribing the whole of John Donne's *Elegie: Going to Bed.* It's the one with the line of prepositions: *Licence my roaving hands, and let them go, behind, before, above, between, below.* He continues with *The Imperfect Enjoyment* by Lord John Wilmot. It's only an excerpt, but there's enough.

> *Her nimble tongue, Love's lesser lightening, played*
> *Within my mouth, and to my thoughts conveyed*
> *Swift orders that I should prepare to throw*
> *The all-dissolving thunderbolt below.*
> *My fluttering soul, sprung with the painted kiss,*
> *Hangs hovering o'er her balmy brinks of bliss.*
> *But whilst her busy hand would guide that part*
> *Which should convey my soul up to her heart,*
> *In liquid raptures I dissolve all o'er,*
> *Melt into sperm and spend at every pore.*
> *A touch from any part of her had done't:*
> *Her hand, her foot, her very look's a cunt.*

I can only admire Dad's schoolboy savvy in grubbing up a poem about premature ejaculation from someone I haven't even heard of; but I can see Mum might've been disgusted to find it – and even the others, possibly – copied down. But was that sufficient to turn her off men? No way. There's also another excerpt over the page: from *The Ballad of Reading Gaol* by Oscar Wilde. It's a little diversion from Dad's main stream.

Yet each man kills the thing he loves,
By each let this be heard,
Some do it with a bitter look,
Some with a flattering word,
The coward does it with a kiss,
The brave man with a sword!

And then after a few more empty pages I arrive at an entry written like a diary.

Saturday 4.2.61 *Linda*

Letter from Birmingham in the post. Have been conditionally accepted. Makes up for the U.C.L. letter. Home soccer game vs. Gunterton, which we won 2-0 with goals from Pete Vale and an own goal. Afterwards Baz told me he is back with Pat and would I make up a four again with Linda. Pat's dad not keen on her going out with him alone. Said I would. Biked on into town and bought 'Good Time Baby' by Bobby Rydell at new Disc Jockey shop. Afternoon with K and TV. Rovers lost 4-0 away to Rotherham and drop into relegation territory. Didn't stop for Juke Box Jury. Mum shampooed my hair and I changed shirt & trousers. Baz called at 7pm in the Velox. I sat in back with Linda who was nicely perfumed and wearing a dark green blouse and green tartan skirt. Into the Majestic where Baz bought the tickets, two double seats in the circle. Saw 'Saturday Night and Sunday Morning' with Albert Finney. Very naturalistic X for sex in Nottingham with violence too. Second feature was ironically 'Linda', and preferred by Linda. A boy meets girl story set in Brighton. Baz and Pat were snogging but we just held hands. Think she would have liked more but I want my first kiss to be with Alice. In the dark I tried to imagine it was her next to me. Coffees in the Wimpey after and I paid. Home and she kissed me on the cheek as I got out. At least it wasn't on the lips. Need to avoid her. Two months till Easter and chance to try for Alice again.

So while Dad was longing for Alice he had a Linda longing for him: a spurned admirer probably hoping a love story involving her namesake would prompt a kiss – but it never came. I made my play for Sarah Rivers at that age. The double seats had gone by 83, but I went for the Majestic and the Wimpey as ports of call en route to the bus shelter at the end of her road for our snogging and petting. Dad was too ascetic to take the chance of some practice. Anyway, Sarah moved well upmarket, marrying into the Mumby Haulage clan – Ulcethorpe's royalty. She can't complain about us drifting apart. I turn over the page, expecting the next entry to be about Alice. It is.

Wednesday 5.4.61 _My babe in the woods!_

Did a day's work in the kitchen in just the morning, wallpaper stripping, washing all the paintwork, and painting the ceiling. I'm getting quite a proficient interior decorator! A fried egg on toast and a change of clothes before biking out to Hackby the quieter back way. Waited near the track into the wood. It was nearly 4.00 when she came, wearing a black cabled jumper and pleated grey skirt. The dog barked but she hardly showed any surprise when I stepped out. Said I'd wanted to see her and talk to her for ages, and if I couldn't ask her out, could I meet her there sometimes? She said I already had, hadn't I, but it couldn't be for long or she'd be found out. We walked up the track to where there was a pile of logs to sit on. She misses B.G.S. as her school is all girls and very strict, but keeps in touch via her various girlfriends here. I told her about going to University. She wants to study medicine. Conversation was easy, although the dog Gem was a nuisance. All too soon she had to go, but said she could be there tomorrow at about 3.00 and would tell her mum she was going for a longer walk. I sat on the logs and watched her go, my babe in the woods. She was cool on the surface, but underneath I think she was as excited as me. Got soaked in a shower on way home. Changed back into painting things and had time to dry clothes in front of gas cooker before Mum in. She pleased with my décor progress. I joyful with my Alice progress so TV and radio wasted on me.

At last they've spoken – apart from on the phone. I'm pleased for Dad. He deserved to get something back for all the effort he put in. I turn over the page.

Thursday 6.4.61 Seventh heaven!

The day only began at 3.10, or 2.30 when I arrived in the wood and knew I was near her. She was arrayed in a tight black jumper with a tartan dress like a gymslip over it and the black stockings. She smiled her special smile and let Gem off the lead so he wouldn't interfere. She let me hold her hand. She wanted to know how long I'd been keen on her, and could hardly believe it when I said, and how I'd come to be in the woods yesterday. She knew more about me than I thought, including my going around with Pat and Linda last year. I said that was all finished and Baz had set it up anyway. She would have come out with me when I phoned, but her dad is old-fashioned and sets silly rules. He was born in Poland and they are Catholics. I asked to kiss her but she said not yet. I must prove myself first. I can write to her at school next term, Stuart Hall at Dunborough. Next week she's away on holiday so tomorrow is our last day. The dog came back whining so we walked down the track to a gate into a field. There's a footpath across to a lane, her 'longer walk' and another way for me. She was backing the gate and I was very close but resisted the temptation. All the time we chatted on about books (she's reading 'Great Expectations') and films (she'd seen Tony Hancock in 'The Rebel' as well) and pops and how she hates her school and misses Gem. We walked back, she checking her watch. Her dad was at home and the longer walk

157

takes 45 minutes. "You can see me tomorrow, Alan," she said, using my name for the first time. "Same time, but only for a few minutes." And she clipped Gem's lead on, stepped out into the lane, waved and was gone. Home in good time. Evening in seventh heaven with my thoughts. She's my girlfriend. I can write to her. I might kiss her tomorrow.

So, what happened next? I turn over and face a ferocious attack. The first words jump out at me, snapping like the heads of Cerberus: *I've killed her*. I flinch, but there's no escape. I have to read on.

> I've killed her, the one I love. I can't take it in. It was all my fault. I don't know how I'm writing this. I don't know how I got home. Mum's not in yet. I can't let her see me like this. I've got to calm down. I feel awful. I've made some tea, and I thought writing would help to get it straight in my head, but it's all shaky. I wanted to kiss her so much before she went away, and then the dog jumped up. But I wouldn't let go and she started to struggle. Afterwards I was rooted to the spot in horror. The dog barking up by 'Two Elms' brought me round. I think I was crying. I must have run up the track and over the field to the bike, but I don't remember. But the rest is horribly clear. My life's not worth living now I've lost her. I've destroyed all my hopes.

I let go the breath I've been holding to keep me steady, and gulp in more air to read it again – and then again. And the repeats ease my breathing and loosen knots at the back of my neck. I've found the answer, and it's this sickening tale. Poor Mum; she discovered a black heart under the golden surface of the man she loved and thought she knew through and through. On the brink of her new relationship, she'd have recoiled so far I can see how she fell into misandry and despair. What did Pam say? 'She couldn't trust herself to judge men'. Ivor would've had no chance after that.

But I think she got it wrong. I'm grabbing at another interpretation. I've no choice. Dad's my hero: one of the Boroughcliff martyrs whose deaths shamed the chemical industry into cleaning up its act. I can't have him destroyed. She must've thought he'd strangled Alice and got away with it. But I won't be the son of a murderer. Haven't I just read Oscar Wilde? *Yet each man kills the thing he loves* isn't literal. I work feverishly on my scenario: the awkward embrace, the pawing dog, the unsatisfied ardour, the slapped face, the angry rebuff. This could be the key that turns through the wards of Dad's words. It's got to be; but how can I find out? I let my eyes pan across to the opposite page.

Friday 21.4.61

Managed to get up before lunch and have written this opposite that, so I must be a bit better. Mum's going to write a letter to school and say I'm leaving. It's a load off my mind. She wanted me to try another week off, but it's pointless. At least she's stopped asking me why I feel so bad. The arguments were making it worse. Wrote the cancellation letter to Birmingham like she suggested. Baz called after tea to see how I was, but he was too full of Pat to need any answers. It wasn't what I wanted to hear. I need to forget all that. Rang K to apologise for the last two Saturdays. Said I'd go round tomorrow for the match. Rovers are safe now. Faggots, peas and mash when Mum in. Then I sat watching TV all evening. Mum said we'd go out to cinema tomorrow to cheer me up. 'The Greengage Summer' and 'Les Grandes Familles' are on at the Odeon. I tried to look enthusiastic.

And I try to stay enthusiastic about my theory in the face of Dad's depression. But just because I might get over a dumping without too long down in the dumps doesn't mean his blues weren't due to Alice casting him off. My key might still fit, and one letter suggests how to test it: K – K for Keith, Dad's footy fanatic friend. Can I find him? Might he remember something to prove me right? Turning over I see two more of Dad's diary entries about trying to get on the employment ladder – with Westminster Bank and Carr Components. He fails. It makes for more sad reading to finish his little book.

No, not a little book, but a little time bomb ticking away in a box or a drawer for fourteen years before exploding in Mum's face. Why did he write it down – something so incriminating, whatever the facts? OK, why did I write about the pits of my life in my diary: Wednesday 16th October 1985? To spread anguish and turmoil into the familiar pattern of lines on a page, a day all sorted and tidied away, that's why. If Dad was like me, it was his way of trying to move on and leave his tragedy behind him. He didn't think about posterity reading it, and neither have I. Diaries are for secrets – or were then, before Myspace and Facebook created a generation of self-publicists collecting artificial friends and neglecting their real ones – and once written they're part of you, and not easy to throw away. What would Lou think about me if she read about Amanda and what I did that day?

I take another dose of punishment for my sexual transgression – the tepid bath, the Germolene on my bum, the stinging – and bed down in the spare room. I bury my face in Lou's pillow to breathe in the faint scent of her, and wonder if I'll confess.

SEVENTEEN

I've three variants in my mind for the spelling of Keith's surname, and leaf through The Phone Book to see who might match up. There're ten Wainwrights including a K, no Wenwrights, and two Winwrights with no Ks. And Borrowdale Avenue sounds familiar.

It's been a good morning, redeeming a restless night. I don't know what kept me awake, but I wasn't short of causes: bizarre extra-marital sex, my sore buttock, the guilt, Dad's confession, Ivor Hughes' attentions – and that's not counting the wailing wind and the steelworks clang. It's a wonder I slept at all. But now I've e-mailed, form-filled and phoned my way to feeling back in control, if not exactly normal.

I've also given Lou the full monty on my time with Ivor – but not yet on my full monty afterwards or what I've found out since. I swig the rest of my midday cuppa and finish a biscuit before ringing.

"Is that Keith Wainwright?"

"This is Mr Wainwright, yes."

"I'm Michael Paine, Alan's son."

Silence. I must've stopped his metronome and thrown his rhythm out. "Right," comes at last, but nothing more.

"We used to go to football together."

"Yes."

It's time I set the tempo. "Look, I'd like to come and see you. Do you mind?"

"What about?"

"About Dad. I know we haven't met for years, but you were his best friend. I want to ask you about him."

"Well, I don't know."

Why's he so chary? "Please, Keith – for his sake."

"Where are you?"

Ah! Maybe I've got my foot in the door. "At Kilvert Road. I'm sorting things. My mum died last week."

"Yes. I saw it in the *Argus*."

"I could come now."

And then he opens up wide. "No, come at one-ish. We'll have a bite to eat together."

Pleased at having talked my way in, I fritter away half-an-hour on the Beeb and Times websites before setting off. It's only a ten minute drive to Gunterton, Ulcethorpe's rival to Bardby as premier leafy suburb, but I go downmarket through Froderby first – past the terraces of red brick houses looking like prison walls from the end of each treeless street, and built to keep sweating Victorian steelworkers sweet. You can still get a solid house for 80K here, but fronting an artificial tenfoot formed by the closed ranks of parked cars.

57 Borrowdale Avenue seems to have contracted since I was eight, but the garden's grown – not in acreage but into a jungle. He should leave a machete by the gate. I have to wend through wind-gusted whips of branches on my trek up the mossy path. The bell seems mute, but my rat-tat-tat brings a shadow to the frosted panes, and the peeling door opens to the extent of its chain. I don't remember ever getting beyond the doorstep before; Keith was always ready or we met him somewhere else. He sizes me up through the slit, looking for a recognisable development of whatever image is in his head.

"Come on in, Michael." It's a positive ID for him. But when he opens the door I see a flabby, balding, anaemic stranger in a dirty pullover who shaves without a mirror and probably follows football from his armchair now. "I hope kitchen'll do you. Dining room's me archive."

And so is the hall, it seems. I follow him past stacks of the boxes that packs of A4 come in. The kitchen's tidy but as much in need of a facelift as Mum's.

"What're you storing, Keith?"

162

"Me memorabilia."

"Footy?" I hardly need to ask.

"Mm. Now, beans on toast, tinned soup or I could do you an omelette?"

I choose the omelette to spare me from more of what I've been eating at Kilvert Road. "Do you still watch Rovers?"

His answer's a surprise. "Oh, yes, home and away. Never miss – not even when they dropped into Conference."

"I always look for their results, but I've started following West Ham now. I go to the odd game. It's my nearest Premiership team."

"Founded eighteen-ninety-five; record crowd forty-two thousand three hundred and twenty-two; record win ten-nil versus Bury in nineteen-eighty-three; record defeat eight-two versus Blackburn in nineteen-sixty-three…"

"You should be on *Mastermind*, Keith."

"Well, I don't know. Me general knowledge isn't in same league – not like that black bloke winning last year with football. Sit down, why don't you. You can give me your coat. It looks like Alan's."

"It is – or was. I inherited it. A bit of re-stitching is all it's needed."

He nods and takes it from me as if it's a mink stole, not an old Spitfire jacket, and hangs it under the stairs with other coats. I'm wondering if I dare ask what bumph he's accumulated that fills a whole dining room and half a hall – it might release another outflow of stats – but he moves on from facts to feelings.

"You know, holding his flying-jacket then were very special. When you lose a relative people are sympathetic. When you lose your best mate, nobody cares. We were together near on twenty-five years. I never really got over it; never wanted anyone else as a pal." He sniffs and then turns to hide his face in the larder and the fridge.

I don't reply. I don't know what to say. But if he's distressed, I'm surprised. If my turning up thirty-one years later in Dad's flying jacket turns him back into a snivelling mourner, then a best mate is a lot matier than I realised – unless Keith's releasing the grief of a bereaved lover. Mm. Maybe for him their meetings were like dates; those Saturdays the fulfilment of his lonely lovesick week. Anyway, gay romance is not something I know much about.

And I don't know much about best mates either, for that matter. I've never had one. I don't think Jay Yates qualifies. If he had, wouldn't I have followed up to find out what happened to him and not let him disappear like that? Yet I was starting to get comfortable with the idea of a friend by then. I suppose talk of a nervous breakdown scared me off. He's Borough Librarian now, according to what Mum told me she'd read in the *Argus* last year – the same summit of provincial respectability Grandma Paine's father reached before the war, but a strange peak for an IC chem eng dropout.

After can opening and egg breaking with his back to me Keith recovers. "I'm sorry about your mum. I don't think I said on the phone. You caught me out of position. Brown bread all right with yours?"

I watch the three minutes of manoeuvres to serve baked beans on toast and a three-egg omelette with bread and butter simultaneously. If I hadn't been blessed by Lou saying yes I think I might've got stuck in a solitary groove like Keith. I'd never have been satisfied by anyone else either. Second best comes nowhere for me.

"I usually have a beer now. Will that do you?"

"Yep, fine. You're nifty in the kitchen, Keith."

"I don't know. I've had a few years practice since me mum died, anyroad. I carry on with her recipes just for meself. I don't rate those ready meals. This is first time I've cooked for two."

He takes two bottles from the fridge and gets an opener from a drawer.

"I like this because it comes from where it should. Most of them foreign lagers are brewed here; the labels don't mean a thing."

And as he pours Beck's down the inside of a tilted glass I feel my pity flowing out as well. This shy man with his desiccated life dedicated to football once had my dad as his soulmate. Now he's a recluse communing with the contents of his boxes. Yes, with those long ago Saturday afternoons of TV sport or watching Rovers so very special for him I feel more hopeful about my quest. We pick up our knives and forks and I kick off.

"How's your memory for nineteen-sixty-one?"

"Do you mean nineteen-sixty/sixty-one or nineteen-sixty-one/sixty-two?"

So he thinks in football seasons – a sort of Julian calendar. "Sixty/sixty-one – April."

"Rovers had a late run that saved them from Third Division."

"How about Saturday April 8th?"

I'm certain his pause is simply for swallowing. "We lost one-nil at home to Huddersfield Town."

"Do you remember anything else?"

"Barry Jones missed a penalty."

I need to switch Keith to the other wing. "Anything about Alan, I meant."

Now he does have to think, but not for long. "He never turned up. When I gave you the score something clicked. He always let me know. I rang him later and his mum said he weren't well. It's all coming back to me." He saws off another mouthful.

"And when did he come back to you?" But he's not to be rushed and so I add a filler. "You do a mean omelette, by the way."

"I'm glad it's to your liking. Well, that were for next home game a fortnight later: two-nil versus Plymouth Argyle."

"Did he say what'd happened?"

"Not as I recall. I were just pleased to see him again. But he'd changed."

"In what way?" I try to sound relaxed.

"A lot quieter, like. He'd decided to leave school, so he should've been a lot happier. I were, when I left. It weren't till he met Marlene that the old Alan came back."

"So he was down for a long time, then?"

"Oh, yes. Right down in the mouth."

It's not what I wanted to hear. Clinical depression doesn't fit my theory. But I don't give up yet. "Did he talk about girlfriends?"

"No. He knew I weren't interested."

165

"He never mentioned an Alice – or Linda?"

"No, I've just said. That were something for his other pals. I were only a bit of his life." He stops, yet in my head I hear, 'But he were all of mine'.

He busies himself with another mouthful, and having heard his tone of testiness as a yellow card I've no option but to swallow my disappointment and do the same.

* * *

We part with the handshake avoided when we met. I know he plays *Championship Manager* on his computer, adds to his archive via eBay, files his stuff to a system of his own devising, has a run of Rovers programmes from 1946, watches Sky Sports on a 40 inch TV and much much more. I asked, and he enjoyed the telling. He knows absolutely zilch about me. But if I've been his first-night audience of one, I'm not complaining. My selfish, self-invited guesting into his lonely life has been to his advantage, not to mine – and I feel glad for him. With my arms raised to ward off the lashing branches, I'm a surrendering fighter pilot on my way back to the gate. And after the thoughts deferred by all Keith's lecturettes, I'm surrendering my position on Dad's escapade in the woods too. There must've been more than just a slap in the face there, literal or figurative.

In the calm of the car I watch the gesticulations of the Borrowdale Avenue trees. What had Dad written in that poem? *The final solution: consummation.* With his amorous intentions frustrated, might violence have mutated to violation? Is my only choice now between a dad who was a killer and a dad who was rapist? The weight of the realisation compresses me into inertia. I can't move. It's like the seat belt's locked up – but I haven't put it on yet. I can't hear – the wind bending the branches or the L-driver botching a three-point turn. I can't even think. Well, not forwards, only back. What comes next? How do I shred the past? I'm in hibernation mode, waiting for someone to press a key.

My mobile rings; someone has. It's my traffic sage Paul Charter with more feedback on his swansong – today, a working lunch at Tanker-freight's Tilbury offices. I feign I'm on the move and promise to call him back. But it's my call back to the world of action, and away from stupefying speculation. If what happened that afternoon in Hackby is as bad as I fear, it'll be in the *Argus*. Now I know what to do next. I phone Paul from the multi-storey in Coke Street. It's mainly good news: 3-1 to us, although I shouldn't see it like a football score. That's Keith's fault. We're cooperating, not competing. But they wouldn't budge on the fleet value, so there's a write-off needing sanction.

"I'll sort that when I'm back, Paul. Thanks for all the work you've put in."

"You getting it all sorted up there, Mike?"

"Yep. Everything's under control. House clearance Thursday, then I'm away. Can't wait."

"See you Friday, then."

I should be a salesman. Everything under control, my arse. How do you squash emotions back in their boxes once they've escaped? Grief, guilt, horror: I've suffered the lot since Lou went. And that's not counting the compassion let out by Ivor and Keith – or my flirtation with one of the seven deadly sins. What's happening to me? I've always been able to keep everything buttoned up. I stick my ticket in my pocket, zap the car and skitter down two flights of granolithic stairway.

Ulcethorpe's Central Library isn't so central now, but it has had accolades for innovation – presumably for more than just a shape to satisfy a pharaoh. It'll be my maiden entry into this high-tech polyhedral successor to Carnegie's gothic endowment to the town. Today the paved square in front belies the piazza status sought by planting mature trees with circumferential seats and borders of laurel and aucuba. Pigeons are strutting unworried by the eddying litter and I soon discover why: Tuesday 0900–1400. Fuck, fuck, fuck it. The National Lottery might've funded the capital cost, but the Metropolitan Council can't afford to open it all day. I've another eighteen hours of not knowing – although when I do know, I don't know how much better off I'll be. I walk on to the *Argus* offices as a desperate remedy, to be told what I could've told myself: there's no public access to newspapers from forty years ago there.

"Try the library," the young lady brightening the foyer with her purple hijab advises. I bite my tongue. But at least I've time for a detour to Andersons to sign their house sale agreement now.

On the way I swap the Corus-tainted wind chill of High Street for some air-conditioned cosseting in the Eastvale Centre in the search for a cup of tea. The Centre is another maiden entry, but I knew what shops to expect before coming in. I could be almost anywhere in Britain, and even the premature Christmas muzak isn't a surprise. It's depressing, but I've accepted these cloned malls up to now. But pacing the arcade today, my mood is steering my eyes towards a different view.

This is retailing without a heart, without a soul: identical units defined by their brand and their logo; where individuality and authenticity have been kicked out of the window to give marketing a free rein to entice in the shoppers for standardised stuff mostly made thousands of miles away. Clothes, phones, sportswear, stationery, cosmetics, health food, jewellery, whatever: the hidden persuaders all use the same box of tricks. I pity the staff on minimum wage propping up these hollow shams. I've never thought about them before.

I sit in Starbucks with my Earl Grey, feeling disorientated, sad and lonely, and phone Lou for comfort, like a homesick new boarder ringing his mum. She's packing up her painting tackle before jogging round the short circuit before it gets dark. I tell her I'm off to the estate agent but would rather be panting by her side.

"Why not come home tonight, sweetheart, and drive back up to-morrow?"

"I'd love to, darling, but there's just too much to do." I would and there isn't, but I'm the sphinx bolted to the pedestal and watching that pyramid.

"Go out for a meal, then."

"Not on my own."

"Well, with somebody. Isn't there anybody there you know?"

"No, no one." Well, not in the way she means – and I'm not going to try contacting Jay Yates, even if it did all happen after he left.

"Go and buy some steak and a bottle of wine then. Promise me."

* * *

Back in the tired old Kilvert Road kitchen I stick my steak in the fridge but leave the spuds, toms and mushrooms in the carrier. I need a sog in front of the box to contemplate my inheritance – the stigma not the money. I think I'd give up the cash if that'd blot out the other. How can I match my good memories of Dad with what I fear I'll find out tomorrow? Did he have the tragic hero's fatal flaw? I can't remember anything bad about him – not even the short fuse I've come by that sets off my micro coprolalia. How could a failed kiss have turned him violent? Even when I was that age the girl still played the princess and the boy the respectful suitor. He must've known the rule: you only get what you're given – or couldn't he read the signs? That power's swapped over now; it's more like the prince and the showgirl. Conditioning by media-flaunted norms and aspirations has made girls very vulnerable. I'll soon be worrying about mine.

I haven't a clue what I've been watching, but the news is now leading with Iraq again. I retaliate with the remote to avoid any further depression. The TV sits on the yellowed melamine of the wall unit cupboard they used for their records, which is yet another place I need to sort out. Their collections – Mum's easy listening and Dad's post-war Brit stuff – are kept apart by a bellows of buff document wallets. When I pull out this barricade Mum's records topple over to rest on Dad's. I stack the rubbed and grubby wallets on the coffee table and read the neat titles along the fold of each flap: CAR, HOLIDAYS, BANK, PURCHASES, UTILITIES, RATES, TELEPHONE, MORTGAGE, HOUSE, EMPLOYMENT. I've already had Mum's filing system out of the dining room sideboard for processing. This is ancient history: the pre-disaster imprints of my fallen idol.

I leaf through sheaves of bills, letters, accounts, statements and agreements to build a pile of paper for the recycle box, and throw the cardboard aside for the green bin. There's just one foolscap sheet I keep separate: Andersons' particulars for a *solid and spacious semi-detached dwelling* being offered freehold for £2,450 o.n.o. I'll compare it with what they say this time round – a little test of their competence, to check they're earning their fee. If 10 Kilvert Road is typical, I've calculated – by going to the laptop to do it – that house price inflation here has averaged 10.2% per annum over the forty years.

Now it's time for the final folder: EMPLOYMENT. I pull out the wads of payslips before clutching the P60s, notices of coding and a few other papers. And it's a folded sheet in amongst the latter that hooks my eyes and opens my mouth and dries my throat and converts me into another Michael – the avenging angel.

EIGHTEEN

In a TV drama I'd already be in the kitchen choosing the sharpest knife – or in the shed unhooking the washing line by torchlight, or in the bathroom counting Mum's accumulation of paracetamols, or in her bedroom stuffing tights into my pocket. But real life's less hyper. Maybe I'll want to stab or hang or poison or garrotte Sir Smart Alec Masters again later, but for now I'm sedating myself with Côtes du Rhône and googling my way to familiarity with his lifestyle and career. Dad's redemption certificate is on the dining room table alongside the laptop. I pick up the copy of his memo to read and admire for the nth time.

Performance Intermediates UK
From: A. Paine, Shift Supervisor
To: A. Masters, Works Manager
cc:
Date: 15.6.74
Subj: Oxidation reactor bridging pipe

With the loss of Mr. Stevenson I should like to urge you to seek a professional opinion from a specialist outside the works about the design of the 20 inch bridging pipe now under construction to join R102 and R104. Although I do not have any engineering qualifications, I believe from my A level science and looking at books in the Technical Office library that what is proposed is under-designed.

Because the pipe has a dog-leg, the expansion bellows at each end will be out of line. When it is pressurixed there will be sideways forces on the bellows for which they are not designed. This could strain and distort them in a dangerous way, either damaging the assenbly or even causing a rupture. It might be made safer by anchoring the new piping with proper rigid supports, but I have been told that the pipe will rest in a cradle made of scaffolding. This is mot a proper support.

I realise it is important to get back into production as quickly as possible, but what we are doing may be storing up more problems for the future. Please accept my suggestion as constructive, and not critical of the sterling efforts everyone is making.

A. M. Paine

He typed it – I say he, because of the mistakes – with a second sheet of printed memo paper backing the carbon instead of a plain flimsy. Probably done without thinking, it gives me damning evidence as a result. Every blank sheet of that paper was carbonised itself in the holocaust two months later. And the company name went up in smoke as well, to let Phoenix Intermediates rise briefly from the ashes. And if that's not enough, I've gold plated the provenance with a couple of agreements rescued from the coffee table pile to prove to the world how *A. M. Paine* signed his name. Thank God he signed on the copy too.

I feel as if I'm walking a tightrope. Dad's own sterling effort to prevent disaster has redeemed him and steadied me pro tem, but I still dread overbalancing at the library tomorrow. He didn't spot the bending moment that jack-knifed the pipe, but his forecast of the squirming bellows is brilliant in the circumstances. It's more whimpering than whistle-blowing, but in 1974 and in his lowly position I don't think he could've done much more – other than tell someone he'd written it, and not just slip the proof into a folder for posterity to find.

Without the qualifications to match his acumen Dad hadn't any power. He fell at the status hurdle safety people have to clear to get advice accepted, because our track records are so hard to prove. You can't better a goal of zero accidents, or quantify all those prevented – truisms that don't mix easily with fashionable performance indicators. Having success measured by the absence of failure always bugged me in CSS. The irony is that Dad did discover his success, worse luck.

For yet another time I picture him in that control room before it imploded and ignited; but now he's raging on top of the agonising and praying. Yes, raging against that self-seeking bastard Masters, the man who probably tossed his warning into the bin. Poor Dad paid the ultimate price for having his theory proved. It's the most ghastly scenario, for which I intend to make Smart Alec squirm like those out of line bellows. He's not going to live down Boroughcliff this time round. And I've got just the man to help me. Ivor Hughes has come on the scene as if cued by serendipity. I've always believed in self-sufficiency and the weakness of relying on someone else – but not now, not for this. He'll be pleased.

The synergy of empty glass and empty stomach prompts my move into the kitchen. And it's a welcome break from the turmoil, boiling, baking and frying myself my little feast – although there is an ingredient missing: the primitive satisfaction I've found in cooking to feed others that turns a task into a pleasure. The thought brings an unexpected sympathy for Keith and Ivor, destined to cook just for themselves for evermore. Yes, I'm warming to the idea of letting Ivor host me at his home some time.

* * *

On the other evenings I've had TV suppers slouching on the sofa, but with tonight's posh nosh I sat upright in the dining room opposite the laptop. And Emily's text took my mind back home, away from reeling all over the place here. I treated myself to visualising my Three Graces: Lou clearing the kitchen and worrying if the ECO program will clean their dishes properly; Emily in bed reading stories in funny voices to her toy animals; and Hannah isolated from the world practising her

Skriabin and Ravel exam pieces before tomorrow's lesson. I'll phone Lou and Ivor in a few minutes with my news, but now I'm back at the computer with my coffee reviewing the bio I've assembled in Word.

SIR ALEC MASTERS, CHIEF EXECUTIVE, ATOGAS
Childhood:
- Born 1942, Sleaford, Lincolnshire
- Son of an RAF Group Captain
- Schools: Winchester House, Brackley; Oundle
- **Universities and qualifications:**
- Christ's College, Cambridge – BA in Chemistry 1964, MA 1972
- Harvard Business School – MBA 1969
- **Employment:**
- ICP, Teesside, 1964
- Mainz Chemische, Frankfurt, 1969
- Performance Intermediates, Boroughcliff, 1972
- Mainz Chemische, Frankfurt, 1975
- Atogas, 1977 to date, Rotterdam, Baton Rouge and London.
- **Honours and awards:**
- Knighted 2002
- Fellow of the Royal Society
- Honorary Fellow of Christ's College, Cambridge
- **Directorships and Trusteeships:**
- Universal Banking Corporation
- The Rankine Foundation
- Bate, Armitage & Ross
- The City Orchestra
- AAGU
- **Other:**
- Married twice, divorced twice, five children
- Recreations: sailing, vintage cars, and early music

Ivor called him my bête noire yesterday evening, but he's my enemy now, the man defined by my bullet points – though not yet shot by my bullets. Not even his affinity with early music saves him. It's an impeccable pedigree to flesh out the man with the fleshy Machiavellian face grinning from the Atogas website. He's an elusive enemy, too: no phone numbers, no addresses. And at Atogas House he'll be Minos on his throne with a labyrinth of protection. But Ivor's sure to know how we navigate the passages to reach him and pull him down.

The urge to speak to Lou soon tugs me across the hall to the sitting room and the phone. I want to hear her voice. It'll be my sweet course, and far better than any of the M&S desserts I chose not to have. Having dialled our number I plump down on to the sag bag beside the unit with the receiver in my hand.

"Hi, darling," I say, when she answers.

"I hoped it was you."

"What were you doing?"

"Flaked out with my feet up and that book about Degas and Whistler you got me. You stopped me nodding off." I hear her yawning.

"Sorry. A hard day?"

"It's always more of a strain when you're not here."

"Mm, I suppose so." It's the technical things that bug her because they still remain a mystery, however many times I explain. "Girls in bed?"

"Emily's gone; Hannah's doing her Bournvita. Did you have your steak?"

"Yep, Hereford fillet, but I didn't really taste it. Louise, I've found out something here about Dad: he warned the works manager about the pipe that burst and killed him."

"How do you mean?"

"I've got a copy of a memo he typed two months before the disaster, asking for the design to be looked at again. He forecast what happened."

"And nobody took any notice?"

"He only sent it to his boss: the guy who's now top dog at Atogas, if you remember; the bully I can't stand."

"Oh, Mike, sweetheart, that's awful." The sound of her solicitude is better than any sedative. I wish she were here with me now. "What can you do? It's a pity you've left CSS."

"I've beavered away into his background on the Internet. Next I need to work out how to get at him."

"For what, sweetheart? Nothing silly?" I hear the catch of alarm in her voice.

"No, not silly. I want a public apology, at least – if there aren't any legal moves I can take. He wrecked our lives – and all the others. You know Omega's mantra: all accidents are preventable. Well, Dad offered that bastard the means to prevent not just any accident but the goddam Boroughcliff disaster, and he funked it."

"You don't know that. You haven't heard his side of things. And he didn't know there'd be a disaster. You're seeing it all with hindsight." Lou always sees the best in people. It's her mantra.

"But he's a chemist. He might not have known about the piping mechanics, but he could've assessed the consequences. He should be made to pay."

"The Ivor you talked to last night – can't he help? He'll know what to do, surely, from what you said." I can hear a mixture of glee and relief.

"Darling, you're brilliant; I'd thought of that too. I'm going to phone him next. I'll talk to you again afterwards. Is that OK?"

"Yes, go on. Best of luck."

I haul myself up to bring in the memo and extract his card from my wallet, reading for the first time: *Ivor Hughes, Safety Consultant and Writer, 41 Parkside Road, London N2 8AZ.* He didn't say if he planned to go back there today, but I try the 0208 number first to find out. I'll stay standing for this call – flopping wouldn't be right.

After counting eight rings I'm expecting a recording when the live voice responds, "Hughes here."

"Ivor, it's Michael Paine."

"Noswaith dda, Michael. You've been exceedingly quick."

"Quick?"

"In finding something out. Or is that not the reason you're ringing?"

176

I halt to sort my answer. "Oh. I see what you mean. I'm still investigating that. No, I'm phoning about something else I've found out. I hope you can help with it."

"Fire away. Very glad to be asked, I am."

I tell him about the memo and he asks me to read it out. Then there's silence.

"Are you there, Ivor?"

"Yes, sorry. I'm trying to take it in, that's all. It must've knocked the stuffing out of you. I'm going into my sitting room. I'll think better in there."

"Well, actually it fired me up. I want him to confess in public that he ignored Dad's warning, and own up to the manslaughter of sixteen men. How do I go about it?"

"You go about it with a lot of care, Michael. It's David and Goliath, and there's only one stone for your sling. But you've come to the right man for help. I've had the odd dealing with Sir Alec. You mustn't underestimate him."

"I don't. He walks on water and catches bullets in his teeth blindfold. I know."

"Almost. But your discovery's come at an interesting time. Atogas is my next project. See, we writers are addicted; we don't wait to finish one thing before planning the next. Is their environmental and safety record due to Masters or despite him? That's the theme."

"I can tell you the answer," I snap.

"Yes, Michael, I understand how you feel. But I'll decide on the basis of research and evidence."

"My dad's memo is evidence, isn't it?"

"Of course. I wasn't suggesting otherwise. You know, it's not so long since I was at Kew at the PRO and made some time to look at the records of what Masters actually said to the Boroughcliff Court of Inquiry – a prelude to my inquiry, see; his first utterances in the public domain."

"And?"

"I'm speaking from my memory so this is a paraphrase, but when asked if he'd considered taking external mechanical engineering advice, he said no. He'd full confidence in his own staff to design and construct the modification, and there'd been not a single dissenting voice."

"The fucking bastard. So he lied, as well as ignoring the warning." I realise I'm shouting in triumph, but it's premature so I lower my volume. "Sorry. I got carried away. But what do we do about it?"

"Look, when are you driving home?"

"Thursday afternoon or early evening."

"Can you make a detour by here? I can see the memo, and I'll have time to think of a plan. I'll feed you."

So, he's going to be hosting me sooner than I expected; and the thought of being taken care of is strangely comforting. I'm in his hands and I'm happy to trust him. It's a novel feeling for Mr Self-reliant. "Yes, I'd like that. And you're very kind."

"Have you got a satnav in your car?"

"No, but I've a London A to Z."

"Good. You'll find me. Leave the M1 at Junction two."

"I'll manage. I'll call you when I'm on the way. And I'm really glad I phoned you."

"Me too."

I drink my bedtime milk with a Paxman harangue on Newsnight for company and a much more sanguine blood flow to my brain. I'll sleep tonight: the wind's dropped somewhat, my bum's much easier, the guilt's receding, and I'm Dad's avenger. My urge to strike back for him is still boiling like the cyclohexane that once exploded to take him away.

After pointing the remote and putting down my glass I lounge back on the cushion. It's a mistake. Fears submerge no deeper than crocodiles eyeing their prey. As my head droops and my defences drop, the dread of Dad striking at me in the library tomorrow resurfaces. Then my waking thoughts morph into dreams: I'm Howard Carter waiting to breach the pyramid and discover the legacy of the tomb.

NINETEEN

My mobile's attempt at *Für Elise* interrupts my breakfast. It's Adrian Tankard, my Brentfield superintendent. My joke about his apt name when we first met sunk like the weight on a dip tape. Maybe that or his failure to get my job has made him into a sourpuss – although Paul did say he could be a bit difficult; and from a guy with a view of humanity like his I suppose I could translate that as 'an awkward bugger'. Still, he's a key man in my team. The sooner I find a slot for a one-to-one so he can let off any steam and clear the air the better. I can't succeed in a job with discontented staff.

"Sorry about troubling you on vacation, Mike, but I need to consult."

Vacation? What's he talking about? He knows why I'm away. Maybe he thinks it should be vacation and not compassionate leave. "Go ahead, Adrian."

"I want full twenty-four hour working from two more VMS mechanics on the main T27 pump. We've only the one guy a shift contracted. I need to tell VMS this morning."

I wait for further explanation, but his flow's stopped like the pump's. "Adrian?"

"Yes."

"Can you give me some background?" I think he wanted me to supplicate for the extra info to bolster his position.

"T27's heating oil. It's full, but the other HO tanks are low. Demand's high this time of year so if the standby fails we might be up shit creek."

I feel he's setting me an initiative test, but we are over budget on maintenance and I did tell him to rein back on extras. "Standby's up and running?"

179

"Yes."

"Well, transfer T27 into one of the others when you can. Is the pump in the shop yet?"

"No."

"We'll review it tomorrow, but don't authorise them today."

"OK, Mike, your decision." I'm sure he wanted to add, 'It's what you're paid for.'

"Adrian, while you're on, I want to review the E and I maintenance service we're getting from Contech and why they're slipping on the testing schedules. We could do that one morning and then go out to lunch for a chat. I'd like to hear your ideas on how we optimise the new set-up. Put up some dates when you ring tomorrow, OK?"

"Suits me, Mike. Good idea. Talk to you soon."

For an ex-CSS guy, getting behind with the safety interlock verification programme is like a priest disobeying one of the Ten Commandments. Whereas fleet management is a sensible offload, contract maintenance might've been a step too far – as Network Rail decided after Potters Bar. We can't buy in commitment to our culture any more than government bribes make dedicated teachers. With process control relying on computer software these days, and control rooms looking like call centres with only keyboards, screens and telephones on the desk, it's reassuring to have belt and braces with the hard-wired shutdown system in the back room. I reckon Contech don't ever think beyond breakdown repairs. They don't understand us – but I do think Adrian understood my peace offering and will think about coming over to my side.

* * *

There's a welcome glimmer of sunshine as I drive to the library. I'm pleased; I need all the good omens going. But stepping from the multi-storey into the wind tunnel of Coke Street there's still enough velocity from the Steppe to send me shivering into the pyramid. After admiring the ground floor panorama of hotel foyer, Internet café, bookshop, and reading room all combined, I venture into a glass cylinder to be elevated in the central core as fast as Jay Yates' rise to be in charge of it all. He might be in the building now, but I shan't look him up. There's that slight risk involved; and, anyway, with Ivor's friendship in the offing I don't think I can harbour more.

Reference is on the mezzanine, a stratum where book browsers seem to be extinct. Certainly there're none to be seen at the shelves, but a flourishing species of screen-staring mouse-trapping student types is clustered at another array of computer terminals intent on the Internet. The young lady wearing glasses at the desk looks like a model in a Specsavers ad, but she deflects wolfish attention with a bookish look – sombre clothes, frowning face and hair pulled back into a bun. Maybe there's a dress and hair code in the staff handbook to perpetuate the stereotype. Anyway, I'm relieved to find I've no wolfish attention on offer today.

When I announce my quest for old copies of the *Argus* she's all eagerness to assist, springing up to guide me to the deserted local studies section in the corner. The index, cabinets and viewers are soon shown and the routine explained; but then she can't resist advertising their other microform resources – censuses, registers, directories and many more – hoping to tempt me into beavering away with the twigs of my family tree, not realising I'm here to investigate the trunk.

At last she retreats to let me try my hand at researching, and the red ring binder labelled *Ulcethorpe Evening Argus* tells me the microfilm number for April 1961. I open the cabinet drawer feeling like a spy with a microdot camera about to reveal a dark secret to the world – fearful, yet eager – and exchange my black plastic dummy box for the white carton holding the film. At the viewer I'm all fingers and thumbs, but finally the spool is mounted and the film threaded and I'm rotating the little handle to open the window on to all our yesterdays.

After about a minute I've wound the film forward to Saturday April 8th and wound myself into a state of gut tugging anxiety – but then

I let out my pent-up breath. The *Argus* headlines are national and innocuous: SCHOOLMASTERS VOTE FOR PAY INCREASES. I can only see the top half of the front page, but the lead story is from Blackpool: a conference debate on how the reduced economic status of schoolmasters is lowering the value pupils put on their teachers. Plus ça change… I raise the image to view lower on the page – and turn the screen into a magnet and my scalp into a pincushion.

SCHOOLGIRL'S TRAGIC DEATH

A beautiful and brilliant young student has been tragically killed. Alice Krysztowczyk, 14, of Hackby was struck down yesterday afternoon only a few hundred yards from her home. Her injuries were consistent with being hit by a car. We understand Alice had taken her dog Gem for a walk as usual into the nearby woods. She was found at the roadside by her mother Mrs. Doris Krysztowczyk, 35, who called an ambulance. Alice was pronounced dead at the scene.

In a statement released through Trent Valley Constabulary last night, Mr. and Mrs. Krysztowczyk mourned the loss of their "beautiful and talented daughter, our only child, so suddenly taken from us", and prayed for God's help in coping with their grief. They went on to ask the driver of the car to come forward "so we may understand how the accident happened. We have already forgiven him or her".

Formerly a pupil at Bardby Grammar School, Alice started boarding at Stuart Hall, Dunborough, Suffolk in September last year, where she "shone at science and games and relished the academic rigour". She hoped to study medicine at university.

Alice's father Andrzej Krysztowczyk, 54, came to Britain in the war with the Polish Air Force as a navigator, and flew bombers with 300 Squadron from RAF Hemswell. Afterwards he stayed on to marry a local girl and form with a colleague the electronics company Elco, which has premises on Trentholme Road.

At the family bungalow in extensive grounds on the edge of the village curtains were drawn today, and the doorbell went unanswered. Neighbours spoke of the delightful family, and their shock at the loss of a girl so loved and admired by everyone.

Inspector David Nash told the Argus that the police were fully committed to finding the perpetrator. He wishes to hear from anyone who saw a grey saloon car, possibly a Vauxhall, driving at speed through Hackby and on the road to Atterthorpe at about 3.15 yesterday afternoon to contact him on Ulcethorpe 12399.

I speed read with increasing relief. I know it's selfish, but I don't care. Dad's not guilty – at least, in the eyes of the law. The hit-and-run merchant did it. She must've run out after the dog or to get away. I'm sure those words in the diary would fit. There's also a picture, and Alice stares out at me via the coarse dot matrix of the time, apparently from a school photograph. Her allure shines through the obscuration of old technology with a disconcerting familiarity, before I reason why. She looks like Mum as a girl, judging by the photo archive I've been rescuing from the sideboard and scrutinising again. And I think she's the girl in that secret photo that Mum found and then must've thrown away. I'm not sure that calling fourteen-year-olds sultry doesn't smack of paedophilia, but they both had a certain sexy something. I can understand Dad being besotted and chasing after her to Linda's chagrin. He must've been absolutely gobsmacked when he set eyes on the ripened reincarnation at Brown and Beasley. Mum rescued him from the same uncharted quagmire that sucked her from Ivor's rescuing arms. It's a second ghastly irony.

Why didn't Dad ever confess to Mum? Maybe he was going to but never found the right moment. Or maybe he could never face up to what he'd done wrong – not so much the struggle for a kiss as scooting off and never saying anything, and leaving Alice's parents to grieve without any notion of the truth. Or did he think Mum would want him to tell them – even after however many years – and he couldn't cope with that? And why haven't I ever owned up to Lou about my Alice episode with Amanda Rose? Because she'd want me to make restitution too?

A reluctance to lose sight of my salvation makes me read the report again, but slowly, studying each word. *Krysztowczyk*: I'd glossed over that as unpronounceable. But this time the surname is not only pronounceable but also familiar. The pins are being pushed back into my head. Kryshtovchvk is my best attempt on the sound, and the word is written on the label of that top flat doorbell. Doris is the clue. While Dad's Alice resisted him, her cousin Karol's Alicia invited me. If only it'd been the other way round. I shiver at yet another of life's not so little ironies.

I continue my reread: *her injuries were consistent with being hit by a car*. Only consistent with? Have I jumped the gun? I'm certainly jumpy again. But no, it couldn't be; there's that Vauxhall – and an inquest to come to prove it. And for the first time, at the thought of Alice, not much older than Hannah, laid out in the mortuary as the silent witness, I have a flush of sympathy. It shows me a picture of a distraught Andrzej hugging a weeping Doris – still shuddering from the shock of finding Alice's mangled body – with their hopes wrecked and their lives foundering. Did they ever recover from the trauma of that senseless and sickening death? And how would Lou and I cope, without God's help, behind the closed curtains? I pull out my hankie to wipe my eyes, and resolve to visit Hackby to find where it happened; where Dad's eagerness and Alice's modesty and the Krysztowczyks' fogeyish rules were the leitmotifs of a tragedy.

It takes an hour's eyestrain to find the short column on Alice's inquest and dispel my lingering concern. The phrases that stick out are *multiple injuries, struck by, striking against*, and *accidental death*. I'm happy to accept that the pathologist and coroner got it right. The grey saloon never gets another mention, and I'm not inclined to peer any further ahead for it.

After a quick rewind of the film on to the feed spool, and the little

ritual of the black and white boxes, I saunter over to thank Miss Spex
– but she's looking up into a face from my past: the face of the man I
wasn't going to look up. There's no doubt who's leaning towards her
with hands apart on the desk: my mate for that year at IC and the
brainbox from Trentholme, Jay Yates. I slam on the brakes, but he's
already turned his head at my approach. Fuck it! There's no avoiding
him now. I'll have to make the best of it. On I go.

"If it isn't Jay." It's John really, but all his stuff was marked J.A.Y. I
hold out my hand as he straightens and shows off his giraffe neck.

"Mike Paine. You've barely changed – and I'd know that scar anywhere."

"You likewise – and I'd know that scowl anywhere."

"Touché. I shouldn't be scowling. It's nothing personal."

"I know, but you always did – one of your defences." His handshake's
a bit limp but his face is welcoming now.

"You're in charge here, aren't you? My mum read about you in the
Argus."

"Not quite – just the assistant. I hope she's got second sight. Excuse
me, Kate; this is a friend from my student days. I'll be back in a minute.
Let's talk over here, Mike. I could show off my office in the apex, but
I'm on the way out."

I follow him to a row of armless armchairs guarding the rails on to
the floor below. We plump down on two at one end.

"How did you finish up a librarian?"

"It's a long story. What are you doing in here?"

"That's a long story, too." We smile and shake our heads, but neither
of us knows what to say next. It's the awkward silence that forces me
on. "I'm sorry I never made contact, Jay. I thought about it."

"Don't worry. I wasn't in a fit state, anyway. These things happen;
but I've got the answer, Mike."

"As you always used to say."

"Did I? What I mean is, now we have made contact, if you're free
tonight come round for a meal. My dear wife's out. We can have a
proper powwow before she's back; reminisce about South Ken; trace

our routes from there to here. How about it?"

My resistance to his renewed friendship and the thought of IC reminiscences prompt a polite excuse – but I hold my tongue. My default position is shifting. I don't want to seem churlish – and it's a better option than another solitary evening at Kilvert Road. "If you're free." I must've paused long enough for him to sense I was lukewarm. "I mean, perhaps you're still local and you've got other commitments."

"No, no, I'm not local and I've no commitments. I'd really like to come, Jay." Well, I'm willing to come; and he always needed reassurance.

"And you won't mind meeting Sarah Rivers again?" We turn further towards each other like mirror images, but I'm quizzical while he's twinkling. "She's my wife, you see."

"But how?"

"I'll tell you this evening." And he smiles again.

"Well, congratulations, Jay. But this is weird – first you, then her."

"Sometimes life's like that. It's not just in novels."

"And will she want to see me?" I ask, stalling. He's right; we've crossed into Mills and Boon territory and the eternal triangle. I don't know that I can cope with both of them at once.

"Why not? I'll phone her, anyway. She's never said anything slanderous about you – just the opposite, really."

"You said she'd be out?"

"Yes, and probably back quite late."

I suppose I can manage a brief encounter, with her lateness giving me an easy way out; and I don't want to disappoint him now. "OK. If she's happy to see me, I'm happy to see her."

"That's settled then. 308 Bardby Road. We're in the book if you need to ring. Seven-thirtyish?" We stand up together and there's rather more power in his thin fingers for this handshake.

"See you later," I say, echoing his farewell.

After being blown back up Coke Street I give a demo of my driving skill, manoeuvring the Beemer out of the multi-storey via its tight hairpins without a scrape (it's not only Minis that have supersized since the 70s). But then I drive out to Hackby on autopilot, breaking one of my safe driving strictures to leave space for thoughts of Sarah and Jay. I don't have a thing about ex-girlfriends, but I can't stop highlights of my first love flashing through my mind. The romance didn't survive our higher education separation, but we'd been tied by a string of firsts until then – although not the premier one, denied by her inhibitions. It must be over fifteen years since that last sheepish encounter in Heatons. Now we're both separately tethered, some polite eyeing and sniffing can't do any harm. Yes, I should think Jay's a good foil for her – and she for him.

He and I converged in 84 because our tracks to the Smoke started so close. Our yellow-belly origins paired two edgy freshers finding their feet, and then we stuck to each other in the labs. Self-interest's like superglue; he had the lightning mind and I had the adept fingers. He was swotting himself up the first class ladder, but fell off with a nervous breakdown in the third term, no-showing to a chem eng practical – heat transfer coefficients, I think – and I haven't seen him since. He might not have been as keen a drinker or partygoer as the rest, but I still liked him the most.

Despite *Imperial Matters* and an alumni focus office I've never fished for anyone from the efflux of my year – and no one's looked for me either. That's not a surprise; my self-reliance is seen as self-satisfaction in many people's eyes. I think friendship's mainly a food for the needy, but there're one or two others I'd be pleased to see if I didn't need to keep the lid on that can of worms. I ponder names and recapture faces until alerted to the present by the 'HACKBY Please drive carefully' sign.

Hackby matches many local villages, with boundaries pushed out in the 60s by rural ribbon development now enfolding infill estates. I slow down to 20 but see no bungalows with *extensive grounds*, even by the Lilliputian standards of today. A left at the church brings similar results, and then I try the Atterthorpe road with its old brown brick and terracotta pantiled cottages nucleated by the Fox Inn. There are four larger bungalows before the derestriction, but a complete

187

absence of any trees. I turn round again by courtesy of another field entrance and cruise back to the T-junction. There's only the turning to Pellingham left.

And it's promising. After the 'Single track road with passing places' warning I see a battalion of conifers on the right dug in alongside the lane; and opposite, beyond a paddock, another mixed company of trees sufficient to shield a house. I drop down to second and crawl past an open gate. In two seconds of sideways viewing I'm convinced the spacious bungalow on view was once Two Elms – the name Southmead on the varnished diagonal of tree branch the forced consequence of Dutch elm disease. And the anticipated track into the wood appears on cue to make me stop the car in the first of the passing places just beyond.

I'm an unbeliever in all religious formats, but as I stand close to the killing place in watercolour sunshine I half expect a spiritual experience: some enlightenment to see Alice's death as the central motif of a complex design instead of the outcome of a random clustering of events. But there's no aura: only the tempting Le Mans straight of the lane skirting the firs, and the wind's moaning failure to penetrate their branches. Whatever the Krysztowczyks suffered, the ricocheting shards from that horrific impact certainly paralysed Dad, and then years later Mum. They each had a route mapped out for them and couldn't take it. OK, it's only his failure to grasp the nettle that sets the scene for her to do the same. If he'd gone back to school and on to Birmingham and then left Ulcethorpe behind, she wouldn't have come into the picture, and I'd not be standing here now. I suppose what actually happens is the grand design: the zigzagging reality coloured in on the infinite feint pattern of possibility.

I stroll into the evergreen gloom, treading between the crusted ruts on the hundreds and thousands of the fallen spruce needles – the route they took hand-in-hand the day before disaster struck. The track's dead straight, and a hundred metres ahead is the gate. Am I seeing things? This can't be happening. I must be having a mystical moment, after all. Their contiguous silhouettes are up against its bars. The shock jump-starts me into acceleration, anxious to dispel the illusion – and then I release my breath. There's no illusion to dispel. The truanting pupils clasping and kissing there are real. I hear her hissing, "Sean, there's someone coming," above the wind's whine, before the gate opens and they're off across the field. This must be Hackby's Lovers' Lane – well, for the last fifty odd years, at least. When I take their place at the gate he's shoulder-hugging her along a trampled path between the winter wheat to some other blissful retreat. If Dad had kissed his Alice here they might've had a blissful future too.

But flights of fancy aren't my thing, and I've had a surfeit this morning. As I walk back along the resinous cut through the wood my mind's feeding on more solid and immediate fare: Mum's freezer dole-out to the neighbours and Mrs B, buying some wine for Jay, clearing the house. More planning – now, that is my forte. There shouldn't be anything more to worry about in Ulcethorpe. Jay's not likely to want to know anything about my time at Imperial after he left. I decide to try the Fox for an early lunch and commune with Lou. It's time I turned singing detective and told her what I've found out.

TWENTY

"I think I'll take that little Chinese bowl, if that's acceptable, Mr Paine," says Mrs Ruston. "I've always liked it."

"Yep, fine. Anything."

"Did she, like, mention us in her will, or something, if you don't mind my asking, love?" asks Mrs B.

"No, only me I'm afraid; but I think she'd have liked you all to have a memento. It's my idea." So here we are, with my plans for the frozen food handout extended to this tea party and little giveaway. It's a sympathetic compensation for them missing out at Owerston Hall.

"Very nice thought, Michael," says Mr Furr, from the swivel chair. "I'll let Rose choose ours."

The three ladies are lined up on the sofa, lifting bone china cups with cocked little fingers. I'm stuffed into the sag bag backing the TV.

"Well, that brown bowl with a lid like a chicken in the kitchen would be nice. You know, the one for eggs."

"What's your choice, Ruth?" I ask.

"I've been thinking, love. Might I have that lovely photo frame? I think it were old Mrs Paine's. I know you're in it now, but it'd just suit my Colin – if you're not taking it with you, of course."

Four pairs of eyes focus on the art deco art of the silversmith, so I look that way too, and wish I could wipe away my school portrait's cocky smirk.

"No, you have it – the photo as well. I've others to take home."

"Ooh, you are a star – just like then. I reckon it's autumn term nineteen-seventy-five. I've got one up of our Wayne when he were ten with that blue background – it's when your mum went into her decline."

"But wasn't that nineteen-seventy-four – the year of Boroughcliff? I know we didn't arrive until nineteen-eighty-one, but I assumed Marlene had been in that state ever since being widowed." This is Mrs Ruston betraying her schoolmistressy past with a drizzle of vinegar.

"Well, as it happens, Beryl, you're wrong," says Rose Furr. "She'd started to get over it by the following summer and looked really radiant, bless her."

"Aye, a real feast for the eye, she was."

"Dennis, please! Don't take any notice of him, Michael."

"But, he's right, and I'm not offended," I say, with a benign smile.

"Michael, Louise and me were only talking about it at the crem – how she bought a gorgeous dress to go out with a journalist." Mrs B announces this to Mrs Ruston like a confidante with inside information.

"Is that the one who came round once when I was in here?" asks Mrs Furr. "A big, fair haired, good looking chap, as I remember."

Mrs B swivels round to Mrs Furr to offer correction. "Oh, no. He were sitting behind us on Monday – small and dark; though I never met him at the time."

"Well, this chap was a journalist, that's for certain. She said. It was all a bit unpleasant, so that's why it's stuck in my mind."

"Unpleasant in what way?" I ask.

"It's a long time ago, Michael. It's more a feeling I've got than anything."

"See if you can remember, Mrs Furr," I urge.

Promoted to the centre of attention, she concentrates like the medium at a séance.

"I was sitting here one afternoon and the twins were on the carpet. I think I'd had a test at the clinic or something, so Marlene had looked after them. It wasn't a regular thing. We were neighbourly, but not that close. She went to the front door, there were voices, and then I looked round to that doorway and he'd come in with her, with his

191

arm round her shoulder, squeezing her up close. He must've gone when he saw me. She didn't say much, or I can't remember what she said – but she was upset. He was a journalist, and he'd been bothering her... That's all I know."

She finishes, leaving us agape and wanting more. Well, I certainly do. Mr Furr is first to intrude on the hush.

"So who was it, Michael?"

"I've absolutely no idea," I reply. But I'm lying; I do have an idea. I can see him in my mind's eye: the big, fair-haired journalist lounging at a desk in the office Ivor's taken us into. What the fucking hell was his name?

"He sounds nasty," says Mrs B.

"If she had someone like that wanting to barge into the house and manhandle her, it's no wonder she became withdrawn," declaims Mrs Ruston in fierce tones.

Her perception could be splined to mine, but she hasn't got the backstory for context. A thirty-year long tunnel transmits the dimmest glimmer, but it's enough to show a more plausible cause for Mum's blighted life. Her reading of Dad's admission was the initiator, and now I see what catalysed her ultimate reaction – and ruined any second chance Ivor might've had. If only Rose Furr's snapshot wasn't so fuzzy.

The ladies' voices are now unleashed, topping each other's tales of boorish men they've known, and leaving Mr Furr to swivel and twiddle and giving me the chance to think this revelation through. And as my imagination sharpens the image, I'm being chilled and heated at the same time. The big picture's clear now, and it's sickening: Mum's cringing and the hunk's crowing. That fucking lady-killing bastard has pestered and hunted her to exhaustion. She's trapped, and too weak to struggle or too ashamed to call for help; or maybe she fears disbelief or censure – the attractive widow leading the young man on. He was thwarted then, but on another afternoon she gave in as the only way she saw of getting out.

On another afternoon – and with a shiver and a tingle I'm seeing something that fits: the back door locking me out, Mum coming down upset and angry and smoking, and me taking the blame. That's when it happened – or one of the times; there might've been more. I'll never know whether her escape was quick or protracted, but the scars and bruises of it never healed. She was shafted into her shrinking anxiety and shrivelled depression. It all fits. I'll have to tell Ivor, whatever the consequences. I need to know the name of that blonde monster. He's the one to blame.

* * *

I've heard enough we-ought-to-be-goings and it's-time-I-wents, so I bring their coats in from the dining room for distribution and bestow the bowl and photo frame. Then I lead out into the kitchen for the china chicken and the freezer share out.

"Is that Marlene in there?" asks Mrs Furr, eyeing the pale oak box I left on the worktop. "We haven't had a cremation in the family," she adds, excusing her ignorance.

I move it, so she can read the little brass label better. "Hold it, if you like."

She lifts it a few inches, as if it might be booby-trapped. "Ooh, it's heavy. I thought ash was light."

"Wood ash is," corrects Mr Furr. "But that's the bones, not the coffin. Shall I unload the stuff, Michael?" And he squeezes by to reach the freezer in the corner when I give him the nod.

You'll need a nicer container than that, I think," says Mrs Ruston. "I've got Edward's ashes in a Minton vase."

"I'm going to scatter them. I was going to do it at the crematorium before going home, but I've had second thoughts. And I want to involve Louise and the girls."

"You want somewhere that was special for her," she continues. "I'm not sure that Ulcethorpe is the right place, dare I say."

"Why?" I ask.

"Because she came to loathe it. The only good thing that ever occurred in Ulcethorpe was your birth, she told me."

"She never said that to me," I say.

"Isn't there somewhere in Danbury or nearby?"

"I'll talk at home about where she liked to go most. There's a deserted chapel by the sea – that's a possibility."

"There you are, then." And her wise and wizened face crinkles with a smile to reward my change of heart.

I grab the bag of plastic carriers from the hook behind the pantry door, pass them over to Mr Furr and ease into the dining room.

The distribution is soon completed and I shepherd my visitors out of the front door. Now I'm watching their laden traverse of the tarmac, floodlit through the sitting room and dining room windows; I want to prolong this possible last sighting of Mum's few friends. Between the bulging privets Mrs B and the Furrs turn to nod, but Mrs Ruston plods solidly on across the road. Again I salute the Furrs on their reappearance up their garden path as Mrs B disappears into the shadows, and then look over at the stooped silhouette of Mrs Ruston in her doorway as she turns on the light. I wave but she doesn't seem to see the silhouette in mine.

Back indoors I draw the curtains and slump on to the swivel, intent on reflection. The cracks in my foundation are spreading by the hour – and the smooth ashlar that's been my face on to the world is splitting apart. I built on the firm basis that Dad's conventional life ended in a disaster with no one person to blame, and Mum's grief calcified into an unbreakable shell. Since I was nine those two facts underpinned the construct of my life – until now. The weight of evidence for the full story has crushed them. Alice's killing, Dad's dropping out, Mum's lookalike-ness, Dad's acumen, Masters' treachery, Dad's killing, Mum's renaissance, Ivor's love, Mum's retraction, Mum's violation, Mum's depression: eleven chapters defining my parents' ruined lives.

Mum, Mum, why didn't you ever tell me – even if only that you hated it here? And why didn't I ever ask why you were like you were, and try and understand it? Maybe just one admission or one question would've been enough to break our shells; and then tears might've flowed with kisses and hugs – and a torrent of pent-up love. But we never came close, and it's too late now – but not for my third spasm of sobbing. What a waste, what a waste. Secrets are cancers. Their insidious ramifications infiltrate like divisions of malignant cells. They destroyed Mum's life long before the carcinoma took over.

The phone rings and tugs me up from my dismal reverie. It's been next to the TV forever, the ABS plastic degrading from off-white to near yellow.

"Hi, sweetie. How was your tea party?" It's Lou, so I sink into the sag bag.

"It went well. Easier than I expected – not that I've washed up yet."

"No more nasty surprises?"

"How did you guess?"

I recount Mrs Furr's prosaic words verbatim: the unpleasantness; the big, fair, handsome journalist; the squeezing close; the bothering. As permanent as Mum's brush-off words for Ivor, they'll always be replaying in my mind. "It made me feel sick. But it's the ultimate explanation for Mum's behaviour – not the grief, not the diary, but this bastard overpowering her. And that's a euphemism. I could use more brutal words."

"OK, I admit it looks bad, but you can't rewrite history. Your mum decided to keep it a secret. Even if misguided, you should respect that."

"In your position I'd say the same. But I'm in the house where it happened – and probably because it happened. She'd have moved her life forward otherwise, to somewhere new, I'm sure. Mrs Ruston said Mum came to hate everything here, Ulcethorpe and the house. She kept that a secret too. If only I'd known when I could've done something about it. Secrets, bloody secrets. I'm going to tell Ivor about his rival. I'm sure it's the guy he shared his office with. I'll talk to you later darling, I'd better get on."

I get up, start piling the crockery and then slump back into the swivel. I'm no depressive, but that doesn't mean I don't have gloomy moods. Still, after another half-hour of feeling sorry for myself I'll be ready to soldier on. Yes, and brave the chance of Jay Yates raising the spectre of Amanda Rose.

TWENTY-ONE

The Yates residence is the between-the-wars one-off I've noticed on previous drives past here: an Abbey National umbrella roof with dormers, ground floor eaves, and a rectangular bay window at each front corner. Jay gets up in the morning in one pyramid and goes to work in another. The house looks unaltered since built, but the front garden's a defoliated pavioured parking lot. Alongside a Honda Civic, I'm still leaving room for two or three more. I pull a handle to disturb a real bell and wait with my offering: the priciest red Bordeaux I could find in Threshers.

"Evening, Jay. Something for the table."

He scans the label. "Mm, looks good. You must be psychic; I'm doing steak. I didn't think you looked like a veggie. Give me your coat."

If he recognises my pilot jacket from those old times he doesn't say, but carries it over to the rear of the hall. His cords and striped shirt stretch him even thinner.

"Nice house; unusual," I say.

"It suits us – all the space downstairs, and only two bedrooms. We don't have any children. Come into the kitchen while I open this."

I follow into a shabby chic ambience of stripped pine, distressed paint and quarry tiles, all cosying up to a gleaming green Aga. While he rummages in a dresser drawer for a corkscrew I lean my bum against the king-size table that still leaves a generous surround for cooking activities on its boards and at the other work surfaces.

"Sarah's out, you said?"

"Yes – Sally to me. She's at a case review in Hampshire. I mean, she was. She's on her way back now."

"Case review; that sounds legal," I suggest.

"She's a social worker. We're both loyal council employees."

"You were going to tell me how you came to be a librarian."

"Yes, when we're settled. Let me concentrate on this first." I watch his hand twisting and tugging at the corkscrew. I should think he could span an octave and three. "I expect you're married, Mike – with two point four children?"

"Yep, to Louise, but only two point zero girls."

"And a chemical engineer?"

"Yep."

"So life's arrow's on target – I mean, what you might've forecast back in eighty-four has come to pass?"

"Not exactly. My mum died last week; she was only sixty-three. I didn't expect that. It's why I'm here."

"I'm sorry, Mike."

He stretches his elongated fingers towards a tentative touch of my arm, and I nod my thanks with another of my buttoned-up smiles.

"Since when, the arrow's fallen out of the sky," I add. In fact, I've felt threatened by a whole Crécy-load of archers.

"How come?"

"I'll tell you when we're settled."

"Mike, I'm sorry. I mean, I haven't offered you a drink or anything. What will you have?"

* * *

In their 1950s-decor sitting room I've been sipping tonic water to lubricate my account of the arrows of outrageous fortune. "And then after I left you I drove out to Hackby and found the crime scene, complete with two kids in the wood playing the lovers."

"You're joking?"

"No. A boy and a girl skiving off school to canoodle – quite an eerie moment, as if I hadn't had enough by then."

And that's enough of the soap for Jay. This afternoon's instalment is still sub judice – and of course the Polish episode I didn't broadcast.

"I should think so. But you seem to be made of tough stuff, Mike. I'd have cracked and been off to the doctor for sticking back together."

"Medication?"

"Yes. Well, more medication. I mean, I'm already a junkie." Lounging on the sofa, all that betrays the angst cramping his life is a tremor in the hand he stretches for the occasional cashew or crisp.

"Were you taking stuff at IC?"

"Good Lord, no. I didn't know I was a nut case then. I mean, that I'd a genetic predisposition, but no one had told me. No one said, 'Your Aunty Flo died in an asylum'. She was never even mentioned. I don't blame Mum and Dad for that. It's not the sort of thing you tell your kids, is it?"

"No, not then. But we've explained my mum's anxiety and depression to our girls. I think she had a genetic flaw too, but we always linked it to the bereavement. Maybe we got that wrong."

He nods. "Yes, it's different now. Disability, diversity: it's accepted. It's one of the things that tip the balance in favour of the present over the past."

"You're an optimist, then, Jay?"

"Yes, an always anxious optimist."

I match his smile. I'm taking to him – his open stance on his affliction, for one thing, and the considerateness permeating his charm. He's changed a lot from that workaholic student. I've hardly shifted at all.

"I admire that," I say. "So what triggered your breakdown?"

"Pressure… and yet more pressure – from my dad to be the best. And then I simply seized up: I could barely read a sentence, let alone write one. They referred me to a medic and I was packed off home."

"I didn't see any signs."

"The practicals were easier. I could piggyback on you."

"And you never thought of coming back?"

"Yes, I thought of it, but whenever I did, panic attacks came too. Then

199

I got consolation from accepting I'd never wanted to be a chemical engineer in the first place. The illness let me steer a different course, despite it not being as easy then as now. Fortunately I didn't have any powerful motivation to keep me on my original track – certainly not the sort you had, Mike."

I pause as the word penetrates: motivation. "Boroughcliff, you mean?… Yep, I suppose it has driven me."

Yes, he's right. My life's been programmed: to get the entry visa; to cross the frontier; to discover the country where Dad perished; to show my accreditation; to be appointed legislator, inspector and judge; to be a sort of Moses and lead the inhabitants to an accident-free land. So why have I sold out?

"That's set you thinking," he says, leaning for more nibbles and breaking into my reverie.

"Yep – about my move out of corporate safety. Boroughcliff did push me along that road for a purpose, but I came to see it as a dead end."

"Because you'd achieved your goals, if you'll excuse the jargon?"

"No, Jay, I can't claim that; the goals never are achievable. You could say, it was for all the wrong reasons, the selfish ones: money, status, control. I wanted better proof I'd succeeded in life. But safety has to be a dead end – or an infinite groove, if you like. The Ivor character I mentioned is confined in safety consultancy and campaigning because it's always work in progress; there's always unfinished business. And it's only with long-term commitment that you can accrue the kudos to cause radical change. I only sprayed a few exhortations on the walls like rail-side graffiti. And now I'm thinking I've been a smug bugger, with my U-turn and early exit."

"I'm sorry if I've upset your apple cart."

"Don't apologise. Something's crystallising because of what's happened; because of what I've found out." Yes, I've been betraying Dad.

"Another tonic, or shall we eat?" he asks.

* * *

We're dining in their minimalist enclave of beech, glass and chrome when Jay lobs his grenade. "Did that Amanda Rose stay the course?"

I was hoping she wouldn't get a mention. I take a refill of claret. How much does he need to know? More to the point, how little can I tell him?

"No. She died: took her own life, I'm afraid, in her second year."

His eyes, the colour of faded denim, lock on to mine, either surprised by my words or the cool way I said them. He won't know I thought up the answer in advance. He takes a gulp of the water he's careful to alternate with sips of wine.

"I thought she might've been unstable. It takes one to know one. She was a flirty piece, the only girl on the island."

"She'd come from an all girls school. The shock must've gone to her head."

We resume our steaks in companionable silence. Maybe he'll be satisfied with that.

"You weren't tempted, Mike? I mean, went out with her after I left?"

No, he isn't. My discomfort level's rising, but I don't want to purge it by lying to him. Maybe forty-eight hours ago I would've done. It seems I am changing, after all. I take my last mouthful and deposit the knife and fork.

"I still had a girl of my own, remember." It's my last attempt at evasion.

"What, after the long vac?"

I hear polite disbelief. I was a common denominator in their lives then; they're sure to have exchanged notes. There's no escape. I look up into his face for a last and unwarranted check on his probity. It's my turn for an open stance on my affliction; time to show all three stumps.

"Jay, I haven't told this to anyone, how I was involved – not even Louise. It's a roll-out of my new anti-secrecy policy. You OK to be my confessor?"

His eyebrows rise, lifting his drooping eyelids clear of the pupils. "Yes. If you think I'm up to it and it'll help you. I'm the one that goes for counselling, not gives it. But don't feel you have to."

"No, I want to – and thanks. It'll be a dry run for both of us."

I feel flushed, and realise my arms are quivering and my fists are clenched like when I got excited as a kid. But it's not with excitement now – it's fear. I'm a non-swimmer on a high board steeling himself to dive in. I didn't think the decision to share my secret could hit so hard. Is this how therapy works? I take a series of deep breaths to steady myself and get back some control.

Jay's quick to notice. "Take it easy, Mike. I'm your confessor, remember, not your judge."

He carries on chomping his steak while I take more time out to think through my synopsis – my version of the truth. Amanda's will never be told. Now I have to begin.

"Well, with my romance with Sarah fizzling out that summer I went back to IC with no special defences. I think Amanda saw me as a challenge: a fanciable guy who'd ignored her. Anyway, she started coming on to me, but I didn't respond. To be honest, her reputation scared me – not her morals, or lack of them, but all the experience she'd acquired. I'd never… you know, quite gone the distance with Sarah, so didn't have any form. I dreaded a cock-up, if you see what I mean."

This brings a smile to his face as he chews.

"Especially if it got disseminated," I add.

His smile widens, appreciating the etymology.

"I'd moved out of hall into a student let in Putney. One Wednesday afternoon I got on my train at South Ken, and just before the doors closed she darted in to sit next to me. She'd been lurking, of course. Could we talk? Why did I avoid her? Had she upset me? She hated friction. Couldn't we be friends again? On and on, and quite manic – as if we'd been an item and I'd dumped her. Anyway, by Putney Bridge I'd become amenable. I'd had a District Line ego trip, I guess: a sexy girl desperate to lap up my words and other guys on the train (none I knew, fortunately) looking envious. She invited me to tea and I said OK. She had a flat near Barons Court station that Daddy had bought her – more as an investment than a present for good A levels, I should think. On the way up Fulham Palace Road she was on to me like cling film, so you can guess what happened next."

"You came of age?"

"That's one way of putting it."

"And quite understandable, Mike, thinking back to those flashing eyes and generous lips."

I nod in response, thinking more of the generous sex: my tentative etude in the bedroom with her as teacher, and my bolder playing during our duet on the sofa. "And that's the sum total, Jay. I saw other girls as potential soulmates, but not Amanda Rose. She'd thrust herself upon me, and there'd been no development. We started with the climax, and the only option was repetition – repetizone, as we musicians say."

"And did you?"

"Repeat, yep. But I didn't stay that night – or any other. We'd decided on a stratagem: her flat to be the love nest for our daily assignation, with no coming and going together, no staying over, no meetings elsewhere, no recognition in college. I don't remember who suggested it, but it felt like adding cayenne to hot peppers. I pranced off that evening with the spare door key feeling like her personal stud and greedy for my next performance."

"But it didn't stay like that. I mean, she wanted more?" Jay's free to examine me now he's finished his steak. I know he's sympathetic, but I'd prefer a grille or curtain in between for the next bit.

"If more is less, yep: less sex and more intimacy. She wanted our relationship to move backwards, I suppose. If it had run normally – you know, meeting, fancying, dating, chatting and getting affectionate before the sex – everything might've been different. Within a week she'd told me about her family and explained all things Jewish; and she cooked meals for me and wanted to know the ins and outs of my life. It wasn't a route I wanted to take. I saw it more like one of those holiday flings – not that I've ever had one – loving the sex but not the girl. Then she asked me if I'd go and meet her parents the following

Sunday. I felt steamrollered and had to dig in my heels. I said no way; and they wouldn't want her dating a gentile – a clever excuse, I thought. It was either more of the same or nothing. She cried and tried to persuade me. She loved me. How could I be so cruel? She couldn't live without me – and lots more in that vein. She had a tantrum and I walked out. 'Don't go, Mike; you'll regret it', were her last words. She didn't appear for lectures next day. I reached the flat by one o'clock. I'd been due to go early anyway, it being another Wednesday. I found her dead in the bath with her wrists cut."

He's at a loss for words; and I've never been able to lose that image, even after twenty years of trying to wash her blood from my hands: the raven haired mermaid set in the cold carmine lake, the kitchen knife smearing the white tufted bath mat, and the two letters propped behind the beaker on the glass shelf.

"Mike, I'm sorry," he says at last; and, after another pause, "You couldn't have known. You shouldn't feel guilty."

"You haven't heard the worst yet, Jay. After standing transfixed – probably for only a minute or two, but it seemed like an hour – I started calculating. I didn't touch her. I put the letters in my jacket pocket. I scanned the flat for anything incriminating. I put the key back in the kitchen drawer. I listened at the letter box before letting myself out. I walked back to Putney like a cool dude. I took the matches from the kitchen, and I burnt both letters outside the back door without opening them."

"They were suicide notes?"

"Yes, I'm sure: one to *Michael* and one to *Daddy and Mummy*. I didn't want to read what she'd written to me, and I couldn't risk them reading the other. Then I had the torment of imminent discovery: the police wheeling in forensics, and the press releasing their ferrets. Maybe she'd asked her parents about me going there. But nothing happened. Our liaison had only lasted a week, so I'd barely left a trail. The coroner decided on suicide while the balance of her mind was disturbed, according to the notice Prof Enderby put up. I could consign it to history, I thought."

"But you couldn't? I mean, the guilt wouldn't fade?"

I shake my head. "Not quite. It was the scene in the bathroom that wouldn't fade, even though I could blame Amanda for it. I didn't feel remorse then. I suppose I was too shallow for that seed to germinate. It grew later though, and now I think destroying their letter was the worst thing I've ever done."

"It's not so awful, Mike," he says, trying to anneal my stress. "She'd taken her life, but yours was all to come. Perhaps being a witness at the inquest would've ruined yours as well."

"That's very charitable, Jay. I hope Louise will see it the same way. You see, it's all recorded in a diary – my last; I stopped writing them that year. I don't want her to suffer through a misunderstanding like my mum. It's ironic isn't it; my dad left Alice's parents in the same state of ignorance I foisted on Amanda's. We stole their truths as if we were just pinching a jigsaw piece they'd never miss. We'd never met them, but that was no excuse."

He nods. "Will you tell Louise?"

"I don't know."

I look down at my plate. At least I've told someone – but don't feel any better for it. There's been no relief valve lifting to ease the pressure of remorse. It's not that Jay could've absolved me – no one can do that – but his generous compassion hasn't even lessened the shame. And as a trial run for telling Lou, it's been a failure too. I can see Lou wanting to know a lot more about Amanda; wanting some conception of that other version of the truth before she forgave me. I think I'd feel a lot worse after telling her – and frightened about any expiation she might want me to make. I'm not ready for it yet. I look up at Jay, who's waiting like a bedside nurse for a patient's recovery. "Thanks, Jay. You've been a great help. Shall we talk about something else?"

TWENTY-TWO

After the cheese board came the cafetière, but we returned to the retro room for that. Jay's retrodden his path to Sheffield and an MA in Librarianship for me, and then galloped ahead on a hobby horse to explain how the Library Association went acronymic into CILIP with the Institute of Information Scientists… Anyway, Hannah's text brings him to a halt and jacks up my eyelids again.

"May I read that one as well, Mike?" His interest in the girls, and disappointment that I don't carry their photos, is rather touching.

"Maybe I should translate. Her texts are more abstruse." I falter once or twice in reading out, "*Hi Dad. Jack Aymes wants to date. He's tonk. Mum says not yet. Next birthday poss. Hope to see you tomorrow. Love H.*"

"Twelve, you said, so she's probably as mature as that Alice all those years ago. I mean, physically, but perhaps emotionally as well. Childhood's shrinking, Mike. You should hear Sally on child exploitation by big business. This Jack's the first of a whole series of boys coming into their lives whom you'll be worried about."

As I drink more coffee I hear the sound of a reverse-gear-whining and exhaust-pipe-burbling duet outside the window.

"That's Sally," Jay announces. He jumps up and scoots out to welcome her home, leaving me sitting tensed and ready to spring to attention. I look round the room at the sepia photos of old Ulcethorpe they've framed as my way of trying not to listen to their private moment in the hall.

"Hallo, Michael." She's in the doorway sooner than I expected, and still with her coat on. Jay's chaperoning behind.

I'm on my feet ready for a handshake. "Sarah. It's good to see you."

206

But her familiarity draws my hands to the cashmere of her sleeves and my mouth to the makeup on her cheek.

"She's going to have a bath, and join us for a nightcap," explains Jay.

Sarah offers a slight smile and a nod of confirmation before turning away to Jay's fussing assistance as she takes off her coat and scarf. I'd been on edge expecting an awkward greeting: long-separated lovers smothering libido with decorum. But at the crunch she became my old friend married to my new pal.

"There." Jay soon reappears, radiating glee now his prize bloom is in water. "What do you think? Is she how you remember?"

"Different; better. You're a lucky man." It's a white lie. "Why don't you tell me how you two got attached?"

"We met nearly eight years ago. I was on the ref and tech desk in the old library and she asked if we could get *Working with Sexually Abusive Adolescents*. It's the sort of title that sticks in your mind. She filled in a request form and explained about being in social services, so could I e-mail her on the council intranet when it came in? That started a little electronic correspondence. When I saw her in the Arts bar one Saturday evening soon afterwards I thought it was meant to be. I asked her out, she said yes, and we progressed from there. I won't treat you to the details. How about you and Louise?"

The resume of my artful wooing has led us to the artful doings of Damien Hirst, Rachel Whiteread and the rest, and a friendly argument on conceptual art. Jay's trying to convince me of Shedboatshed's merit as the latest Turner winner when he sees Sarah listening in the doorway.

"Come and sit down, Sal. I'll get your whisky. I'm just rabbiting on."

She takes his place in the chair opposite mine, flipping her slippers off as she tucks her feet on to the cushion. In pyjamas and dressing gown, minus makeup and specs, and with tousled hair, the hard woman might be the soft girl I once thought would be putty in my hands; but I feel like putty in hers now. She smiles an invitation for me to say something.

"This is strange. I set out this morning to discover skeletons and finish up with old friends."

"And two for the price of one, Michael." And then she adds, "You've filled out," half closing her eyes to focus.

"As a person, I hope." She's drawn in, tightened up.

She smiles. "Probably; but face and waist too."

"Too much sitting around."

"I go to a gym," she says, before Jay's return with her drink brings a non-sequitur. "I'm sorry about your mum. John told me upstairs. God, I need this." She raises the glass and sniffs. "Mm, it's good."

"I thought I'd get a malt in. It's Jura – on offer at the Co-Op." He folds himself like an anglepoise lamp to sit at her feet. "How did the meeting go?"

"Michael won't want to know about that."

"I wouldn't mind," I say. "Social workers get a bad press. Tell it to me as it is."

"You sure?"

"Yep." My nod seems to please her. Jay's the beneficiary: she fondles his hair, although keeps looking at me.

"My job's chairing reviews on the progress of the kids we care for: fostering, education, health, aspirations – the lot. It's like a six-monthly check-up. Today's was for a boy in Hampshire."

"But why so far away?"

"The foster carers moved. It's no reason to break up a happy family."

"The local council doesn't take over then?"

"Well, yes and no. But the aim is continuity for the child, Michael."

I'm impressed. "So that's put before cost effectiveness."

"Let's say the welfare of the child is paramount. That's our maxim. But… Well, you know; there are budgets."

Yes, this curled up night-attired woman sipping her dram, who wouldn't be moulded as I wished and lacked any compensating charisma, has come far – to self-assurance, for one thing. It's not only the child protection policy that's impressive. "Is he an orphan, the boy?"

"God, no. That's rare these days. Single mother, unknown father, abusing stepfather, drugs: that's more the mixture now. But he's doing well. The referral came in time. He was telling me about his riding lessons. It's fantastic to see the change, even since I first met him."

Sarah's untying my blindfold to show a parallel world of inadequate or abusive parents, child centred interventions, foster carers, healing and hope. A world that's unseen until a rare tragedy – a Victoria Climbié – prompts a tabloid witch-hunt; and where, as in accident prevention, a thousand hallmarks of success can be effaced by the single failure the public get to hear about.

"So is foster caring the norm? Aren't there children's homes?" I ask.

"Not many now, Michael. Perhaps places for one in ten. Some looked after children can't actually cope with a family environment, but fostering's used for nearly all of them – and there's enough countrywide to fill a very big stadium. I'm all in favour, providing we don't skimp on assessments. I don't like kids being institutionalised."

"Are foster carers allowed their own kids?" I ask. Our talk has sown a seed in my mind.

Sarah wakes up to the implication. "You're not thinking of fostering, Michael?"

"We hadn't been; but who knows, after tonight. Louise has been saying our lives are too comfortable. Up to now I've been answering, that's the way I like it. I think she'd be keen. A lot would fall on her – and the girls. I suppose there's fostering info on websites. We might be trying the Essex County Council one when I get home."

"I hope you do. There's always a shortage. How old are your girls?"

"Twelve and ten."

"They should be all right. I'd like to know about them, but I'm going to have to go to bed. John can tell me what you've talked about in the morning."

She gives him her now empty glass and steps into her slippers. I'm standing too, at the other end of the hearthrug, my hands and face at the ready for however we'll say goodnight. And like a canny chess player she deftly replicates my earlier gambit before darting away, leaving me with the scent of lavender bath oil and memories of similar elusions long ago.

* * *

Outside, the familiar clang from Corus is being blown by with a whiff of coal tar, but at least the wind's screened my windscreen from frost and I can reverse out straightaway on to the empty clearway. On the amber-flooded road I have the feeling that I've let a hitchhiker into my car and he's hijacked the controls: an interloper who's making friendships, empathising with the elderly, confessing sins and contemplating care for disadvantaged children while I'm in the back seat. He'll drive me home tomorrow and present Lou with a transformation at the door. But no, it's me, starting the tricky climb down the cliffs of my private island to replace the 'Keep Out' signs with 'Visitors Welcome'.

Jay's a find, but Sarah's an enigma of variations: poised and uneasy, pleased and disappointed, relaxed and abrupt; and all the time re-examining the old specimen slide I've slid into her microscope. But there's nothing to stop me seeing Jay, is there? I've given him my card anyway, but guess it's the geography that'll keep us apart – unless… If I make that comeback in CSS there'd be visits to Whittonsea in my diary again, so opportunities to reappear in Ettisham Park and Bardby Road if I want them – although maybe not at Owerston Hall. My mind's a whirligig of indecision: 'will I?', 'won't I?', 'maybe', 'sometime'.

I half-circle the Station Road roundabout and cross the railway bridge to the rhythmic pound of bogie wheels over points on the track underneath. Maybe it's steel to Sheffield or coal to Newcastle. I went goods train spotting at Barnetby with Ian Ivatt and his father a few times when I was Dad hunting after Boroughcliff. It's the Mecca for rail freight anoraks now, according to last week's *Argus*. And I've got Ivor now if I want him, thirty years late. At least I'm pretty certain about that – although maybe less as a dad and more as elder brother.

TWENTY-THREE

Mum's clock radio buzzed its last 10 Kilvert Road wakey-wakey when I was already up, dressed and stripping the spare room bed. I'd opened the curtains to yet another reminder of Dad: the window reveals still un-wallpapered, just as he left them that day in 1974. I'm washed and shaved and on to the last two Weetabix now. Properclear are due at eight-thirty, and I want the things I'm taking to be out in the car by then.

The hour soon passes with my busy accumulation: four boxes of wrapped breakables to accompany the photographic archive, the jewel box, Dad's testaments, Mum's concertina file, the Knit It carrier, the casket and a chair. It's the one Grandma Paine gave me for my bedroom long before I knew about Regency sabre legs. Mr Holmes sucked his teeth when I warned him off it, so my taking it has probably put at least £50 on his bill.

The clearance crew arrive soon after I've vacated the crumbling tarmac, and reverse their Luton van up to the front door.

"Here we are, ready, willing and able; one, two, three, go," announces their tubby shaven headed leader, like a punter keen to be first in at a car boot sale. "I'm Donald, by the way. You got all your bits out?"

"Just my luggage and laptop left. Is that going to be big enough?"

"Oh yeah. A lot of that bedroom stuff packs flat. Don't you worry, Mr Paine. Leave it to the experts." And as we walk through the sitting room he adds, "You don't even have to stay here."

His invitation to escape prompts the idea of a pilgrimage to soothe my conscience, and after Adrian's call to concede the T27 saga's over and the pump's being refitted, I give Donald my mobile number and set off. 308 Bardby Road's a lure as I drive past, but my glance across

211

the road shows a car free frontage. It's a similar situation alongside the cemetery railings. The raw morning has deterred even the most devout grievers and mourners so far. After saluting the gatekeeper snug in his lodge, I hunch my way into his domain of stone death certificates and trudge the old route.

It's an expensive memorial, with its Carrara marble headstone and kerbing for the quartz chippings. Maybe a guilty Performance Intermediates paid. The grave brings no visions of Dad, but I see a youthful Mum tending it – bending with flowers for the urn that's long gone. After she stopped visiting, I came with Grandma Paine sometimes when I went for tea after their schism. It needs flowers now, but not the stiff stalks from a florist. No, something permanent to soften the stony stare of the slab: a mini herb garden or a lavender bed or a rosemary bush with forget-me-nots and bulbs. Lou will know, and maybe the council will do it for a fee. I've brought the camera with me and take a couple of photos from different angles for her and the girls to see.

Grandma's monument takes more finding: the route's not programmed in my mind, and the stone's horizontal like the entrance to a crypt. But at last I'm rereading the wordy pall I had chiselled into grey granite to her precise written instructions (including lower case throughout).

Here lies the body of

Agnes Ruth Paine

Born 3rd March 1906
Died 8th November 1990

Daughter of Albert Hothersall,
chief librarian of this borough, widow
of Leonard Thomas Paine (1902–1944)
and mother of
Alan Michael Paine (1943–1974)

"Durate, et vosmet rebus servate secundis"
("Carry on, and preserve yourselves for better things")

I didn't tell Jay about my librarian antecedents, Agnes as well as Albert, but it can wait for another time. I had to look up the Virgil – as she must've done to immortalise the erudition she always professed – and I've always taken it in the singular and as aimed at me: not to fail like the other men in her life. It's a hard admonishment, but I try. I aim the camera and press for more memento mori pics.

* * *

"Two phone calls, Mr Paine," says Donald, sweating through the dining room with a carton of kitchenalia. "I'd have rung if you'd been much longer. Andersons the agents, and a Mrs Yates. I jotted her number down. Here."

I respond alphabetically and arrange to host Anderson junior at two-thirty so he can admire Donald's team's thoroughness and take a set of keys. Now it's Sarah's turn.

"Hallo. Sally Yates."

"It's Michael, Sarah." I'll stick with her old moniker.

"Oh. Hi, Michael. Thanks for ringing back. I'm working at home this afternoon. I thought you might like to come round for some lunch – say, one o'clock." I'm slow to reply, and the pressure of silence forces a justification. "We barely had a chance to speak last night, did we?"

It's true, we didn't talk, other than about child protection. Still, it's a surprise. But they come as a pair. If I see Jay again, I'll also see Sarah. It might be less awkward in the future if we have a heart-to-heart now. These social mealtimes are when the revelations come: Ivor, Keith, the oldies, Jay. What will Sarah bring to the table?

* * *

I'm treading the bare boards still unsure of my part: the bereaved son. With no script and director, it's all improvisation. For me, wandering through the bare rooms is less an indulgence in nostalgia than filling in time. As the Paine accumulation was compacted into the white van, so Mum released her final hold on me. With the evidence of her existence eliminated – and when we've scattered the ashes – she'll fit neatly into a special file in my mind. I'll be free from always measuring what I do against an objective set to please her. I can grow into my own man. Yes, but what is that man going to be?

After checking my watch I decide it's time to leave. I'll get there a polite five minutes late. But driving off, my thoughts are further forward in today's future down in Finchley than in the next companionable hour.

I park next to Sarah's blue Focus and jerk the bell.

"Come in. I'm running late," she says, to explain her breathlessness. I follow her into the kitchen where a Waitrose carrier lies limp on the table, having surrendered most of its contents.

"Any help needed?" I offer, hanging my Spitfire rig from a chair back.

"No, it's just salmon and new spuds. Let's have some wine."

After her apologies for the Sauvignon temperature, we take our glasses and return to the past: last night's places in the 50s armchairs and a question that spears back to 1985. "Why did you ditch me, Michael?" She follows her strike with creature comforts – a gulp of wine and slipping off her heels to curl up on the cushion.

"I thought it was mutual. You didn't seem so very keen."

"I was keen enough. Perhaps I should've showed it more; but with a dad like mine it's no surprise I was reticent."

"And after a year in London I didn't want to be tied to anyone from here."

"Thanks."

"But you found someone else."

"Several someones, thanks to a brother in the rugby club. It's called being on the rebound. I bounced into bed with all of them."

"And married one?"

"The first who asked."

"You didn't love him?"

"God, no. Like I said, I was on the rebound. And Stu was a Mumby with a silver spoon in his mouth. He wanted a trophy wife, and I saw my chance as a gold-digger."

"A marriage of convenience."

"I thought so; but I was wet behind the ears." For the first time she looks away from me, and blinks down at her lap. "I could never measure up: in public, too chatty and forward; at home, too selfish and lazy. Sluttish was the word he used. Then he got a taste for corporal punishment." The glistening behind her specs lenses is unmistakeable now.

"I'm sorry." Was her suffering my fault? Indirectly, yes, I suppose; but I don't see why I should take the blame.

"I thought I'd escaped spankings when Mum got rid of my dad. I went back to her and the bank job until I saw my purpose in life. After I enrolled for the diploma in social work at Hull I never looked back." She forces a smile as she lifts her head. "Now tell me about a happy marriage."

* * *

Forgetting to lay the dining table prompted her to serve here in the kitchen; and her rush to a third glass of wine moved her polite inquiries towards an inquisition in search of our marital flaws. It's not been easy, her forcing answers like a kid wanting to shake a pound out of a money box and me being cagey so she only got a few pence. Her chair scrapes on the tiles, and she takes our plates over to the beech drainer behind me.

"You don't see it, do you Michael?"

"See what?"

"This." And before I turn to see what she means, I feel what she means. Whoosh: hands on my shoulders, a collision of heads, lips thrusting for my mouth; and then she's on my lap with arms encircling, and it's

215

proper kissing. I can't say it's not pleasant, overpowered and imprisoned in less than five seconds flat: branded with lipstick, injected with saliva, and anaesthetised by alcoholic breath. But it's time to resist. I grip her shoulders to prise us apart.

"Sarah. No."

She sighs in my face, and flicks her specs behind her on to the table, not caring where they land, grinning as if we're already sexually complicit and she's locked us in a cell and it was the key she threw away. And now she's licking her lips to soothe the bruises – or anticipating the work ahead.

"Don't tell me you're not keen. I can bloody feel you."

"I can't help it. I'm a man."

"God, you don't have to tell me. The one I thought I'd got over, until last night. And I laughed at a girl at work for shagging with a bloke off Friends Reunited. Let's go upstairs." And with her weight off my thighs my erstwhile lap dancer practises for the tug of war.

"No. Stop."

She lets go. "In here then. It's one of my fantasies." And she sits on the table, gesturing to emphasise its extent. "A special offer for my special man: full submission and no holds barred." And with this raunchy invitation she kicks off her shoes and undoes her jacket to show she's serious.

And it is time to be serious, but with words not deeds. I stand and grip her upper arms, prompting her to tilt her head back and close her eyes in expectation of what's not coming: my ultimate exploration of the girl who once liquefied my dreams. "Sarah. There's no future in this."

Now she's searching my face. "My crystal ball's different." And she unbuttons the neck of her blouse.

"Stop."

She obeys, but only after the little bow between her bra cups has come into view. "You see how I do what you tell me." And she adds a come-to-bed try-me-out smile.

It's not easy resisting full-on seduction, I'm discovering, but I think I'm doing OK so far. This is a million miles from Alicia's supine passivity.

Anyway, I continue my refusals. "Jay loves you; I love Louise. In other circumstances it might be different, but I'm not going to betray them." And yet I don't want to hurt her.

"God, haven't you ever been unfaithful?"

I prevent myself saying no. "Once." But I don't admit to it being on Monday night.

"Well, double it. Don't worry about John. He has to turn a blind eye to my peccadilloes."

"This isn't a one-off then?"

She shakes her head. "It's my fitness trainer at the moment."

"Why, when you've got Jay?"

"It's because I have got him. He's the loveliest man, and I wouldn't want to live with anyone else, but he can't rise to the occasion. You know... It's his pills."

"Can't you do something?"

"I bloody am doing something."

"That's not what I meant. For him: Viagra or something."

"We've got a modus operandi. You could be part of it – make up for the past." But it's she who's trying to make up for the past. She stares into my eyes desperate to see tunnel vision, and rams home the brutal instruction, "Fuck me."

I flinch. She's ramped up the voltage of her electromagnet, but the attraction's not enough to pull me into her unfathomable well of needs. I've passed the test; I shake my head. "No, Sarah. It's not going to happen. And if you sit quietly I'll tell you why."

I release her arms and sit beside her on the table to offer a hug. She leans against me and we're flaccid together. I couldn't be more exhausted if we really had been wrestling.

"I'd like to be your friend. I want to be Jay's friend. I want Louise to like you both. They're new streams in my idyll, as you called it; but if I did what you ask they'd run dry."

Her voltage drops to a gentle wheedle. "But just once; they wouldn't know."

"I'd know. My cheating on them isn't an option – not now. Secrets and lies are the worms in the rose bud. This week I've been converted: I've read chapters from the book of Revelation."

"Good for you; but don't preach. I can't change my ways so easily."

"I'm not asking you to. I'm just explaining why I said no when an attractive woman offered me her sacrosanctity."

"Silly. And that's definitely not the word for it – if it is a word – the way I carry on." But she gives me a quick kiss on the cheek to seal our platonic reversion, and after a pause says, "Perhaps it is unfair to John. He was the first to show me the softer side of men: the caring, considerate side. I wouldn't have married again otherwise. And now I take advantage of it to get laid by blokes that don't count, other than as dildos. God, it's ironic, isn't it. Why can't he be hard too? Let's have our raspberries and cream."

* * *

I kiss her mouth like a brother might, and she closes the door on our session of attempted relationship redesign. I don't know if she'll tell Jay about our one-to-one; and it not being a soap opera, he didn't come home and catch us. Although I spoke of my CSS return, I've made no plans to visit. His erectile dysfunction wasn't raised again, but maybe she'll ponder on her two-timing: her worm in the bud. And if he knows how she's getting fulfilment, it's high time she stopped rubbing her spice into his wound. Poor Jay; in his situation even I'd be depressed.

Reversing the car from the house broadens my view of their façade. Behind it I've seen they're in trouble, and I'm driving away and leaving them to it. But what else can I do? Despite what I said to Sarah, I don't see a future for me with them as yet. Her coming on to me has barred my way to Jay. It's disappointing, but... Maybe she'll change and fess up; they'll work something out; he'll get in touch. Who knows? I might just have enough stamina to change myself, but there'll be nothing in reserve to help anyone else.

TWENTY-FOUR

On the M1 I've stayed with Radio 3 in the sedated inner lanes, steering clear of Classic FM's ads ad nauseam and the hurtling hyper-linked convoys in the outside track. Although the route's been free of crossroads I've been thinking my life has reached one – or a more bewildering cloverleaf of turns.

Over an overpriced tea and pastry at Leicester Forest East I stare out as the last dregs of sky light leak away and a munching face looks back in through the black screen of the picture window: the hero of *A Week in the Life of Michael Paine*. It's an account of profit and loss, although I haven't read the final chapter yet. The balance sheet seems loaded with assets: not just the 120K, but his burgeoning friendships and thinking about other people's needs. It's a surge of sensitivity just sprung. But the liabilities stack high too: the aftershocks of bereavement, confessions of guilt, urges for revenge, pitfalls with Sarah and Jay, the trauma of restructuring his life. They're like unstable rocks which could topple to make white water in the stream. He might drown. And did I say a week? The poor guy's been turned inside out in half that time. Fucking hell, I don't think I can I cope.

After phone calls to Lou and Ivor to pinpoint my position, I relieve myself in the gents, fill the car with non-Omega diesel (slap on wrist) and zoom up to 60 on the slip road in 8 seconds like the brochure says. Ivor, bach, here I come.

* * *

Frazzled more by three miles on the North Circular than ninety minutes on the motorway, I needed the soothing of Glenn Gould playing Bach on a CD for the last leg of the journey; and the relief of getting to Parkside Road in one piece smothered my mini worry about intruding into Ivor's life. Have I mistaken the signs; or is it a last-ditch defence after opening the gate for him to come into mine?

Car space is at a premium, but down at the end of the road I locate a 525-sized slot and park close to the closed park gates. I emerge to the amplified rattle of a train on a girder bridge – a train extruded from the Northern Line tube, I guess, or one about to burrow underground – and walk back uphill between bay-windowed late Victorian terraces whose house prices have probably gone stratospheric. Agents must be pushing them up above half-a-million now. The wind's hardly a whisper here – it's been dropping all day and our latitude's two degrees further south – and I'm getting an earful of my heavy breathing instead. Maybe I need a fitness trainer more than Sarah.

"Noswaith dda, Michael. You found me all right then. In you come."

He's opened the door on to a tiled floor, a chenille curtain, brass stair rods and an aspidistra on a stand – the scenery for another hospitality performance. But it can't be a performance; there's no artifice. The broad smile, the friendly gleam in his eyes, the simultaneous hand shaking and shoulder pressing are utterly real. Why was I worried? He does want me, and sent out consistent signals – at the crematorium, in the hotel, on the phone. It was just my defective receptor at fault. And yes, I'm glad. It's a good feeling – because I want him, too.

"That's the evidence, is it? Give it here while you take your flying jacket off." And then the red plastic wallet's back in my hand as he hangs my coat on the hallstand. "Tonic water? I got some in."

He ushers me into his front room where smokeless fuel is glowing in the grate. "This is cosy," I say. Other than his TV and hi-fi, I'm surrounded by a clutter of stuff from before the Great War, arranged without the artistry it deserves. Lou let loose in here would enjoy herself adding style to the substance. He returns with the drinks (whisky for him) and plonks into the leather chair on the other side of the hearth.

I don't know if his black shirt and trousers are smart casual evening wear or to show he's still in mourning.

"Shall I take a dekko, then?" he asks, pointing to the wallet on the arm of my chair.

I pass my precious papers over well clear of the heat from the fire. "The other two are just proofs of signature."

After his perusal he twists to lift the memo to the standard lamp behind. "That's good: watermarked paper. Another proof if we need it. I said we can't be too careful, if you remember. And she never saw this, my Marlene?"

I can recognise the heartache now, as he says her name. God knows how he'll take my news. "It was tucked in a file. She didn't add to Dad's system; started one of her own. So, what's your plan?"

"I thought I'd get my publisher to contact the Atogas press office and set up an interview. We'll mention my book and lay it on thick that I want Sir Alec to have every chance of putting his side of the story. He'll smell a rat, of course, and want to see all the questions in advance. And he will – except one."

"Which is?"

"Whatever you want it to be, Michael. You'll be there, see. You'll be my assistant, working on the book with me."

"Brilliant." And it is. Whatever else follows, I'll have the pleasure of seeing his face fall and his mouth gape.

"I thought you'd like it."

But my tremor at asking the one question will set off an avalanche. Do you remember Alan Paine? What did you do with his memo? Why did you ignore it? What did you think about him? Why did you lie to the Inquiry? What do you feel about the lives you took? Do you care about the grief you caused? Will you make a public apology? How? When? Yes, the questions are easy; but Smart Alec's sure to obfuscate with a set of politicians' answers.

"I do," I say. "But he's not likely to cave in with a mea culpa on the spot, is he? It would mean admitting he'd lied under oath."

"No, no, he won't. Not if he's the man I take him to be. But we have to give him the option, see. He might choose to act dirty, but we'll be squeaky clean. It's my first rule of campaigning: only fight from the moral high ground."

"And the second?"

"Only use weapons that are licensed. There's where many groups fall down. You have to keep public opinion on your side; it's your greatest ally by far."

I nod at my sage. "So what's next for us?"

"We take one step at a time, Michael. You can't have your afters before, as my nan used to say. See, the dynamics of our first encounter will dictate what strategy we follow. Now before I forget, I'm going to copy these. Come up and see my den, if you like."

He leads upstairs to a rear bedroom fitted out for his work. The alcove bookshelves either side of a chimney breast devoid of its fireplace are chock-a-block, and the table's spread with a feast of printed words in magazines and newspapers piled up high. In contrast, the desk shows off bare scuffed leather, except where the computer, scanner and printer ply.

"So this is where you try to prove the keyboard's mightier than the sword," I say.

"Yes, where I'm happiest... No, let me put that another way: where I'm least gloomy; where I feel my life's not been completely wasted."

As usual, I'm at a loss for consoling words to deal with a depressive – even after thirty years experience with Mum – so while he manipulates the desktop technology I turn away to investigate his books. *Zeebrugge: Learning from Disaster* catches my eye, a tilted coping stone on a haphazard paperback wall. Picking it up reveals the memorial list of the dead on the back of the dust jacket – almost two hundred names. That news in 1987 made an impression even on my callow consciousness. It was on a Friday night during a pub crawl, but I hadn't registered the death toll as so high. *Lessons in Corporate Responsibility* is the subtitle. Yes, and still to be learned, as Ivor's soon to tell the world.

He sees me putting it back. "I wish we'd commemorated the Boroughcliff dead with a list on our book. Still, there's the memorial in the church. Anyhow, two sets of copies, one for you and one for me."

"What about the originals?"

"We won't be using them until we need to. I'll keep them out of harm's way at the bank."

"I hadn't thought about any skulduggery." Maybe I am in a TV drama, after all.

"No, of course not. But you have to think of him as the Duke of Atogas: the fierce ruler determined to hold on to his empire and very willing to instruct the secret police. But we'll be en garde." He looks at his watch. "There's still half an hour till our casserole's ready. Let's go back down."

In the sitting room I slip my copies into the folder, and wish I could slip myself somewhere safe too. But it's time to own up to the black secrets of the Paines.

"I've got things to tell you, Ivor; things I've discovered."

"About Marlene?" He sits forward, his hands clasped as if in prayer. "Fire away. All ears, I am."

I suppose the first part won't be so hurtful; and I explain about the diary and journal, and Dad's fixation with Alice and their secret rendezvousing. "But then the next day's entry's written by a nervous wreck. It hit me for six, so I can imagine Mum absolutely gobsmacked. It starts off, *I've killed her*." He flinches as if a lump of Coalite's fallen on the rug.

"He couldn't have – not literally?"

"That's what I thought, but I think Mum took it straight. It's not clear what happened from what's scrawled, but he tried to kiss Alice and she resisted and her dog jumped up. You can read it several ways, but death by strangulation's one."

"And you think that's why she... she threw me over?" My terrier image of him comes back: he not only suffers the black dog, he is a black dog, eyeing me soulfully as his master in the hope of a kind word.

"I'm sure. If she felt half the turmoil that struck me, I can quite see her rush to shutter the windows and bar the doors against another man she hardly knew."

"Yes, I see: a terrible shock – for both of you. But he hadn't killed her had he, your dad? You're far too easy."

"No. Well, not directly."

And as I tell him how I wound my way to elucidation in the library, his focus lengthens to a point beyond my face.

"So, filed in the cuttings library – just up the corridor from my office – was the answer to the question she never asked. My salvation it might've been, if only she'd told me. How could she take those words as gospel truth for the rest of her life – never question them, never make any investigation?" He deflates into his chair, his head lolling back to look up to the leaf and garland ceiling centre, as if following its convolutions will lead him to the answer.

"I thought the same, Ivor. I could understand what she did in the heat of the moment – the emergency shutdown – but then the questions must've buzzed away like bluebottles in a window. Why didn't she let them out? You'd have been let back in."

"We'll never know."

"I said, I thought the same, but only until I heard about…" My rumble strip does its job and I brake in time. "I've still something to tell you. It might be hard to take."

"I'd better have another whisky, then. I'll get you another tonic, shall I?" He exits with a brave smile to replenish our glasses, and I think about my opening line until he's back on stage.

"There was another reporter who knew Mum then, wasn't there? A big chap with fair hair. He was in your office that time you took us there." Now I've warned him, I'll wade straight in.

"Dave – Dave Fletcher. He covered sport. But he didn't know her. Well, he'd been at the party at Ravenby Manor, and they had a dance I think. Why?"

"I had a party yesterday: afternoon tea for the neighbours. Mrs Furr from next door remembered an incident from about that time when you knew us." And I continue with the voiceover for the little scene that's been re-running in my imagination like those intrusive BBC TV trailers: the ring of the bell, the forced entry, the hug in the doorway, his stage fright and quick exit, her abashed admission of his bothering. Ivor crumples his face in disbelief.

"Poor Marlene… That's his style… But no, he wouldn't have." I'm silent, waiting to see the implication suffuse like blood through grazed skin. "Whoever it was, she'd have been devastated. Whatever he did, she'd have crawled into a hole."

"But are there any other suspects?" I say.

"No. It's him. It fits."

"How?"

He takes a fortifying slug of the whisky. "Dave was a tyke both ways round: a Yorkshire Don Juan. Fletcher the lecher, he was known as. He liked to brag to me about his conquests. Reports from the cunt front, he called them; for my training, he said. A woman a week wasn't unusual. Only once he went quiet on them."

I'm the one sitting forward now. He looks down into the sparkling glass for comfort.

"Before the party and after, it was. He met his match in Janet Smith. She was one of my fellow thespians, and brought him along to it. That must've been a week or more after he first met her. He'd kept quiet for obvious reasons. Afterwards I asked him how he was getting on, and he said they'd split up. I don't think much splitting was needed. She'd been playing him along, see. I'm sure I told him about my brush-off in sympathy – or else he asked me. We weren't buddies, but friendly enough. His eyes must have lit up thinking she was available. That was a busy time for me with my scoop, but I don't think he had any news about his women for a bit after that."

He has another drink, and deserves it after a speech that seems to fix Dave Fletcher firmly in the frame for indecent assault or worse. OK, the incentive of Janet's rejection and the window of opportunity are only circumstantial proofs, but with ID and witness statements we should get a conviction. The telephone's ring brings me to my senses. "Excuse me, Michael," and he goes into the hall.

What the fucking hell was I thinking of? What conviction? What prosecution? What arrest even? Where is the bastard? What did he do? His silence tells us nothing. He could hardly brag to Ivor about a success with Marlene Paine, and if she fought him off, so to speak, he'd have kept quiet about that too.

Ivor's laugh, not heard before, invites me to eavesdrop. I'm glad there's someone to lighten his gloom.

"I won't forget, but I'll write it on my calendar if you like. I've got my own supper party tonight. I'll tell you about it, but not now. Eightish, then. Nos da, Marie."

I wait while he marks up his date. He looks less doleful when he comes back. "Sorry about that: my new editor inviting me to a little do on Saturday. It's the second time she's asked me to one. I said no before. Now, where were we?"

Maybe he feels released to freedom too. "I was about to ask what happened to this Dave."

"He got the push. Kay Wilson wrote and told me after I left – she was the girl at the *Argus* that got me into my drama group. There was a complaint by Pauline Cage. The features editor's secretary, she was: a perfectionist. She stayed on one evening too many, and he tried to have his way. She must've had some steel in her. She gave the Old Man an ultimatum: either Dave went, or she went to the police."

I've got that sick feeling again, and it's not the teatime pastry. "That's pretty damning evidence, Ivor."

"I know. I'd rather not think about it."

"I'm sorry I've landed you with this as well as the other, but I had to know."

"Of course you did. Don't apologise."

I don't know which of the monsters disgusts me the more – Masters or Fletcher. Never mind, I need to get even with both. "What happened to him after he left?"

"I don't know. Back to Batley, I suppose, or somewhere like. If he's still writing, he didn't move up any grades." Ivor's staring as if he can see my cogs turning, and fears I'll drag the anchor of my escapement and unwind. "You've no hard evidence, Michael. Dave thought he was God's gift to women and got used to an easy ride. In the end he'd forgotten how to climb down. Of course I'm sad and upset; but let sleeping dogs lie."

Yes, he was a dog. If we're going to beard Masters in his fortress, who says I can't collar the lecher in his kennel?

TWENTY-FIVE

I almost skip down to the car after our au revoirs. I'm on the last lap. We'll talk next week about the action plan: our entrée to the sanctum sanctorum at Atogas House, and my return to the ninth floor of Fenchurch Tower. I think my resolve to get back into CSS relieved the pangs I'd caused him with my earlier news. I don't think his whiskies and beers would've been enough.

I hope it's the park gates and not my motor magnetising the hooded little gang with their cans.

"Here comes the pilot," raises sniggers.

"Is this your Beemer, mister?"

"Yep."

"We've been looking after it. You don't want it scratched. It's quality."

"No, you're right. Thanks. I'd do the same for you. Night, lads."

It wasn't really a threat, but might've tipped me into their trap and forced a handout. Anyway, I don't hang about to test them, so have to postpone the map reading and my call to Lou. After retracing my route back on to High Road, a glaring parade of eight-till-late shops backdrops a space to stop. The A-Z confirms twelve miles of more A406 torture before rescue by the A12.

"Hi, darling. I've just left Ivor's. Be with you half-eleven or earlier."

"I might not wait up, sweetie. Do you mind? I'm really tired."

"No." But it's disappointing.

"But wake me when you come to bed if I don't hear you." That's better.

"Love you, Lu-Lu. Night night."

The North Circular stresses less at this later hour, but still offers a stiff test with its variety mix of junctions. I count twelve of them before I'm on the home straight. And having made good time, I make a spur-of-the-moment decision as the M25 crossover looms. It diverts me up the slip road to traffic lights at red, which then release me on to the roundabout for more of the same. At the last set Glenn Gould ends the final Aria from the *Goldberg Variations* – the movement played at his funeral in Toronto in 1982, and what I'd like at mine. I turn off the CD and turn my mind on to finding the right turn off the A1023.

It's Ivor's fault. He's become my personal guru. Spot audits, he said, when we spoke in the bar, and my gear's in the car. It's been on my mind with my career volte-face: the safety police. Tonight I'll go in with two hats on to show how it's done and maybe prove the benefit, although I don't expect much amiss – not at an Omega site. I'll check permit sign-offs, the operators' log sheet, equipment lockouts, today's loading sheet, the watchman's log. It shouldn't take long. I don't know which of our operators will be on shift tonight, or if they'll remember me. There'll only be the two plus the contractor backup. In fact, I haven't met everyone there yet. It could be an interesting meeting.

Stockley Lane flanks a palisade of fence panels, pine and larch lap. Behind is the once small 60s housing estate which Adrian said spread our way in the 80s, as if to keep up with the Joneses when Brentfield expanded. In front of me the shelter belt of live pines and larches screens the depot, but not the aurora of floodlights above. I turn right at the T-junction to motor between the trees, as up ahead a car emerges from the left and comes my way. That's Stockley Lane too, but a two-mile straight and my route to the gate. It's Omega's replacement for the obliterated original: a pair of lines ruled forty years ago on the layout plan. We don't do wiggles and bends. What's he doing, the silly bugger? Sorry, fellow traveller; I mustn't forget my defensive driving. My beams are dipped but his are flashing like strobes at a rave. And he sounds his horn on the way past to give a demo of the Doppler Effect. He's warning me of something – but what? Animals on the loose, an accident, a speed trap? I'll soon find out.

After I've turned the corner I see a bank of fog. It's a still night now, but this is the first I've seen. It's strung out across the road like a white voile curtain from our metal railings on the left and into Warfield Business Park on the right. I slow and switch my fog lights on to drive through with care – only unlike the other lucky driver I don't make it. The engine races, stupidly I brake, and then it dies. Fuck, fuck, fuck it! Can I coast it? No. There's just enough momentum to make it on to the verge.

Yes, it's fog – but it's fucking petrol fog. I can smell it. What the fuck's happening? And my mind's made up for me, I don't know by whom: not to try and restart the car and risk an ignition and be cooked to a frazzle, but to get out and investigate – because I can. I don't risk asphyxiation. My vehicle policy not only put fire extinguishers in all company cars, but a Draeger escape set into site management team motors. And mine's on the back seat, cleared from the boot when I stashed the heirloom loot. But it's still gut wrenching to reach for the orange bag – not the twisting round, but the clutch of fear. At least I don't need the helmet. But I need my mobile; and have I got my access card?

Now I'm a hoody with my can – of air. The breathing's easy; or would be if I could slow my lungs down. At this rate I'll never get ten minutes out of it. I try and relax before opening the door. On the road the cylinder adds weight to the millstone already around my neck. This is my site, and there's been an almighty shitey cock-up. If it's not sorted I'll be dead and buried – one way or the other. I walk steadily along the kerb like a beachcomber in a sea fret – only it's the bloody vapour from winter grade petrol. I know the data off by heart: vapour pressure 70 to 100kPa; butane content 7 to 10%; flashpoint minus 40C. That's the theory. Please God, don't make this the practical and let it all catch fire.

After only sixty paces but what seems like an aeon I'm in the clear – well, out of the fog. I scamper another fifty metres just in case before taking stock. After easing off the hood to sample fresh air, I reset it to conserve my supplies. There's a smell but I can breathe OK. I look back as the creeping petrol stratus explores the sleeping business park. When did that place creep up on us? The three tanks I can see floodlit behind our railings aren't misbehaving. The source must be further inside the site. I listen hard for anomalous sounds. Is that splashing? What the fucking hell's going on in there? The driver of that car or one of the operators might've already phoned for help, but I can't rely on it, so I poke 999 on my mobile, anticipating the 'Emergency – which service, please?' before it's said.

"Emergency – which service do you require? Police, fire brigade or ambulance?" I didn't get it quite right.

"Fire brigade."

"I'll put you through."

Hurry up.

"Fire control here." Now it's a guy. "What number are you calling from?"

Bloody hell. "I'm on my mobile."

"Can you give me the number, please?"

How many more stupid questions? OK, I know they're not stupid, but they're bloody infuriating. I rattle it off.

"Can you tell me what's happened?"

At last! "There's a massive petrol leak in the Brentfield fuel depot. Vapour's spreading west into Warfield Business Park. It's formed a fog. You can see it. We'll need foam to blanket the spill."

"To do what to the spill, please?"

"To blanket it: a foam blanket."

"Thank you. Is there a fire?"

"No, not yet."

"Who are you, sir?"

"I'm Michael Paine, Omega distribution manager. It's one of my sites. Staff may have rung up already. There's a codeword, but I don't know it. And there'll be response protocols."

"Where are you exactly?"

"About two hundred metres north of the main gates on Stockley Lane.

I'm going down there now. You should come in from the south. My car stalled in the vapour cloud up near the Warfield Road junction."

"Thank you, sir. The first fire engines should be at the gates in about ten minutes, at five past eleven. Please leave your phone switched on."

I shove it back in my pocket. He didn't say if they already knew – but why the bloody hell not? I jog on, holding my orange bag to stop it jumping and bumping like my heart. Now I'm at the gates. Although the hinged ones are open, both barriers are down – defensive grids like railings without the spikes. The watchman's not in the gatehouse, so either he's investigating already or somewhere out on site doing his rounds. I dial 333 on the phone in the little box to ring the control room and ask what's going on and get the barriers raised. They've got CCTV in there, so could be watching me – or better still, doing something about the leak. Brr-brr... Brr-brr... Brr-brr. And so on. There's no reply. But why the bloody hell not?

I stick my card in the reader and click through the turnstile. Ahead is the top-heavy toll plaza of tanker loading stations – empty now because we don't fill on nights with only a skeleton staff. I need to be round to the left. Hang on. Slow down. There should be local controls for the barriers. Yes, there is. Bugger: the green button doesn't fucking work. And it's the same story with the other set. There must be an override.

I'm jogging again and looking along the access road between the perimeter tanks and a separate block of four. The lower vista is hiding behind the white cloud a hundred and fifty metres away. The splashing, as clashing as laughter at a graveside, is unmistakable now. I notice T27 painted on the nearest of the foursome – my test case from yesterday. I passed that; it's a good omen. I'll recce further along and try and suss out the problem – my second detour of the night. And am I glad I made the first? I think I am. The agonies of all this are bringing me close to Dad – as close as being in his skin. God, let me be a hero for him. Don't let me be incinerated. Dad, I never imagined it half as bad as this for you.

I'm puffed – or panicking. I slow to a speedy walk alongside the bund wall, but can't put a brake on my breathing. In the gap through the quartet I can see one of our monsters, a 10,000 tonner for unleaded. It's only the central slice, but the view's normal. There's a second as big on its far side. At the corner I stop and stare up the next road – and it's clear all the way to the trees. I'm homing in, but what am I going to see? I venture forward with the Draeger set at the ready. Christ! I can't believe it. No wonder I could hear the splashing: it's not a leak but a goddam full-scale overflow. The second giant T11 is spewing out petrol as if it's being force-fed – which it is. I expected a pump seal failure or a blown flange. What I'm seeing is the 500 tonnes an hour coming down from Wiremouth or Whittonsea gushing out of the top vents: a twenty metre cascade all round thundering into the bund like Niagara Falls. And the spray's tremendous. It's the evaporation from that making the vapour cloud so large.

I turn and run. What the hell's gone wrong? We've got level measurement and alarms on the screens and cameras snooping and operators watching. We've got high level switches and automatic shutoff valves and direct phone lines to the refineries. And tonight they're all useless. There's no way this should be happening; it's surreal. Worst-case scenarios are for emergency planning. I've thought about them in my job, but in this nightmare I'm actually living one. I need to stop the flow before the cloud ignites and flashes back and we go up in smoke. I know stats say there's a better than evens chance of safe dispersal, but I don't know what goes on in that business park. How long have I got?

Now I'm outside the admin and control block, puffing as I hoick open the door. In the hallway the clock clicks from 11:00 to 11:01 as I lasso a coat hook outside the gents with the escape set. I could do with a slash but screw the stopper in more. And I've got a real vindaloo sweat on as I scurry down the corridor. In fact, I feel goddam awful.

"What's going on?"

Yes, what is going on. There's no one in the control room to fucking answer me. Their paraphernalia's spread all about, but they've abandoned ship. And I'm a helpless wreck without them; scuppered by control technology that's cutting edge – except the phones. I grab at one of them and the handset clatters on to the desk. I'm shaking. For God's sake keep calm.

"Is that Wiremouth – the control room?"

"Aye, it is."

"This is Brentfield. There's a massive overflow. You've got to stop the transfer."

"But we've no transfers on right now."

"Well, it must be Whittonsea. I can't tell. I've just arrived here. The fucking crew's gone missing. Ring Whittonsea for me. I need to get the gates open. It's Michael Paine."

"Aye, don't fret. I missed the name though."

"Paine. Michael Paine. I'm in distribution."

"Right. I'll get straight on to it. Good luck."

Good luck. It's OK for him in ordered calm up there – OK for everybody that's not here. For Lou and the girls tucked up in bed. Oh, Lu-Lu, why didn't I go straight home? Please God, save me for Lou. Stop it. Stop it. Being a wimp's not helping. Get back on the ball.

Are they in the mess room? No, I've just run past there. But I go back out anyway, and look through the window in the door. There's a sandwich box on the table encasing an apple and a packet wrapped in foil. Why can't I see into their minds like that? Have they done a bunk in panic? Are they busy somewhere unaware? Think. Think. They might be in the workshop talking with the VMS mechanic, or with the Contech technician in the E and I block, or getting something from the stores – but why would they go together? Or they could be in this building somewhere I haven't looked yet. I lope back to the entrance. The offices are dark and silent. The gents is empty, the cubicles open. I try the ladies and put on the light: nobody. I turn right and right again. There's no one up this end, and just the switch and interface rooms to come. The electrical panels reassure – their rock solid tradition. Although I'm straight in one door and out the other, I see some isolating switches locked out and tagged. Yes, we can avert disaster with that sort of control. It's part of the world I know.

But in the interface room between two rows of connection cabinets is part of a world I don't know, as shocking as the spewing tank – no, much more. Two men are face down on a camp bed, their naked and taut bodies bent on a rhythmic interface of their own. I swear no emergency planning anywhere in the world has ever dreamt up a scenario like this – not just dereliction of duty, but hedonism on the grandest scale. And it's not just the one fucking the other; they could be fucking Omega into kingdom come. Their heads twist and their limbs slacken. Maybe in flagrante delicto they're even more shocked than I.

"Get up. There's an emergency – T11's overflowing." Their khaki workwear and Y-fronts are piled together on the floor. "And put some trousers on."

"Who the fuck are you?" asks the penetrative one. The other's turned his head away.

"Adrian's boss: Michael Paine. No more fucking questions; just open up the gates. I've rung nine-nine-nine." But they stay stuck together, I suppose in shame. "Come on. I don't care what you've been doing, as long as you get back on the job in time. I'll wait in the control room."

But I don't. I'm boiling and I'm shattered, so I go out for a breath of cool air. What's that? Yes, sirens. They're better than any music I've ever heard. And the splashing's stopped. Maybe we're going to be OK. I've just time for that slash. I turn and then there's the flash. I can't see anything; I've been blinded. And next comes the deafening deflagrating roar. I put my hands to my ears as the blast wave blows me over. My foot twists and my head crashes on to the concrete step. And now I'm being bombarded by flying debris; I'm being stoned to death.

TWENTY-SIX

"May I play the piano, Daddy?" Hannah's come into the sitting room where I'm lounging with the Sunday papers.

"Yep, but you won't have long. He'll be here soon. Do you want me to go out?"

"No. I need to learn to play with an audience. Do you want to choose something?"

"OK... How about something Grandma Paine liked? Scott Joplin?"

"Yes, she did. All right."

It's Mum's birthday. I didn't feel under any pressure to commemorate it; but when I told Ivor where I'd hoped we'd scatter her ashes he said he'd quite fancy seeing St Peter's Chapel where she liked to go. Of course, we couldn't scatter the ashes after that second cremation. They merged with the ashes and residues of everything else in the car as my Beemer blazed to a burnt out shell. We lost our photos of Mum in her prime and Dad, and Dad's poems and last diary, and my Guernsey and the rest of the things I brought from Kilvert Road.

Anyway, today seemed the right day to invite him, so he's coming to lunch. And now with the news from Friday, we've something to celebrate. There're articles in both papers, but I pick up *The Observer* which has the longer of the two. I've read it once already, but want to savour it again – this time accompanied by *Maple Leaf Rag*.

END OF TERM FOR MASTERS

ATOGAS ANNOUNCES DEPARTURE OF CHARISMATIC CHIEF EXECUTIVE

Sir Alec Masters will leave Atogas at the end of the month by mutual agreement. A turbulent eighteen months of damage limitation has failed to placate institutional investors and arrest a falling share value, and few will be surprised at the news. His successor is widely predicted to be Operations Director, James Walsh.

Friday's announcement paid tribute to Sir Alec's charismatic leadership over the last seven years, a period of company expansion by strategic acquisition. However, the successful consolidation of disparate cultures and standards seemed to elude him. This was most graphically demonstrated by the chaotic circumstances of last year's explosion at the Lescolonnes refinery in Louisiana in which twelve employees were killed. As a result Atogas suffered fines equivalent to £7.5m imposed by the US Occupational Safety and Health Administration. And a flurry of litigation by the bereaved will take considerable time and sizeable funds to settle.

Sir Alec Masters' career has progressed to a remarkable zenith by way of the nadir of his association with the Boroughcliff disaster thirty-two years ago. Site manager at the time, he has never been shy of citing his rise from those catastrophic ashes as proof of exceptional talent and mental toughness. However in recent weeks those claims have had a hollow ring.

The company's statement avers that the allegation made by safety campaigner Ivor Hughes that Masters lied to the Boroughcliff Court of Inquiry is totally without foundation, and played no part in his departure. Mr Hughes is seeking a public apology from Sir Alec for those deaths and injuries in 1974. The matter hinges on a warning memo sent by an employee later killed in the explosion, and whether Sir Alec received it. The Mirror newspaper's front page on Wednesday claimed that the site manager's secretary in 1974 has been located in Melbourne, Australia, and is prepared to make a statement. We shall see.

In leaving a year early Sir Alec will forgo bonuses, share options and pension uplifts amounting to almost £2m. In a separate announcement yesterday accountants Bate, Armitage and Ross said that Sir Alec had resigned the directorship he has held there since 2001. Other sinecures may also be under threat if the Boroughcliff allegations are substantiated.

Yet although we've won a battle, we haven't won the war. Still, we've got a red top fighting with us, thanks to Ivor's contacts – although there's no further news from the front. Ivor said he knew Smart Alec would never own up from the moment he showed him the memo. His face had all the expression of a reptile, apparently – a basilisk even, with what would've been going through his mind. And out came the cunning words, 'Very interesting, Mr Hughes. I wish I'd seen it at the time'. And I wish I'd been there to see him – but I wasn't well enough and yet didn't want my ailments to delay the great day. Hannah's now moved on to *Wall Street Rag*. I wonder how the traders will react to his sacking – leaving by mutual agreement, my arse.

He's the only monster left now Dave Fletcher is dead. My search of Yorkshire newspaper websites came up with a 2004 obit that had to be his, and words that have stuck to me like burrs: *Former Echo reporter David Fletcher, 56, has been found dead at his home in Batley; an inquest will be held, although it is understood that there are no suspicious circumstances; he joined the sports desk in 1996 after working on various regional newspapers in Yorkshire and North Lincolnshire, and retired two years ago due to ill health; he was unmarried.* They might've added: *he was a serial womaniser and ruined at least one victim's life.* But he didn't outlive her, which is some consolation, and it let me off the hook – although if he was living I've no idea what I might've planned. To set up a confrontation, maybe, aiming to see him contrite; but after so long would Mum have merged with his hundreds of other conquests – even a thousand and two, like Don Giovanni – and left no special imprint in his mind? 'Marlene Paine? Who was she?' If he'd said that I might've felt like murder. Or would I have followed Ivor's advice and let the dog lie? Thoughts about him wrecking her life, and exactly what happened, keep taking over my mind like starlings pecking at a fat ball – thoughts that are scripting a horror movie in my head.

Hannah stops in mid phrase. "He's arrived, Daddy."

"Right. Let's go and meet him."

I pick up my walking stick, let Lou know by a shout from the hall into the kitchen, and then we're on the doorstep as Ivor emerges from the Mini. It's his second visit to Danbury this year – one more than Lou's mum and dad have achieved, although they do have further to come. He's been a hit with my Three Graces and I'm hoping the two of us are about to build on our rapport.

"Hallo, Hannah. This is for you." It's wrapped, but looks like a book; and he's holding another parcel and a bunch of freesias, presumably for Emily and Lou. "Nothing for you, Michael," he says, as we shake hands. "Just keeping in with the women, I am."

"Quite right, too."

"How are you? I see you've still got your stick. No delayed PTSD?"

"No."

"What's PTSD, Daddy?" asks Hannah.

"Don't worry, sweetheart; I don't think I'm the type for it." I turn back to Ivor and wave the walking stick. "This is only for reassurance now, and the hearing's slowly getting better."

I might not have contracted PTSD, but my exposure to the biggest explosion and fire in the UK since Boroughcliff certainly contracted my focus – from grandiose Paine management ambitions to personal pain management strategies. I suffered a depressed fracture of the skull, a broken foot, tinnitus and multiple bruises after the short-lived blindness from the flash – and two weeks in hospital followed by convalescence ever since. At the beginning I despaired of ever finding a comfortable position, but now I'm well on the mend.

"Anyway, come inside and say hallo to Louise," I add. "Emily's playing at her friend's, but she won't be long."

We're soon settled in the sitting room with our pre lunch drinks.

Hannah's drinking a fizzy cordial and is already absorbed by her present, *Mozart: An Extraordinary Life*. I hope it's not too extraordinary for a twelve-year-old, but he is her favourite composer and Ivor's done well in remembering that. He's sipping whisky, sitting on the sofa and I'm opposite with my tonic.

"When's your date to spill the beans on Brentfield, then?" Ivor asks me.

Up until now I've told only Lou and him why the control room was empty. I kept quiet when I gave my story to Omega's investigation committee by a conference call from my hospital bed. The operators must've started with lies before their surprise at being believed.

"Monday week," I reply.

"Well, at least it's only an HSC investigation board behind closed doors. Good for you perhaps, but not for the country at large."

"Yes, I'm surprised – why not a public inquiry?"

"It should've been. I said so to HSC and the minister in the letters I wrote. No fatalities, see. If there had been, the press clamour would've forced their hands. You're going to come clean, aren't you?"

"Yes, the full monty." He smiles at the joke. "And I'm hoping we'll find out why the T11 high level switch failed to operate. It was a month overdue on Contech's schedule, and now I hear it survived and is undergoing forensic examination."

"But if they'd been doing their job it wouldn't have been needed."

"No… They made me think the human factors we plug into safety management don't go far enough; don't include passions and emotions: love, hate, envy, anger, lust. Whether it was love or lust with those two, their antics not only burnt down most of Brentfield, but destroyed half the business park and damaged over a hundred houses."

"But you survived, Michael."

"Yes – unlike my dad."

"I was filling in my editor about how you almost followed in his footsteps, and about how we first met. When she took in the whole story she could scarcely believe it. She wished they published fiction."

"Why?" I ask.

"Because it would make a super novel, she said."

"What would make a super novel?" asks Lou, coming back in and sitting next to Ivor with her pink wine.

"Michael discovering about his mum and dad and then nearly being killed in another explosion."

"I suppose it is unbelievable," I say, before turning to Lou. "Do you think your book group would want to read it?"

"I should think so – if there wasn't too much about industry and engineering. We're all women, remember. Anyway, it wouldn't get published if there was."

"Why shouldn't there be things like that in a story?" asks Hannah, having emerged from her book. "It's what Daddy does."

"Because most readers of stories are women, Hannah, and there's a limit to how many technical things we can take," replies Lou.

"But you won't know unless you're given them to try."

My little budding lawyer might be making a good case, but she's not keeping her cool. I soothe with, "You're right, sweetheart, but it's academic. There isn't going to be a novel."

"No, I suppose not." She looks disappointed.

The doorbell rings. It's sure to be Emily, so Lou asks Hannah to let her in. The side door is unlocked, but she's something of a drama queen with her entrances.

"And ask her if she wants a drink," Lou adds, before turning to Ivor. "What's your take on the situation with Sir Alec Masters, Ivor? This Australian woman, will she want to say anything?"

"If the money's right, she will. I don't know if they've got a Max Clifford over there. But what will she remember? It's one memo among so many, and so long ago. There'd need to be something unusual – like him crumpling it up to throw it in the bin and her flattening it out to file it. We'll see, but I'm not optimistic."

"Well, his resigning or whatever is an achievement. I've not seen Mike so happy for months."

* * *

I parked my replacement 525 where the once Roman road to their fort of Othona narrows and fragments to a stony track for the last half-mile to the coast. I've been building up my stamina with walks around the estate and into the village, but this expedition will be a proper fitness test. Now I'm paired with Ivor behind Lou and Hannah, who are striding arm in arm, while Emily capers on ahead, kicking at stones with her yellow wellies. We're a garish bunch, blazoning five colours of the rainbow with our mix of anoraks. The wind off the sea is chilling my face as it blows Hannah's questions on fostering back past me. Lou told Ivor and the girls about the possibility on the way here. I know I started the wheels turning, but with them speeding an enthusiastic Lou into the nitty-gritty I've begun to feel somewhat queasy. Still, nothing's been decided yet.

"So, how are things at Omega, Michael?" Ivor asks.

My move back into CSS went up in the vast billow of smoke from Brentfield. It would've looked crass, asking to escape the consequences of Omega's worst ever disaster like that. After my weeks of recuperation I'm due to join the logistics task force in a fortnight or so – the team charged with getting what's left of the site emptied of fuel and fixing our distribution network gaps. Adrian's managing the remains of my empire, so he's happy, at least.

"It's all hands to the pumps, apparently – literally and figuratively. It'll be hectic when I start. I'll not just be hiring tankage but auditing the facilities as well."

"So no move back into safety on the horizon. There's a pity." He puts a hand on my shoulder to prove our connection in the familiar way.

"No, and then they want me on the pre-project board for rebuilding Brentfield, if we get the OK."

"Yes. Well, you'll have to wait and see about that. I'm seeing quite a few hurdles before you ever get to the final straight."

"But not necessarily for me, Ivor." And I turn and smile, and put my hand on his shoulder. It's my first time.

"How do you mean?"

"I'm thinking of resigning – changing tack."

"To do what?"

"That depends on you."

Now we're both turned towards each other. "Go on. Don't keep me in suspenders," he says.

"I thought I might work with you: Hughes and Paine, safety consultants – if you want me."

His eyes widen and eyebrows rise. "If I want you? If I had a job to offer, of course I'd want you. But I'm self-employed, Michael. There's not enough money coming in for two."

But I don't let his words deflect my aim. "Not now, maybe. But with my technical knowhow added to the mixture, couldn't we build the business up? I've got a cushion, remember: the money from Mum. I've been thinking I can do more good for society from outside Omega than from within. We've been resting on our laurels. Brentfield's the wakeup call – for them, I hope, and for me, for sure."

"But it's a radical shift – out of all those corporate comforts and the gold plated pension, don't forget."

"I know; I've considered all that." I thought he'd be more enthusiastic. I need to fire more shots – and I've got plenty. I've had three months to stack a pile of ammunition. "I'm really keen to do it, Ivor – and I'm not suffering from traumatic stress. You talked about safety crusading when we first met, and I said I'd done my stint. Well, now I think I've done my stint oiling the wheels of a juggernaut that's lost the humanity that binds organisations together. You say, 'A little fire is a large fire just beginning'; well, Omega became too bloated to see the little fire under its feet. We just managed to keep our shape a bit longer than Atogas and the others, that's all."

"Well said, Michael. You sound like me on my soap box." He stretches a hand behind my back to squeeze my shoulder.

"I'm glad. You couldn't pay me a better compliment."

"Anyhow, let me have a minute or two to take stock."

Thinking about those two guys on the camp bed while I was feeling sorry for myself in the hospital one started my metamorphosis. They were symptomatic. They'd become aliens without any allegiance, only interested in getting through a boring shift in the most enjoyable way. And those at the top in the boardroom are just as much aliens too, focusing on their KPIs, the share price, their bonuses. They've no empathy for the people they employ. And it's not just in petrochem – it's the same all through the corporate world. It might not be a fire or explosion, but the risk of other disasters – health, environmental, financial, transportation – is there too. Yes, I definitely want out.

While I'm willing Ivor to see things my way, I hear Lou saying, "We're waiting to get a date for their assessment. They have to make a visit. It'll be one afternoon after school. Daddy will be at home too." Yes, we've both been studying the charts and planning our routes before casting off and sailing away from our comfort zones.

I held nothing back from her about my visits to the Yateses (not even Sarah's sally on to my lap) – except one thing: my Amanda confession to Jay. I haven't yet found the right moment for a reprise to Lou. I think I'm scared about how she'll react. How could I face up to Amanda's parents, if that's what she'd want me to do? And would it help them to meet that once-selfish guy? And what if they couldn't forgive me?

I won't ever fess up to Alicia, though. I still feel ashamed. I know it's a secret, but why upset Lou for no reason. She'll never find out about that. There was only a cheque number on the bank statement and I didn't fill in the stub. And, of course, she never saw any evidence of my scorched bum so there was no explanation needed there. My secrets are like those little fires, I suppose. Life's full of them, smouldering and then going out. I hope they're not large fires just beginning – like Dad's was, flaring up to burn Mum.

We walk on, scrunching the stones that make me glad I've got my stick. The longer he thinks, the more optimistic I feel. And then he speaks. "You might be right, Michael. I do turn some projects down, see. You know, where I'd be caught out for lack of qualifications, or don't know enough about the engineering. Having you as a partner could be just what I need. What does Louise say about it?"

"She's all in favour – really, really keen. And if we have to keep ourselves afloat with my inheritance for a time, she can't think of a better use for it."

"Yes, I can see that. I'm getting quite enthusiastic. Don't hand in your notice yet, though. I'll give it some more thought and ring you one evening during the week. I've never considered a partnership, but the more I do the more I like it. Hughes and Paine: it's got a good ring. I never thought anyone would want to work with me."

I give his shoulder a gentle punch. "Rubbish."

Now in range of the chapel's magic we stop talking to look ahead. A solitary stone barn standing tall beside desolate mud flats isn't an obvious source of holy aura, but the emanation from this building even elbows aside the atheist in me – maybe because it's not a barn and was built as long ago as 654 by a saint. Hannah detaches herself from Lou. "I'll show you the chapel, Ivor," she says, and takes hold of his hand to lead him to Emily who's already waiting at the door.

I put my arm round Lou's shoulder and guide her past the south wall so we can look out to sea. "It's promising. We had a brief chat. I think I convinced him, but he needs more time to think it through. I'll tell you more later."

She offers me the shortest and softest of kisses in response. "I know he'll say yes."

I pull her closer so her scent masks the salt tang all around. With our shared wavelength, we both know it's not the time and place to talk more now. The low cloud has drawn the horizon close to the shore: a blurred meeting between shades and textures of grey. I remember Mum staring from here, in fine weather or foul – she didn't care. I'm looking

245

ahead to my future, but I guess she was always looking back on her blighted past. Any future for her was gained through my achievements. That weight of expectation has been taken off me now; and yet strangely, with my new freedom, I think I'll be happy to feel I'm striving for her too. I wish we had a better view: a clear sky, radiant light, the horizon in focus, a zephyr breeze, a blue sea flashing its diamonds. Everything in front of us is so murky.

In Memoriam

The men who lost their lives in the explosion at the Nypro (UK)
Limited chemical works at Flixborough near Scunthorpe at 4.53 pm
on Saturday June 1st 1974

John Barrett, 43

Ward Bradshaw, 19

Terence Carter, 35

Michael Clark, 26

Kenneth Crawforth, 33

Roland Cribb, 35

Thomas Crookes, 53

James Doherty, 46

Steven Drury, 27

Ronald Forster, 23

Anthony Freear, 30

Stanley Grundy, 48

Michael Hickson, 26

Edwin Holland, 24

Ian Kidner, 37

Allan Lambert, 25

Denis Lawrence, 48

Thomas Leighton, 40

Geoffrey Marshall, 20

Albert Nutt, 51

John Render, 20

Graham Richards, 30

Richard Simpson, 34

Michael Skelton, 27

Harry Stark, 44

Geoffrey Twidale, 30

Frederick Watkinson, 33

Keith Winter, 24

About the Author

BARRY HOTSON graduated in chemical engineering from Imperial College in the sixties. His first job was at Flixborough, near Scunthorpe, at a factory which exploded disastrously in 1974. By then he was involved with projects for a multinational chemical corporation, and became their European safety consultant before retirement. *Suffering the Fire* is his first novel, in which fictionalised versions of Flixborough and the 2005 disaster at Buncefield bookend the plot.

Barry Hotson
1943 - 2014

Lightning Source UK Ltd.
Milton Keynes UK
UKOW03f0104091014

239842UK00004B/344/P